QUEENS OF THE FAE BOOK NINE

FAE'S RETURN

MELISSA A. CRAVEN

M. LYNN

Edited by Caitlin Haines

For Tia
You didn't know how to stop talking, and we finally listened.

CHAPTER ONE
TIERNEY

L ife wasn't always fair. There was no way to change the unchangeable, no way to alter a future that was set in stone.

These were the thoughts on Tierney O'Shea's mind as she sat in the mouth of a cave with the giant network of mountain caverns the people of Grima had built over the centuries at her back. Her legs dangled off the edge of a steep drop-off. One wrong move and she'd crash against the rocks below, tumbling toward the sheer fall into the turbulent seas.

Somewhere in the distance was a fishing village, where Grimian people bundled in furs to brave the rocky seas, never venturing close enough to the Vale of Storms to even catch a glimpse of the churning maelstrom beyond that dangerous corridor. There was a point out there, far beyond the white caps. A point no fae could survive traveling past.

Yet, they'd planned to.

A chill raced up Tierney's spine, and she pulled the fur Bronagh had given her tighter around her shoulders. The wind up here was unrelenting in its iciness. Yet, to Tierney, it felt good. The cold. The snow-topped mountains. The ice hanging

She closed her eyes, picturing the white fields of Iskalt, the frozen lakes, and the cold stone palace. Home was just a far-off fantasy now during the day, and a haunted nightmare every time she tried to sleep.

Their one chance of reaching those jagged shores was reduced to ash, burned up by the heat of the fire plains. Soon, they'd expand across all of Lenya.

Soon, there would be nothing left of her or the people she'd come to love here.

The ship had been a desperate attempt to reach Iskalt, a dangerous journey that would have provided one last chance to return home and save a kingdom. But for all she knew, if they'd boarded the ship built to brave the maelstrom, they'd have still ended up at the bottom of the endless depths.

A sigh escaped her lips, her breath releasing in a fog in front of her face.

She could already see signs of the encroaching fire plains in the distance. No one knew how long it would take the unseen force to reach this far up into the mountains, but a trickle of water ran the length of the stone beside her. She dipped one finger into the dampness, feeling the melting ice for herself.

"You shouldn't sit so close to the edge." Keir's gruff voice shouldn't have surprised her. He was always telling her what to do, what not to do.

"If you do not wish to see me fall, go back inside to warm yourself by your precious hearth." He'd hardly left the fires since their arrival the week before. Unlike her, he hadn't been bred to withstand the cold, to brave icy winds and damp feet.

"Are you going to jump?"

She snorted a laugh, the harsh sound foreign to her ears. That wasn't how she laughed. There was no joy in it. "Does it matter?"

"No."

One corner of her mouth curved up. "Well, hate to disappoint, but I have no plans of tumbling to my death."

"Shame."

"Jerk."

"Yes." He lowered himself to sit on the bare stone a considerable distance back from Tierney and her daring ledge.

They'd barely spoken since their way to Iskalt was destroyed.

"I could really use some magic right about now." She scooted back and pulled her knees in to hug them to her chest.

"Is the great Iskalt princess cold? I thought ice ran in your veins."

Tierney shot him a scowl. "I'm not cold. But I am hungry. Do they ever eat anything here besides fish?"

"Grima is a fishing kingdom."

"Yes, but can't they also be something else? We're in the mountains. I'm sure there is plenty to hunt."

He frowned. "Sometimes, I forget how little you know of Lenya."

"Oh please then, inform me, great wise one." Tierney wasn't in the mood for lessons from Keir. She wasn't in the mood for anything from him. They stood on unstable ground, both trying to forget everything that happened to them back in Vondur.

Keir let out a huff of exasperation, a sound she'd realized he reserved only for her. Something about that forced her to hide a smile.

"There used to be crystal mines in the mountains," Keir said. "They were probably the deepest and most prosperous in all of Lenya. That wealth, that magic, is how they were able to build such intricate networks of caves without our knowing. I'm guessing this is where they came after we captured their palace."

3

"What does this have to do with food?"

"A few years ago, my father mounted an expedition to destroy the mountain mines. If he couldn't abscond with the crystals, he didn't want Grima to have them."

"But ... by then, he must have known Lenya was running low, that one day magic would disappear from the kingdom altogether."

Keir nodded. "He led one battle at a time. I did not accompany this unit of men, but the story when they returned was that the mines were gone, and ..."

"And what?"

"The best way to beat an army is to cut off their food supply."

"No." She could tell exactly where this was going.

"There is a river that runs down the mountain, providing water to every spring, every lake. My father used a totem to infuse poison into the very land around it so it would leech into the water continuously."

"But the Grimians have magic too."

"To my knowledge, they never figured out what the source of the poison was. But it destroyed the animal population."

Tierney released her knees, resting back on her hands and staring out into the sea. "But the river runs to the sea, and the fish—"

"I do not know exactly, but we always suspect the water dispersing prevented high enough concentrations to affect the sea."

Tierney closed her eyes, saying a silent prayer for the vast amount of creatures killed by that vile man. It was worse than she'd imagined. "How can the Grimian people stand to work with Vondurians, even if it means saving their kingdom?"

Keir didn't respond to that.

Tierney knew being here wasn't easy for him. The Grimians stayed mostly away from him, casting suspicious looks. He was unwelcomed, unwanted. And yet, he was still here. For now. Soon, he'd return to his palace to prepare his fae for what was coming.

And Tierney wouldn't go with him. She'd already made that decision. Her place was not in Vondur.

"Wait." She turned to meet his gaze. "If the mountain water is poisoned with magic, how then do these caverns survive?"

He pushed to his feet and turned.

"You're just going to leave when I asked you a question?"

He looked back at her and quirked a brow. "Are you coming?"

"Oh." She scrambled to her feet. "I guess. Following you into the depths of a cave beats jumping."

"I'm flattered." His mouth flattened into a thin line.

Tierney couldn't resist a smile as she followed. Whatever happened between them, whatever they'd never be to each other, having him here, for the time being, was still a comfort.

Fresh, icy air quickly turned to a damp cold that sank into her bones, the kind of cold she rarely even felt in Iskalt. No velvet carpets spanned the stone floor to provide the illusion of warmth; no colorful tapestries adorned the walls.

Only a few torches hung along the walls when they passed what was called the gathering space. It was the one cavern big enough for meetings and announcements. Now, only a few servants rushed through it to get from one section of the caverns to another.

Keir took one of the torches off the wall and led Tierney into a part of the caves she hadn't yet explored. All light faded until only their torch illuminated the way.

Before long, she heard the distinct sound of water hitting stone. The walls grew bright as they neared the noise, almost sparkling like ... Her eyes widened. Like crystals were infused right into the stone.

As soon as Tierney stepped through the low archway, she felt it. The magic. A rushing stream flowed from a gap in the wall, hitting a pile of rocks before tumbling into a pool of water.

"Keir," Tierney whispered.

"I know," he said. "I was surprised when I found it. The water is like our healing pools, with crystals embedded in the stone beneath. I think that's what keeps it free of the poison."

Tierney stepped to the edge and bent to dip her hands into the water, feeling the power snake up her skin. She closed her eyes, remembering what it was like to have full control over this kind of magic, how empowering it was. How strong it made her feel.

"Be careful," Keir warned as her toes rocked on the edge.

Tierney didn't open her eyes, but her lips curled into a smile. "Careful is the opposite of what we need. Don't you ever just want to feel it, Keir?"

"Feel what?"

"The magic."

"I do." She could picture his brow furrowing in confusion and agitation.

"No." She rotated her hand, not wanting to ever leave this behind. "You use your magic when you need to. It's a battle weapon for you. But sometimes, you have to just feel it, to let it live inside you."

"You speak of it as if it's a living thing."

"Isn't it?" Maybe his power was different since it came from an object outside of himself, but she didn't think so. "When you use your power, do you feel invincible?"

"Invincibility is a dangerous concept in war."

She shook her head and opened her eyes to see her hand dipping in and out of the crystal-clear water. "War is not all of life, Keir. There are things beyond the battlefield that can cause us greater pain."

"Tell that to those who never leave that battlefield."

She did not want to discuss the tragedies of war with a king who knew nothing else, but she would have rather died fighting for Iskalt than live in exile far away from the land she loved.

Keir didn't speak to Tierney again before he left her in the peace of a magic she could touch but not control. Maybe this was a lesson, the greatest of her life. For so long, she'd trained to always have a handle on the power inside her, to not let it take control of her.

But magic was to be respected, revered. Not used as revenge against her brothers, as a way to get what she wanted. In Lenya, they could only use it when it mattered most. Yet, in Iskalt, it was incorporated into every area of life.

Was that wrong?

She was still sitting in the room with the strange underground spring when Gulliver skidded in, his tail flicking in excitement. "Good; Keir said I'd find you here."

Tierney shot to her feet. "Has something happened? What's wrong?"

The smile on his face allayed her fear. "Nothing is wrong, Tia."

"Then, what is it? Spit it out."

"Eavha. She's here."

"What?" Tierney started toward the door. "Keir left her in charge of Vondur. What in the name of magic would she be doing in the Grima mountains?"

"Maybe she came to finally make Keir go home. Wouldn't that be great?"

Tierney couldn't help laughing at Gulliver's eagerness to be rid of the grumpy king. "We can hope." Something heavy settled in her stomach, as cold as these stone walls.

Gulliver continued chatting, but as they reached the gathering space, Tierney left him behind to seek out a certain disobedient princess.

She found Eavha standing with her brother, waiting for Bronagh's arrival.

"What's going on?" Tierney asked.

Eavha grinned when she saw her. "I never thought I'd see you again." She yanked Tierney into a hug.

Tierney patted her back and pulled away. "Okay, but will someone please explain why you're here?"

"We received word about what happened to your ship," she said.

Keir nodded. "I had Bronagh send a messenger on our way here."

Eavha continued, "I know my brother, so I knew he wouldn't come home quite yet, not until he figured out a way to try to save both Vondur and Grima. I want to help."

"But you're supposed to be leading Vondur."

"I told her not to come," Declan grumbled nearby. "But does she ever listen to me?"

Eavha rolled her eyes. "I left Lord Robert in charge. He'll do better than me anyway. Acting as the queen was sort of constricting."

Tierney couldn't fault her for that. She worried she'd feel the same when her father's crown fell to her.

Fae flooded the room, dressed in the furs they'd worn since arriving at the caves. Tierney didn't miss the way they eyed the

Vondurians—Eavha, Declan, and their guards. She didn't miss the tension pulled taut across the crowd.

Grima and Vondur were enemies, fighting for generations. Now, suddenly, they were supposed to work together to fight a new enemy, one that had no beating heart.

"I don't like this," Gulliver whispered.

Tierney didn't either. How long would the truce last? It didn't matter if Keir and Bronagh had developed a tentative trust when their people only knew one another across a bloody battlefield.

"Vermin," a Grimian soldier spat.

Eavha turned on her heel, her eyes finding the man. She was about to open her mouth when Tierney clamped a hand down on her arm. "Don't. That's Captain Norix."

"And why should he be allowed to speak to me in such a way?" Said like a princess who'd only truly known a life of ease.

Tierney had been in war. She saw what it did to fae, no matter their side. "He lost three sons and a brother to the battles with Vondur."

Eavha's entire body froze and, when she turned to Tierney, there were tears in her eyes. "I ... that's so sad."

"That's war," Keir said. "War is sad."

An older gentleman walked toward them with the grace of a much younger man. Tierney hadn't yet met the Grimian swordmaster, but she'd heard stories of the Vondurian warrior who had switched his allegiance. He'd seen what Tierney saw. The Vondurians fought for supremacy. The Grimians fought to survive.

"Your Majesty." Daniel bowed to Keir. "I only just arrived with a fresh wave of troops and was surprised to hear you'd come." There was a question in his gaze.

Keir looked like he wanted to run away right then, like

9

facing the man who'd taught him how to be the warrior he'd become was too much.

"Daniel." Declan stepped forward. "It is good to be on the same side once again."

The swordmaster's weathered face stretched into a grin. "Declan. Boy, you've grown."

"General, now."

"General? Well, I always knew the status of your birth wouldn't hold you back. I'm glad your king here saw the same as me."

His king. A deliberate separation from Vondur. Daniel was making it known Keir was not his sovereign.

Murmuring surrounded them among the crowd waiting for the king. Most of them were soldiers, men and women who'd followed Bronagh from the palace, waiting for their next move. There were also servants, cooks, and a few children.

And none of them liked their revered swordmaster conversing with the enemy.

Enough was enough. Tierney grabbed Eavha's hand. "We're going to see what's taking Bronagh so long." She ignored the gasps at her informality.

Keir stepped forward. "Maybe I should—"

"No." Tierney pinned him with a look. "You stay right there." She yanked on Eavha's arm.

As they walked away, she heard Keir's voice. "I'm still a king, right?"

"Tierney, wait."

Tierney turned so fast Eavha crashed into her. "Are you going to tell me why you're really here? Your brother might buy the whole seeking adventure thing, but I know there's more."

"There's no—"

"Don't lie to me, Eavha Dagnan."

Eavha sighed. "Fine. When we received the messenger who told us you and Keir were here, Declan and I got worried."

"He didn't really try to stop you, did he?"

"Do you think he'd actually believe he could?"

"Good point." One bright spot of staying in Lenya ... not losing Eavha. It didn't make up for missing Toby, but it soothed some of the burn.

"We brought our best warriors with us as guards."

Tierney still didn't understand, and it must have shown on her face.

"Tia, my brother, the king of Vondur, is in a Grimian stronghold with few fae who would support him should they need to. He is vulnerable and alone among the enemy."

"Grima is not—"

"They have always been our enemy. I want this truce to hold too, but I do not trust them. Certainly not with my brother's life."

"So, you came to protect him." The picture cleared, and Tierney couldn't say it didn't warm her a bit.

"Yes. At least, we brought him more guards, but they wouldn't have gained entrance without my presence."

Tierney leaned back against the wall. "What will Bron think of you bringing armed fae into the caverns?"

Another voice joined them. "Bron will think the princess was being smart." Tierney turned to find the queen herself walking toward them. "My fae do not trust Vondur. Nothing I have done or said has changed their opinions. I do not want anyone getting ideas about restarting this war. Protecting Keir is the best way to prevent that."

"My thoughts exactly," Eavha agreed.

Tierney wanted to believe that if she was stuck in Lenya, at least she could live with the Grimian people. She could make a home with Gullie. But if they hurt Keir, no matter how much he aggravated her, that was something she wasn't sure she could move past. After everything that happened, he'd become a sort of friend, one she too wanted to protect.

Bronagh turned to Tierney, echoing her thoughts. "I don't think he's safe here. And with your association, neither are you."

CHAPTER TWO
KEIR

K eir followed Daniel and Veren from the caves down to the docks along the craggy shoreline of Grima. Their situation was nothing short of catastrophic. It was barely perceptible, but the fire plains expanded more each day. At this rate, there would be nothing left of Lenya soon.

"Stop it. You're stuck on the worst-case scenario." Declan elbowed him as they walked down the endless steps, with their confusing switchbacks and tiered offshoots to different parts of the village. He feared he would never find his way back to the caves without a Grimian escort.

"We are living in the worst-case scenario, aren't we?" Keir's shoulders and spine tensed at the reminder of their predicament. Even now, this bountiful village that lay along the busy wharf would cease to be in a few short months. How long could they keep moving out of the burning path that would lay waste to every corner of Lenya? How long before there was nowhere left to flee?

"There's always a way out." Declan gave him a pat on the back and an uplifting smile. But that was Declan. He was always the more optimistic one. "We just have to find a new plan."

Veren explained, an impatient look on his face as he waved them forward. "We will find a solution to our problem. Keep an open mind and it will come to us."

"Here?" Keir frowned at their surroundings. Fishermen were coming in with the late afternoon tide, hauling their nets in behind them. The catch seemed to be failing more and more every day as the boats headed out farther into the most dangerous parts of the seas in search of fish to feed their families and those displaced from the palace.

That had been a blow Keir had not bounced back from yet. No one had. They'd had such high expectations of sailing the great ship the queen had commissioned. The one Keir never got to see. Now, only the charred remains sat in the cove they could no longer access, just a half-day's ride up the coast. There, the waters still churned with the heat of the fire plains, chasing all the fish from the shores into the cooler waters of the deep sea.

That ship was supposed to save them all. And it had taken them months to build it. Months they no longer had. They couldn't wait for another to be built. Which meant they might not be able to reach Iskalt by sea. They might have to find a way across the plains. Perhaps around them, where the temperatures weren't as intense. But could they sustain the putrid air and harsh temperatures for long lengths of time?

"The people of Grima live along the coastlines, where the air is clear of the smoke from the fire plains and life is much easier than in Vondur." Veren marched along the boardwalk, waving to captains and first mates from various ships he seemed to recognize by name. "We've been able to trade easily with those in the west. They send us fresh produce, and we send fish and shellfish. But it's getting harder now as crops are failing and the catch is drying up. If food shortages continue, we'll starve before the plains reach us."

"You have trade vessels?" Keir asked. "With large cargo

holds?" He'd only ever seen small fishing boats in Grima. Not that he was ever in a position to pay much attention to such things when inside their borderlands.

"We do, your Majesty." Daniel walked beside Veren, his hands clasped behind his back. "Coastal trade has been our livelihood for many generations. We even have flat-bottomed vessels that sail up the rivers inland to deliver supplies to the estates in rural areas. We trade with them for grains and sugar."

"I suppose it is easier when you have safe sea routes to navigate from one side of Grima to the other." In Vondur, they had no such routes, and trade caravans over land never fared as well in the face of thieves and highwaymen eager to plunder what they could. It was always harder in Vondur, where the land was unforgiving. They survived on the things they could produce at hand. If they couldn't grow it or make it, they often did without.

Keir watched the sailors unload their cargo holds, which seemed to yield very little these days. He imagined another time when this harbor would have been prosperous with trade. He wanted to give that back to them. And to his own fae. Perhaps when this was all over, they could open up trade routes between Grima and Vondur. That was a future he would love to see.

Though, Keir didn't imagine he would ever get to experience such a thing.

Several young children ran past, hurrying along to the docks to greet an incoming ship.

"Papa!" a little boy screamed, waving scrawny arms in the air as his older sister tried to keep him from falling into the harbor.

"Mind your sister!" a voice echoed across the water.

Keir smiled when he saw a man not much older than himself, standing at the ship's bow as it sailed closer to the docks. The man waved at his children, clearly eager to get his feet back on land so he could hold his family.

They were just fae. Like those who lived throughout Vondur in the villages and towns he knew so well. For many years, he'd fought in a war against the brutal Grimian soldiers. He'd seen slaughter and bloodshed. Warriors to a man. But they weren't the lifeblood of Grima. These fae were. Just as the common folk of Vondur were the lifeblood of his kingdom.

They were all Lenyans. That was all that mattered anymore, and he had to do something to save them from the fiery end they all faced.

"Captain Michel!" Veren called as they approached one of the largest ships currently docked at the far side of the harbor, where the waters ran deeper.

"Ahoy there, Master Veren." A weathered and wrinkled face peered down at them. "How's that fine ship of our lady queen's coming?" The old man scaled down the side of the ship like a wiry young sailor.

"You haven't heard then?" Veren's voice dropped to a funerary tone. Of everyone, Veren had taken the loss of the ship the hardest. He'd worked with the queen's finest builders to bring that vessel to life. All for naught.

"No." Captain Michel's eyes widened in surprise. "Caught by the fires?"

"I'm afraid so."

"She was a fine ship, Master Veren. But she was too big to make it across the Vale of Storms."

"Too big?" Keir stepped forward. This was the first negative account he'd heard of Veren's perfect ship.

"Aye, sir." He turned adoring eyes on his own vessel. "The Wind Runner is light and fast. She rides high in the water and takes a beating from the torrential rains and surging seas. Even when she's weighed down with a full cargo in her belly, she holds steady through any storm. I've taken her out farther than any other captain in this harbor. She handles the rocky seas to the south without incident. I've brought in some of the largest hauls of the most beautiful fresh red sea bass you've ever seen. They only swim around the Grima Shoals. Got a king's ransom for that haul, you better believe it." His eyes shone with delight at having the rapt attention of a new audience.

"The Queen's Maiden was equipped with oversized sails that could capture the winds and keep us moving through a gale," Veren argued. "She was bigger and heavier to keep us grounded in rough seas."

Captain Michel shook his head. "Any shipbuilder would tell you such." He tapped his nose. "But a captain spends his life on the seas. He knows things. Things a builder will never understand about the wiles of the waters."

Keir smiled, the first semblance of hope flickering in his chest. "Captain Michel." He clapped the man on the back. "What do you say to an ale?"

"I'd say lead the way, sir." The captain swept his hat off his balding head, running his hands through what little hair he had left.

"What are you up to, Keir?" Veren walked behind him toward the tavern on the wharf. "The old coot's full of stories, but that's all it is. Tall tales and boasting."

"I have some questions for him." Keir shrugged. "We still need to find a way across the sea or around the plains, but before we do that, I'd like to know more about our options. And now that we don't have the ship built for the voyage, it's going to be a lot more dangerous."

Declan held the door open for them as they entered the musty old tavern that looked to have been there since the beginning of time itself.

Daniel and Declan found a corner table and ordered them each a tankard of ale from the pretty barmaid.

"Captain Michel." Keir sat down at the sticky table, grateful for the dark corner where they could talk freely. "I'd like to ask your honest opinion." He leaned forward, forearms resting on the splintered wood. "What would it take to navigate the Vale of Storms? To cross the maelstrom and reach the shores of whatever lies beyond?"

The captain's face paled. "What did you say your name was again?"

"Keir Dagnan." He didn't see any reason to lie to the man when asking such an important question.

The captain nodded, looking like someone had walked over his grave. "I see. We must be in dire straits indeed if the King of Vondur sits across from me asking for advice." He moved aside for the barmaid to set his tankard in front of him. Taking a long drink, he wiped the back of his hand over his mouth.

"Can I get you, gentleman, anything from the kitchen?" the barmaid asked, making eyes at Veren.

"No thank you, but I imagine we will need a second round before long." Declan slipped her a coin and sent her on her way.

"Surely there must be another way." Captain Michel took another long swig.

Keir tested the ale for himself. He expected a dreadful sour stout, but it was delicious and refreshing. It seemed everything in Grima was of better quality. Even in a wharf-side tavern full of dirty old sailors who just might hold the answers to the questions plaguing Keir's mind.

"If there was, I would not be here." Keir raised his tankard. "I would know your opinion on the voyage we must make if we are to save Lenya." By now, all Lenyans were aware of the ever-encroaching burning lands that had turned their fresh water rancid, stolen their lands, homes, and whatever security they might have possessed in this war-torn land.

Captain Michel nodded, staring at the contents of his tankard. "It's a foolhardy journey. But a ship like the Wind Runner could do it." He finally spoke, all boasting gone from his voice. "She would have to be outfitted for it. Larger sails, taller, stronger mast. Empty hold, packed with sandbags secured to the port and starboard sides to keep her from rolling. She needs a good, strong crew with experience, quick minds, and sharp wit."

"Michel, you bloody fool, you cannot pass over the Vale of Storms with an empty hold." A wizened old man with a long, braided beard slapped him on the back. "You need to weigh her down." He pulled up a chair and joined them without invitation, a pipe clutched between his yellow-stained teeth. "Let her ride low in the water. She'll have better balance, see." His eyes sparkled with interest at the very idea of sailing across the maelstrom most would avoid at all costs.

Michel shook his head. "Hyde, you old charlatan, she'll roll for certain if she's weighed down too much."

"Not if her crew knows how to handle her." Hyde turned his attention to Veren. "You let her have her head as the winds pick up, gather her speed, like so." His hand moved across the table, mimicking the movement of their theoretical ship. "Keep her on the outer edge of the vortex, moving fast with the wind in her sails. No fear. You cannot hesitate when you're on the cusp." His toothy grin lit up his weathered face. "Ride the edge as long as you can, and when the winds turn, you start to break away, let her momentum push you out of the eddy little by little." He gave a loud clap of his hands. "And when you break free, she'll have carried you to the other side, bound for lands unheard of outside the old storybooks."

"You're both dodgy old fools." Another captain

approached, clutching his tankard of ale. "It's impossible. The vale will carry you down to the bottom of the sea, and then we'll all be lost to the fire plains." He grabbed his hat off his head. "Begging your pardon, sirs, but you'd be better off circling the Rocky Seas to the south to reach the other side of the plains. It's a far stretch and slow going, but with the right flat-bottomed ship, it could be done. Successfully so, if you don't mind me saying."

It seemed Veren had told anyone who would listen about the great ship that would save them all. Now that it was gone, they all had an opinion. And Keir wanted to hear every last one.

"Wouldn't she break up if she hit the wrong shoal?" Keir tilted back in his chair, eager to hear his answer. The Rocky Seas were dangerous but not quite as terrifying as the Vale of Storms.

"Not if you're running with an experienced crew who knows how to navigate a small vessel through the narrow passes." The man leaned against the filthy wall, his eyes intent on solving this conundrum. "It's dead stressful out there, but you likely won't drown so much as have to turn back and look for a better pathway a time or two."

"The lads don't have time for that, McCoy." Hyde waved the barmaid over for another round. "The vale is deadly but fast. It's your best bet for reaching help in time for it to actually arrive before we're all fried to a crisp."

"And if they die before they pass through the vale, then we all die. The shoals are the safest route." McCoy turned to Veren. "My crew has gone as far as anyone living. The fishing there is plentiful, and the weather is fine. We've mapped out the best routes."

"And what happens when we try to go farther than you

have?" Declan asked. "What sends you back home when you've gone as far as you can?"

"Aye, we'd have to find a new route around the far reaches of the shoals. We've run into nothing but sandbars and coral reefs we've not yet ventured past. We haven't had reason enough to find a way, but it's there."

"Sandbars?" Hyde frowned, turning to share a look with another captain who'd pulled up a chair in the crowded corner Keir thought would have been a private place to discuss the matter.

"Aye, you could move across the sandbars with the right equipment and crew. Can a man stand on them and keep his head above water?"

"The last time we sailed that far, it was only ankle deep."

"Ropes and pulleys would get you across with a flat-bottomed boat. Especially if she was small and lightweight." Keir didn't even recognize where some of these opinions were coming from, so many had joined the lively discussion.

"It's not far from land." McCoy sighed. "It's possible the temperatures have risen; it was already hot with steam rising and geysers spewing from between rocks. We'd have to plot a new path farther from the shores." He stroked his beard thoughtfully. "I still say it's the best option for actually reaching your destination, but maybe not the fastest if time is of the essence."

"You could be out there wandering around for months while the rest of the world burns," Michel muttered, clearly unhappy the others had butted into their conversation.

"It is an impossible choice to make," Veren finally spoke. "Either way could yield success, or we could all die in the attempt. What matters now is that we make a decision and see it through." He stared at Keir across the table.

"He is right. We must make an informed decision and give

it our all." The captains all launched into another round of debate on which was the best route and how it could be done.

"You don't think we can trust any of this conjecture, do you?" Declan leaned in. "They've traveled these sea routes all their lives, and I know they have much wisdom to offer, but this is a life-or-death voyage, Keir. We need this to work."

"It will." Keir lifted his tankard, draining its contents with a smile on his face.

"What am I missing?" Declan scowled. "You look too happy to have heard the same conversations I'm hearing."

"The point, Declan, isn't in deciding which one is right. They all are."

"How many of those ales have you had?"

"Listen to what they aren't saying." Keir grinned.

"What do you mean?"

"All these men." Keir gestured at the room filled with captains and their crew, all discussing the dangerous journey they would soon make. Because they would be going. Soon. "Not one of them has said it isn't possible."

CHAPTER THREE
TIERNEY

"Absolutely not." Bronagh paced the length of her less-than-elegant room in the caverns. It wasn't exactly fit for a queen, but nothing about this place was. "It can't be done."

Tierney sat quietly on the stone floor at the edge of the hearth, basking in the warmth from the ever-present fire. For once, she didn't voice an opinion. She wasn't sure she had one yet.

Keir let out a huff of exasperation as he faced off with the Grimian queen. "I think you're wrong."

"And you know so much about the Vale of Storms? Tell me, Vondurian, have you ever set foot on a ship?"

"That's not the point."

"Actually," Veren put in, "that's exactly the point. I agree with Bron on this one. Those old coots are just looking for a grand adventure, but they'll end up with a lung full of briny water and fish pecking out their eyes at the bottom of the sea."

"Nice visual," Tierney muttered.

Veren shot her a wink, looking for just a moment like the charming snake of a boy she'd known in Iskalt. It brought her a strange bit of comfort.

Bronagh drew in a breath, as if calming herself. When she

spoke, her tone was measured, careful. "When we began construction on the ship meant for this purpose, we consulted every shipbuilder in Grima. There were five of them, and they were all in agreement on what was needed to cross this particular sea."

"And how would they know?" Tierney hadn't realized she'd spoken until every eye fell on her. "I mean, don't get me wrong, I think what Keir is saying is completely insane, but no one has survived the maelstrom, right?"

"Not that we know of." Bronagh nodded.

"This captain..."

"Michel," Declan supplied.

Tierney continued. "Captain Michel, he's come close."

"As close as anyone living." Keir lowered himself to the settee, his eyes on Tierney.

"So he says." Veren shook his head.

"Hush," Eavha snapped at him. "Tierney is working through something here; let her think."

She was grateful for Eavha's faith in her, faith in the knowledge Tierney would have all the answers. But the truth was, she was as lost as ever. Was this her way to return home? Or just another way to die?

They all sat around the queen's rooms. Bronagh still on her feet, Veren at her side. Eavha and Declan sat together across the hearth from Tierney, their shoulders brushing. Gulliver was silent beside Keir on the settee.

Gulliver met Tierney's eyes in a silent argument.

Don't, he seemed to say.

I think we might have to.

Tia, this isn't one of your adventures. It's dangerous.

She sighed and shot him a look that said, *Everything we do here is dangerous. I don't want to die by the heat of the fire plains.*

Wouldn't that be the cruelest fate of all? The ice princess, who'd always fought for her independence, burning from the inside out as she yearned for her family and the protection she'd always scorned.

Tearing her eyes from Gulliver, she inched away from the hearth, no longer finding comfort in its warmth. When she glanced around the room, she found Eavha watching her with worry in her eyes, Veren studying her.

And Keir, his gaze was the worst. Imploring. Seeking. He needed her to be on his side in this, not to win but to give his fae a chance. There was desperation there.

"Well, we might die," she said.

"Precisely." Bronagh crossed her arms over her chest. "The seas are unforgiving. Without the proper ship—"

Tierney cut her off. "But won't we die if we do nothing at all?"

The queen closed her mouth, and a heaviness settled over the room. These were their choices, and each looked as bad as any other.

Bronagh pinched the bridge of her nose. "I need to think. Can you all please leave?"

Tierney picked herself up from the floor and followed the others out into the hall. She slipped her arm through Gulliver's and pulled him to catch up with Keir. "My room." The words were barely a breath, but she knew he'd heard them by the way he stiffened and issued one abrupt nod.

The hour grew late as they navigated the network of caves, and only a few fae remained awake, mostly guards going about their duty. It didn't slip Tierney's notice that the guard rotations doubled in size the day Eavha and Declan arrived with a host of Vondurians. The entire place felt ready to explode into battle.

Tierney yanked Gulliver into her room, shutting the door

behind them. They'd left Keir to talk to Declan and Eavha for a moment, but he'd arrive soon. "We need to leave this place." She flopped onto the bed she shared with Eavha and groaned.

Gulliver perched on the corner of the hard mattress. "At least they keep the fires burning." He gestured to the hearth. "I've lived in worse places."

Sometimes, Tierney forgot Gulliver grew up in the prison realm before the magic barrier came down. He'd been born to a life of drudgery and starvation in a place where a hearth would have been life's grandest luxury.

Tierney lifted her head. "I miss home."

Gulliver's face fell. "Yeah, I miss my dad."

"We've been treated well in Grima, but I think our time here is over. Not only ours ... if we don't get the Vondurians out of here, I'm afraid of what will happen."

He didn't speak for a long moment. "We've heard stories of the NAME sea, Tia. Do you really think we can cross it?"

She sat up, reaching for his hand. "Since when has there ever been anything we can't do?"

He gave her a squeeze, his tail lifting to tap her wrist. "Now, you're that ten-year-old girl again."

"With one major difference."

He didn't need to ask her what that was. "Your magic."

She sighed. "I need my brother, Gulliver. I need to return to him. I never fully understood it before. We knew he amplified my power, but now I think he *is* my power. Just like the totems are for Lenyans. It doesn't work without him. I will do anything, face any risk, to return to him." And not just for her magic.

A knock at the door interrupted them before Eavha barged in. "You don't have to knock, Keir. It's my room too since we're all packed into these caverns."

Keir and Declan followed her in.

To Tierney's surprise, it was Gulliver who spoke first. "Okay, Mr. Majesty, we're in." He met Tierney's gaze, but this time there was no argument between them, only gratitude. His eyes told her he'd do anything to get them back home too.

"In?" Declan looked confused.

Keir nodded, his expression matching Tierney's determination. The two of them weren't so different. Maybe that was why there was a tension between them, a rage right underneath the surface. It wasn't for each other, but only their circumstances.

This time, they were on the same side.

"No." Eavha gasped. "Tierney, it's a death sentence."

"But what if it's not?" And as they'd said before, staying was also a death sentence.

A smile curved one side of Keir's mouth. "Yes, what if it's not?"

The hike down from the caverns wasn't easy on a normal day, but this morning, the narrow stone steps were slick with rain—an icy blast that soaked through Tierney's clothes, chilling her to the bone. She didn't think she'd ever been so cold, even in Iskalt.

What she wouldn't give for a warm fire in her mother's rooms, a fur wrapped around her shoulders, and one of her mother's human hot chocolates.

Instead, she was traipsing through the mountains of a foreign kingdom.

From her favorite vantage point high in the caves, she hadn't been able to view the nearest fishing village, but Keir told her it wasn't far once they reached the bottom of the pass.

The treacherous climb was the reason Grimians were mostly safe in their caverns.

Tierney hardly slept the night before. She tossed and turned in bed until Eavha finally hit her over the head with a pillow and told her to stop. After that, Tierney found her way to the library, if one could call it such. It looked almost like a war room, with maps lining the walls and a few bookcases holding precious leather tomes, the few that were saved from the palace.

One of the maps showed the expanse of the Vale of Storms with an unnamed land across it that she guessed was Iskalt. It showed the swirling maelstrom, the rough waters. But she wondered how accurate it could have been when no one was known to have traveled that route.

Her foot slipped, and a yelp escaped her, but a firm grip on her arm kept her upright. Keir.

It was only the two of them this morning. They'd left before the rest of the palace woke, before Bronagh could convince them it was a bad idea.

Keir's grip didn't loosen, and Tierney looked back at him.

He released her immediately with a gruff, "Be careful."

Tierney's breath was shallow the rest of the descent. When she hit the bottom, air rushed into her lungs, and she wanted to kiss the ground underneath her feet.

Glancing up, she saw how far they'd come, how far back up they'd have to climb. A lump lodged in her throat. She could do it. Why were there so many ways to die?

Keir wiped rain out of his eyes. "Come on. The village isn't far."

Drops of water dripped from her lips as she blew out a breath and followed him.

By the time they reached the village, her entire body was stiff with cold. She heard the docks before she saw them. Fishermen yelled to each other from the riggings as they prepared to head out for the day. Weather didn't stop them.

Most of the sails hadn't yet been raised, creating an eerie feeling. She'd never been around ships without the constant flapping of canvas in the wind.

"Veren said most of the captains breakfasted at the Lucky Goose while their fae prepare their ships."

"By breakfast, you mean—"

"Ale, most likely."

She rolled her eyes. "Of course."

"Maybe cider on a day like today."

"What ever happened to fae drinking water?"

Keir flashed her an uncharacteristic grin. "Says the woman who likes her wine."

She shrugged. It was true. "Iskaltian wine, though. Not your Vondurian swill."

He ignored her comment. "Ale and cider can be easier to come by in these parts than water fit for drinking. It's less likely to make one sick."

Behind the docks were a line of warehouses and taverns. Beyond that, ramshackle houses leaned together, as if they'd fall without holding each other up.

It wasn't hard to find the Lucky Goose. A wooden sign swung as rain pelted it above a half-open door. Chatter spilled out as they neared. Tierney wasn't sure what she expected to find this early in the morning, but it wasn't a tavern full of loud men and women chatting animatedly and laughing.

As if sensing her surprise, Keir leaned in. "Those who work on boats are a different sort."

They stepped in out of the rain. No one paid attention to the newcomers or the puddles dripping at their feet. It was so very different from back home. When she walked into a tavern near the Iskalt palace, everyone knew.

"He's in the back." Keir wound around tables to a bald man who looked like he'd been sucked into the maelstrom and spit right back out.

"Captain." Keir gave a respectful tilt of his head.

The man looked up, surprise etched into his face. "Why, if it isn't the enemy king. What can I do you for, young man?"

Keir slid into a seat opposite him. "First, you can keep it under wraps who I am."

The man mimed locking his lips and throwing away the key.

"This is Tia." Keir gestured for her to sit in another empty chair. "Tia, meet Captain Michel."

"Pleasure, Tia." He pretended to remove a cap that wasn't on his head.

Tierney liked the man already, but it didn't escape her notice that Keir failed to tell him just who Tierney was. She could use that to her advantage.

"Captain," Tierney rested her hands on the table, "Keir tells me you've come closer to the maelstrom than anyone in Grima."

"Grima or Vondur." He grinned, his vanity successfully stroked. "No one dares stray as far from shore as my ship can handle."

"And why is that?"

"Because I built her for speed but also stability. The trick is not to spend longer than one needs in rough waters. Get in, get your fish, get out."

"And the maelstrom?"

His brow furrowed. "Well, not even I have ventured that far, but we have stories. Waves so big it's like trying to sail up a waterfall, wind so harsh it'll rip a sail right to shreds, if the hull hasn't splintered and dashed to the bottom of the sea first. I

30

would love to see it just once in my life." He sighed, a wistful smile on his face.

This was the moment. Tierney met Keir's gaze, and he gave her a nod. She leaned forward. "What if you could?"

Time froze as the captain stared at her. And stared some more. Red crept into his cheeks. "All of this ..." His breath stuttered on the way out. "All these questions ... You're not asking me to ..."

"Sail through the maelstrom?" Tierney said. "Yes, we are."

Captain Michel shot to his feet. "Are you insane?" His words were so loud all nearby chatter stopped, all eyes turned on them. "All this talk ... It was a fantasy, not supposed to be real. You can't possibly think there's a fae in Grima who'd risk it." He stormed toward the door.

Tierney and Keir jumped up to follow him. This wasn't exactly going as planned.

As they ran into the rain, a barmaid yelled at Captain Michel that he didn't pay.

"Put it on my account," he hollered back, his steps never faltering.

For an old man, he sure was fast. He reached a boat slip and hauled himself onto a ship that looked just as weathered and tested as him. A handful of sailors shouted greetings.

Tierney knew enough not to board a boat she wasn't invited onto. She stood on the dock and yelled to him. "Is it possible?"

He stopped, the rain bouncing off his head. "I don't know."

"Coming aboard!" A woman pushed by Tierney and Keir, bounding with shocking agility onto the ship. She pressed a kiss to the old man's cheek, and Tierney could barely catch their conversation.

"I heard you caused a commotion in the Goose."

"That was my fault," Tierney called.

The woman turned to her, and Tierney saw just how young

she was. She couldn't have been more than eleven or twelve. Not a woman, just a tall willowy girl. "And who are you?"

Tierney was tired of trying to convince fae to save their kingdom without them knowing the full truth. "My name is Tierney O'Shea. I'm a princess from the kingdom on the other side of that maelstrom. And I want to sail through it to get home, but also because if we don't, all of Lenya could be lost."

Keir cursed under his breath, but the captain and the girl looked on with wide eyes.

Tierney cleared her throat. "But you can call me Tia."

"Well," the girl started, "you should probably come aboard."

"Imogen." There was a warning in the captain's voice.

"Da, we owe it to Mama." She twisted a wet lock of blazing red hair around one finger.

The captain closed his eyes for a brief moment. "Fine. We'll listen to you."

Tierney took that as an invitation and climbed aboard. Keir followed her, still not saying a word. It was probably for the best. A few sailors gave them quizzical looks, but Tierney ignored them as she followed Imogen down a set of narrow stairs to where a handful of rooms branched off. They turned left into a kitchen of sorts with long wooden benches.

A young man glanced up from where he'd been messing with the stove. The captain waved a hand, and he scurried out.

"I'd offer you some tea, but this can't take long because we need to head out soon." He lowered himself to one of the benches.

Tierney sidled up next to Imogen. "You mentioned your mother?"

The young woman nodded, wet stringy hair clinging to her cheeks. "This is about the fire plains, isn't it?"

"Imogen, don't," her father pleaded.

Tierney turned to face the girl, taking in her ruddy skin, the way her eyes held no fear. "It is. If we do not act, they will destroy Lenya."

"I knew it." Imogen didn't look pleased with herself. "What other reason would someone risk crossing the vale?"

To get home. But Tierney didn't say that.

Imogen glanced at her father almost in apology. "The fire plains destroyed our village a few days' ride from here. Da was out on the ship. First came the sickness from contaminated water. When the heat came, Mama was too sick to go, but she told me to run."

Tierney's heart ached for this family, for all the families destroyed by the fire plains. She bent so she was at eye level with the girl. "Across the sea is my kingdom. It's called Iskalt. There, we have all the magic needed to drive the fire plains back, to make sure that doesn't happen to anyone else. But we need to get there."

Imogen turned to her father. "Since I was little, you've dreamed of going farther and farther, of discovering what lay on the other side."

"It can't be done." Captain Michel rubbed his face.

"I thought you said you didn't know if it could." Keir shifted his feet, staring down at the man.

Tierney watched them both. "Just because something has never occurred doesn't mean it can't."

Captain Michel looked helplessly from Keir to Tierney to his daughter.

Imogen sat beside him. "Da, what if we could have saved her? Would you have thought it too impossible to try then?"

A beat of stillness passed before his shoulders dropped. "No, I'd have done anything to save your mother."

"Then, let's try to save other mothers, children, our way of life. There is a reason this princess and her guard have walked into our lives."

Tierney almost laughed at Keir being called a guard.

"Honey," Captain Michel said, "that man is a king."

Her brows shot to her hairline. "We've been chosen to help, to escort the likes of kings and princesses across the sea, a sea that is our home. You are the best captain in Grima. They need you."

Captain Michel looked at his daughter, pride shining in his eyes, before meeting Tierney's gaze. "My daughter wants to help, and who am I to stop her?" He stood. "I will not force my men to go on such a perilous journey. Volunteers only. Which means, every person on this ship will have to work."

Tierney nodded, a smile coming to her lips. She couldn't wait to see Veren mopping the deck or cleaning the lav. But more than that, it felt real.

They might never make it, but at least now they had a chance.

CHAPTER FOUR
KEIR

"Stop pacing, Keir." Tierney sat perched on the edge of a flat-topped boulder. The vast cavern was empty for the moment, but it would soon be filled with Lenyans, come to hear the bad news that would confirm all the rumors told in hushed whispers in the corners of taverns and the marketplace.

"We're going to instill panic and chaos if we don't handle this right." Keir leaned against the stone wall beside Tierney. He didn't like the idea of telling the locals about their plans. At least, not all at once.

"We will give them the truth. It's the least they deserve." Bronagh sat in a straight-back chair at the front of the cavern. She made the derelict piece of furniture look like a throne. That was something he would never have. King, he may be, but royal, he was not.

"She's right." Tierney tapped her foot impatiently. "They aren't going to like it."

"They aren't going to trust it," Veren added.

"But they need honesty from their leaders." Gulliver sighed.

"The people will come around." Captain Michel twisted his hat in his lap. He seemed unable to fathom how he'd ended up in this situation. Already, his men were outfitting his ship with everything they would need to make the voyage. He was still quietly looking for volunteers, but after today, Keir imagined he would have more than he needed. Fae were bravest when their lives and the lives of their families were on the line.

Bronagh's people from the palace began to arrive, filing into the room and taking their seats. The Vondurians arrived next, each giving their king a formal bow. They wanted everyone here to know they answered to Keir and Keir alone.

The air in the room was tense. As if at any moment a battle would break out and nothing would stop it.

Keir was so tired of it all. So tired of a war he didn't want Lenya to keep fighting. Tierney was right. They had much bigger problems now.

As the villagers, fishermen, and merchants began to make their way into the back of the cavern, Keir, Tierney, and Bronagh stood together at the front of the room.

They'd rehearsed this part. The people needed to see them as a united front. Neither Bronagh nor Keir should be seen as the 'leader' of this venture.

"Welcome," they said in unison.

"Today, we are not Grima versus Vondur," Bronagh began.

"But Lenyans." Keir stood proudly beside the young queen. "United against the threat that stands on our doorstep."

Whispers erupted all around, and Keir held his hand up for silence.

"It is true," Bronagh said, her voice ringing across the cavern like a bell. "The rumors you've heard, they're all true."

"The fire at the palace?" a lady from Bronagh's court asked.

"Not an accident." Bronagh clasped her hands in front of her, stiff as a soldier beside her. "The fire plains are expanding, sweeping across Lenya, and we are powerless to stop them."

Gasps of surprise and sobs of protest rang out.

"It begins with the water turning foul," Keir explained. "It will make some too sick to leave their beds. Then, the temperatures rise, the air turns putrid, and the earth begins to shake. The ground becomes so hot that fires spring from nothing to burn the land and whatever lies in its path."

"We need magic. Magic will save us!" the villagers cried out, begging for an easy solution.

"Even if we emptied the mines, gathered Vondurian and Grimian reserves, and used every drop of magic we have left in Lenya, it will not be enough." Bronagh reached out a hand as if to soothe her people. "I would gladly sacrifice what magic we have left and live without it if it meant we could save you all. But our magic is weak. It is not enough. We need help."

"Magic has caused us nothing but heartache," Keir continued. "And in the end, it will fail us when we need it most."

"What can be done?"

"Will we be left to die?"

"Why have you brought us here?"

The questions and the fear that drove them tore at Keir's heart. He hadn't let himself feel it for a long time, but he loved his people and this land. He would do everything in his power to save them. Or die trying.

"There is a way to stop the spread of the fire plains." Tierney's voice rose above the din. "That is why we have called you here today." She stepped forward to stand among them. "My name is Tierney O'Shea, and I am not of Lenya. I am princess and heir of Iskalt, a kingdom of ice and snow that lies far beyond the borders of your world. Months ago, a magical ... experiment gone awry brought me and three of my friends here by mistake. In Iskalt, we have great magic. But unlike here in Lenya, our magic is infinite. I am too far from home to use my magic here, but we have access to crystals there. More than you could imagine and—"

"You expect us to believe this?"

"You would share your crystals?"

"What would your people want in return?"

"No one gives away magic for free."

"What will it cost us?"

Tierney raised her hand for silence. She had that same royal quality that Bronagh had. The thing that made all fae respect her and show her deference. The room quieted, and Tierney smiled.

"I come from the four kingdoms. Iskalt is just one of those kingdoms with lands far beyond what you can imagine. We do not use the crystals for magic. We don't need them. To us, they are beautiful stones we use for decoration and nothing more."

"We must find a way to reach Iskalt." Keir stepped forward to join Tierney. "It is our best chance of survival."

"My father, King Lochlan of Iskalt, will gladly come to your aid. My mother is sister to the Queen of Eldur, which lies on the other side of the fire plains to the west. Her other sister is Queen of Fargelsi, a land so green and fertile it's hard to imagine." Tierney turned to Gulliver. "And my dearest friend in the world is of Myrkur, where the Dark Fae live. His father, my uncle, works closely with King Hector of Myrkur, where they already mine crystals to use for trade. My family are all kind, benevolent rulers who have fought hard to attain the peace we have enjoyed for more than half my life. I speak for them all when I say we will never allow the fire plains to destroy Lenya. As long as it is within our power to do so, we will help you defeat this threat and give all Lenyans access to magic no fae should ever do without."

Astonished faces stared back at them. Keir wasn't sure if they were stunned or if they just didn't believe them.

"It can't be done."

"There are no other lands beyond Lenya."

"The seas are too treacherous."

"It is true." Keir's voice rose above the din. "We must first find a way to cross the Vale of Storms to reach Princess Tierney's homeland."

"It is impossible."

"It's too risky."

"What other option do we have?"

"We have no other option." Bronagh joined Tierney and Keir. "The seas to the south are too shallow and rocky to safely navigate. To the north, they are equally treacherous."

"The maelstrom is impossible to sail across."

"So it has been said," Keir replied. "We've all heard the stories of the dangerous seas. We have always been locked inside the borders of Lenya, believing there was nothing beyond our world. But we have never before had such motivation to risk breaking through those borders to see what lies beyond our knowledge. We have nothing to lose and everything to gain."

"If we do nothing, we will all perish in the fires." Bronagh stood taller, her gaze never wavering.

"Who will make this journey?" A man Keir recognized from the docks clutched his hat in his hand.

"We will. I will travel with King Keir of Vondur and Princess Tierney of Iskalt. Together, we will take the risk for you. I will be leaving Prince Donal in command during my absence."

"And I have left my sister and my council in charge of Vondur." Keir nodded to Eavha, sitting among the crowd with Declan and Gulliver. "By now, you have all learned of the treaty that has brought an end to the war between our kingdoms. We cannot afford to be divided any longer. From this day forward, we fight for all of Lenya."

"How do we know you all aren't just abandoning us to our

deaths?" A bold man of Bronagh's court stood among the villagers in the back, looking as weary and worn as the hardest working Grimians.

"Lord Branigan." Bronagh nodded. "You will just have to trust us. We will be asking for seasoned sailors to volunteer to join us. To my knowledge, you have years and years of experience sailing the Grimian seas as a merchant sailor. You are welcome to join us as we risk our lives to pass through the Vale of Storms and around the maelstrom. As we speak, the Wind Runner is being outfitted for our voyage. We will set sail for the shores of Iskalt as soon as she is seaworthy."

Lord Branigan lowered his gaze. "Forgive me, your Majesty. I only worry for my family."

"As do we all." Keir gazed across the audience, trying to give them a sense of peace about this venture. "You all have families you care for. Please know that Queen Bronagh and I care for our people as dearly as you care for your own families. We will not fail you, nor betray you."

"You have our word as your monarchs. We will die before we abandon you all to the fires." Bronagh gave them a look that said they were done here. "We leave in three days' time. May the magic of our ancestors protect you all until we return." She marched from the cavern, her head held high as her people stood to watch her go. Captain Michel and Veren followed her, urging the court to return to their temporary homes.

"Vondurians, you are dismissed." Keir couldn't be seen following the queen, so a military dismissal would have to do. As they all filed from the room, Keir turned to Tierney. He wanted to reach for her hand, but with so many eyes on them, he wasn't sure it was a good idea. His people needed to see him as a king working with the other monarchs, not beholden to them in any way. That was the surest way of losing their support.

"Keir, you can't go." Eavha waited until the room had emptied before she blurted the words, her tears not far behind. Keir had never been able to stand strong in the face of her sadness. "It's too dangerous." She flung her arms around him. "You are all I have left. I cannot lose you."

Her shoulders shook as Keir tried to comfort her. "It's all right, Eavha." He pulled back to search her face. "I am king. It is my responsibility to see Vondur through this."

"Why can't we just take whatever magic we have left and use it to save as many as we can? We could stop the expansion from spreading any farther, couldn't we? We won't have magic anymore, but at least we will have each other."

"And what would you say to all the men and women and their families who couldn't be saved? And what if our magic isn't enough to stop it? Eavha, you know we need help. Not just access to more crystals but real help. Tierney's people have a kind of magic we don't. Not only that, they have information we don't. We won't find the answers to Lenya's problems in Lenya. I have to go."

"I wish you could just be my brother." She sniffed her tears back, stepping into the circle of his arms to lay her head on his shoulder.

"What kind of king would I be if I let anyone else do this?"

"It would make you like Father." She sighed. "And you've always had too much of our mother in you to be anything like him." She gave another sniff and nodded. "Very well." She straightened the collar of his shirt. "You have to promise to return. All of you." She turned to glare at each of them. "Sail through that storm and bring the magic back to Lenya. I will accept nothing less than success. Let's go, Declan. Gullie. We have preparations to make." She pivoted on her heel and stomped from the cavern.

"That girl would make a fine queen someday." Tierney

came to stand beside him when they were the only two left. "It's too bad she loves Declan or I'd introduce her to my cousin. He's heir to Fargelsi, and in a few years he's going to be in the same predicament I've been in."

"Which is what?" Keir asked in an amused tone.

"In the four kingdoms, an heir must marry another royal or the highest of their noble houses. All the royals are related or close enough to be considered family, even if the blood ties aren't there. It diminishes the pool of eligible consorts tremendously. My father was desperate to find the right match for me."

"That's what sent you running to the human realm, is it not?" Keir asked.

"It seemed like the end of my world at the time." Tierney laughed. "My father and his stupid list." She shook her head. "I guess I'd forgotten what real problems were then."

"And now?" Keir arched a brow at her.

"May the magic help us through this." She let out a long breath. "Because we have real problems running out of our ears."

CHAPTER FIVE
TIERNEY

"Be safe." It wasn't the first time Eavha muttered the words, and Tierney had no response. This wasn't a journey where safe was a possibility. They had to be daring, bold, brave. Safe could get them killed, or worse. It could lead them to failure, and a return to face the fae they let down.

So, instead of issuing false promises, Tierney hugged Eavha with all her might, wishing for another life in which they didn't have to part. She wanted to take the princess to Iskalt with her, to introduce her to a world of peace, where children were allowed to play and young women danced and sparred, and laughed.

Pulling back, she gave Eavha one last look before turning to board the Wind Runner. A handful of sailors who'd volunteered for the journey prepared to set sail. It wasn't enough. One didn't have to be a seafarer to know that.

But she was grateful for every one of them.

"Look out below!" a voice called moments before Imogen dropped onto the deck, landing in a crouch and straightening in one smooth movement. Tierney lifted her eyes to the rigging above, wondering where the girl had come from.

Imogen grinned. "Just making repairs."

Great, they hadn't even set sail and the ship already needed repairs. Imogen intrigued Tierney. She'd recently lost her mother, and yet it didn't seem to have dimmed her spirit. Unlike her father, whose trepidation was obvious, the coming adventure put a spark of excitement into her.

"Something wrong?" Tierney asked.

Imogen shrugged. "We'll be fine."

In Tierney's experience, "we'll be fine" was more a statement of hope than a point of fact.

Imogen left to join her father on the starboard side, and Tierney stepped up to the worn wooden rail circling the deck. Her eyes scanned the Grima coastline, wondering if this was the last time she'd set eyes on Lenya. It was a place of great pain for her but also one of discovery. She was a captive, a refugee, and now, possibly, their salvation.

It wasn't the first time she considered maybe her portal brought her here for a reason. Maybe she was supposed to help Lenya.

Yet, it was also a place of shame.

Veren stepped up beside her, and Gulliver joined her on the other side.

"Siobhan could still be out there." It wasn't fair that the three of them had found each other and she hadn't.

Gulliver's tail wrapped around her back. "If she is, Declan's fae will find her."

Veren, standing perfectly still, surprised her when he spoke. "Is anyone else ... sad? To be leaving."

"No," Gulliver and Tierney said at the same time.

"Not all of us were kept in luxury since day one." Gulliver looked down at his hands, and Tierney wondered if the scars of the Vondurian dungeons would ever go away.

"I know." Veren sighed. "It's just ..." He glanced back over his shoulder to where Bronagh was boarding the ship.

Tierney hadn't understood, but she did now. Reaching out, she lay her hand over Veren's. "She's with you now."

"And if we survive this, she will return home."

Tierney had no words of comfort for him because right then she caught sight of Keir in an intense conversation with his sister down on the docks. They looked to be arguing before he pulled her into a hug and held on like he didn't want to let go.

Releasing her abruptly, he clapped Declan on the shoulder, muttered a few words, and bound up the rope ladder and onto the ship. Tierney left Gulliver and Veren to approach Keir. "Everything okay?"

His brow furrowed. "We're about to embark on a journey no one has conquered before. Our ship looks like it has seen better days, and I have to share a room down below with Veren and Gulliver."

"So ... yes?"

He gave her a reluctant smile, and she prided herself on pulling it out of him.

"But really, I meant with Eavha."

His smile dropped. "Just Vondurian business."

She wanted to press, but his expression closed off, and she knew she'd get nothing else.

"Everyone aboard?" Captain Michel yelled. "We need to set sail if we don't want to miss the tide."

Tierney searched their group. Veren and Gulliver were where she left them. Bronagh stood nearby, gazing across what was left of her kingdom. A few of her fae, guards mostly, took up position on either side of her, their golden armor glinting in the early morning sun.

A handful of Vondurians sat on crates near the door to the stairwell.

45

And then, there were the sailors, the fae who belonged on this ship.

Seemingly satisfied, Captain Michel gave the order to untie the ropes anchoring them to the dock.

The ship bobbed in the rippling water as a cool breeze skated across the surface.

"Oars," the captain yelled.

His fae took up position and long wooden oars protruded from the ship, dipping into the water. And then, they were moving. There was no more second-guessing, no turning back.

Tierney walked toward the Grimian queen, the one who'd been against this risky journey. She'd eventually realized they had no other choices before them. Bronagh was a brave woman. Despite her fears, she'd agreed to set sail.

One of the golden warriors moved aside for Tierney to stand next to Bronagh and watch Grima disappear. Neither of them spoke for a long moment.

Finally, Bronagh's voice filled the silence. "I sure hope you're right about what's on the other side of this sea."

Tierney drew in a briny breath, letting it settle in her lungs before exhaling. "Me too."

The first day at sea was a deception, one they'd expected. Calm waters greeted their journey, and as the winds picked up offshore, the captain ordered his fae to unfurl the giant canvas sails. They stored their oars and got to work directing the ship and keeping it steady.

The sails looked like a patchwork of tears, sewn together with odd colored canvas. Yet, they managed to propel the ship forward under the afternoon sun.

Out on the water, the temperature dropped. By nightfall, Tierney could hardly stand it. The only thing worse was going into the warmth down below that smelled like sweaty bodies and rotting sewage.

The ship was surprisingly large, with three cabins other than the main hold. One belonged to the captain and his daughter. The officer's cabin had been given to Keir, but Tierney and Bronagh convinced him to share it with Veren and Gulliver. And the third was for Bronagh and Tierney.

The soldiers and sailors slept in hammocks in the cramped crew quarters.

Tierney sat on near the ship's bow, surrounded only by stars. Noise came from the quarterdeck, where sailors gathered, but Tierney tuned them out, lifting her face to the sky.

"I'm coming home, Tobes," she whispered into the night, wishing a breeze could carry her words. "I'm going to make it." Through the maelstrom and across the uncrossable sea.

She closed her eyes, leaning her head back against the wall, and feeling the night. Not merely hearing it or smelling it. Waves lapped against the ship. Cool, salty air, the freshest she'd ever experienced. Her magic settled within her, content and calm on the sea. Soon, she'd have control of it again.

Getting to her feet, she stepped to the rail and peered down at the dark water, the silver light of the moon casting it with an iridescent glow. In two days' time, they would reach the first of the rough seas at the entrance to the Vale of Storms. Five days later, if their calculations were correct, the maelstrom.

And no one knew how long it would take to reach Iskalt should they survive that.

Tierney yawned, her chin lifting. If she was going to have any energy to face the coming days, she needed rest.

The smell hit her the moment she opened the door leading

to the narrow wooden stairs. Stale air pushed out at her, and she had to fight the urge to stop breathing altogether.

Descending the creaky stairs, she headed toward the berth that promised her rest, but a sound coming from Keir's room had her turning. It was ... laughter.

The door was already ajar, and she pushed it open, stopping at the sight before her. A card game. Keir sat on the edge of the bed, bending over a small table. Veren perched in a shoddy chair, balancing on two legs. Gulliver was on the floor, cards clutched in his hands.

Veren and Gulliver shared a grin as Keir placed a new card down.

"I can beat that." Gulliver slammed his hand down on the table, his cards face up.

Veren let out a hoot. "How's it feel, your Majesty?"

"To lose at a game I've never played before?" Keir lifted a brow.

Tierney stepped into the room, but no one paid her any mind until she spoke. "Since when are you all friends?"

"We aren't." Keir frowned.

"Gross." Veren crossed his arms.

"Since we proved the king here has a vulnerability after all." Gulliver was the only honest one.

"Yeah?" She had to hear about that. "What is it?"

"Cards." Gulliver grinned. "He's actually terrible. He didn't even know that the Eldurian crown beat the Fargelsi flame."

"I hardly know what Fargelsi or Eldur even are." Exasperation rang in Keir's voice.

"A little tip," Veren said, "Fargelsi flames are the weakest of the four flames. Everything beats it."

"Wait." Tierney peered closer. "Who had a Kingdoms deck?"

"I made one," Gulliver said. "I found some Grimian game while we were there and needed a reminder of home."

Kingdoms was a popular gambling game in Iskalt, not fit for a princess. Yet, she'd loved it. Her friends from the village let her join their games as long as no one found out. And when she was with Gulliver and Griff, they played all the time.

"Can I play?"

Gulliver and Veren let out simultaneous groans.

"Why can't she play?" Keir asked.

It was Gulliver who answered. "Because she's a freak."

"Hey." She wasn't a freak.

Veren nodded in agreement. "She can't lose. I don't know how, but Tia wins. Always."

"That can't be true." Keir looked from them to her. "There's too much luck involved."

"I don't always win." Tierney hugged her arms over her chest, trying to remember the last time she'd lost the game. She'd won many sweets over the years, the only thing her friends had to gamble with. But she'd always brought them pastries from the palace.

"Fine." Gulliver sighed.

Veren picked up the deck and shuffled rapidly, his fingers nimble. "Guess his royal Majesty has to see for himself."

Tierney sat beside Gulliver and met Keir's eyes, a challenge in their depths. He wanted to beat her. Tough luck, buddy.

Her tongue poked out to wet her lips as Veren dealt eight cards. Keir's gaze followed the movement, settling on her mouth. Did he want to kiss her as much as she wanted him to? Everything that happened to them in Vondur seemed like some distant past. It was a new world now.

Vondur and Grima were behind them. They wouldn't reach Iskalt for a long while. No kingdoms were keeping them apart out here, only their egos.

49

"Are you two going to stare at each other all night or play?" Veren asked.

Tierney's face heated as she realized they were waiting for her to pick up her cards. As soon as she did, she suppressed a grin. This was going to be fun.

Four games later and Tierney still hadn't lost.

"I give up." Keir threw his cards on the table.

"Told you." Gulliver leaned back on his elbows. "She's a freak."

"Or I'm just exceedingly talented." Tierney sent them a wink. The exhaustion she'd felt was gone now, and she wanted to move. Standing, she started toward the door.

"Where are you going?" Gulliver asked.

"Up top. I can't stand another minute in this horrid room with you lot." Really, she'd have stood a lot worse with them. She didn't know when she'd started counting Veren as a friend again, but even his presence brought her comfort now.

It wasn't until she escaped into the fresh air that she realized she wasn't alone. Keir followed her silently, as if it was the most normal thing in the world. He stumbled as the boat swayed.

Tierney laughed, rolling her eyes. "We've been on the boat all day. Still not used to it?"

"Vondurians aren't meant for the sea."

"Neither are Iskaltians. We're more suited to frozen tundra where we wrestle bears and fight wolves."

His eyes widened. "Truly?"

"No." She chuckled. "The frozen tundra part is true, but the other is just what some fae think of us."

"I have no doubt you could take down a bear."

"Well, thank you for your faith in me." She peered over the edge. "What about creatures of the sea? In Lake Villandi, we

50

have the Asrai, and they can be vicious, but I've heard stories of animals with razor-sharp teeth who can survive in the sea."

"I try not to think about it."

She turned to him. "Why? Is there something the great warrior king is afraid of?"

He met her gaze, hesitating for a beat before lowering his voice. "There are some things."

Somehow, Tierney knew he didn't mean whatever swam in the depths. Her gaze held his like a magic force kept her right where she was. His totem shone like a beacon where it hung from his neck, but the longer she watched him, the more it dulled.

"Keir." She reached out to touch the crystal, the back of her fingertips brushing his chest. "When?"

"Yesterday." He put his hand over hers. "I felt the moment the last of the magic drained from it."

"Why didn't you ask Bronagh for another?" In Vondur, he wouldn't have had to ask.

"Tia, did you notice how almost no one in Grima used magic. I can't remember seeing it there once."

Tierney thought over her time there. Keir was right. "They've depleted their crystals entirely."

"Not exactly. They do have precious few, but they do not use them unless necessary. And Vondur, I didn't want to take a crystal that might be needed to save fae from the fire plains while we're away."

He had no magic. Without a crystal, there was none inside of him. She hadn't noticed Bronagh with a totem either, which meant there wasn't a single bit of magic on this ship.

"Why do you still wear a depleted totem?" she asked, drawing her hand away.

"Because it is a reminder. Even without magic, we still have power." The words were for her and her alone because she understood all too well.

She hadn't realized she'd stepped so close to him until she turned and her shoulder brushed his chest. "Why did you do it, Keir? Why did you save me those months ago in Vondur?" She'd never truly been able to answer that question. He killed his father, risked his life. For her. For Declan and Gulliver too, but not only them.

Keir turned, peering out at the calm water. A breeze blew the hair back from his forehead. "My fae needed a king with their best interests at heart."

"But you never wanted that to be you."

A breath rattled past his lips. "Tierney—"

"Say it, Keir."

He pushed a hand through his hair and closed his eyes. "My father was an evil man. I'd known that for a long time, but it wasn't until you ... what he did to you. I hated myself for the role I played. It gave me the courage to act."

"Why?"

"What do you want from me, Princess?" He turned hard eyes on her, his lips dangerously close to the side of her head. "I gave you your answer."

"Not the full of it." She faced him, the mist from his breath skating over her cheeks.

His eyes searched hers, looking for his own answers and most likely finding none. Tierney didn't even have answers for herself. "I couldn't bear the sight of you hanging," he whispered. "I think it would have ripped me right open."

Tierney would shred just as thoroughly should anything happen to him. She hadn't planned on it, hadn't wanted it, but whatever this was sitting between them in choked silence wouldn't go away.

Reaching out, she gripped his arm, telling him it was okay

to feel things. He didn't have to be stoic and hide his emotions all the time. He could be a king and still be afraid.

Afraid of losing her.

Afraid of losing himself.

Afraid of failing the one position he'd never aspired to.

"Goodnight, Keir." Tierney gave him a soft smile before turning and leaving him up on deck.

By the time she lay her head down beside Bronagh's, wrapped in furs and burrowed into the hard bed, sleep dragged her into its depths like the sea coming to claim her as its own.

CHAPTER SIX
TIERNEY

By the second day, they'd left the calm seas far behind. Even Tierney had trouble keeping her feet firmly planted beneath her, and she had some experience sailing the rough waters of Loch Villandi.

The hour was early, but she couldn't take another minute in the narrow chamber she shared with Bronagh.

"Careful, Tia." Gulliver reached out to take her hand as she stumbled up the last step and onto the rolling deck. His tail snaked around her middle, anchoring her to him and the ship the hopes of two kingdoms rested on.

"Need fresh air." She blew a damp strand of hair out of her face.

"It's only going to get worse, isn't it?" Gulliver clutched her hand, staring out across the surging waves that crashed against the hull, spraying a fine mist of seawater over everything. Pretty soon, they would all forget what it felt like to be warm and dry.

"Much worse." Tierney sucked in a deep breath of sea air. With a new stench of decaying fish on the wind, it wasn't exactly fresh, but at least it wasn't stale human bodies and vomit filling her nose.

"How's his Majesty fairing this morning?" Amusement

It turned out the King of Vondur did not have his sea legs yet. The minute the calm waters diminished behind them, Keir's stomach began to heave and roll with the waves, and no amount of staring at the horizon helped.

"He hasn't stopped vomiting yet. I fear he's in his bed for the duration."

"I will not stay in my bed a moment ... longer." Keir staggered across the deck, his face as pale as the Iskalt snows, his dark hair hanging in limp curls around his face. "I just need to walk around a bit." He sucked in a breath and let out a strangled groan.

"He's going to blow." Gulliver moved them aside, turning Keir toward the ship railing. "Best get it out."

Keir lunged for the portside, emptying the meager contents of his stomach over the railing. Tierney wanted to go to him, but the captain had warned them all to keep to the center of the ship when on deck.

"Your Majesty." A sailor approached him with eyes full of sympathy. "You'll feel better if you stay below deck with a cup of tea and a biscuit or two. Keep something in your stomach and in a day or so, you'll be right as rain." He clapped Keir on the back and went about his duties.

They all had duties to see to. Gulliver was quite good at climbing up into the rigging to help handle the sails and cables. Tierney didn't like the thought of him up there when the seas were so unpredictable, but they all had to pull their weight onboard.

Tierney was responsible for running messages from the captain to the crew, and she helped mend the sails when needed.

Bronagh handled the cleaning below deck and filled in wherever an extra pair of hands was needed. And Veren was assisting the captain with navigation and keeping watch with the other sailors.

Keir wasn't up to helping anyone yet.

Tierney let out a breath when Keir finally backed away from the railing. She didn't like seeing him so close to the edge when he wasn't at his strongest.

"I'm not going to fall overboard if that's why your face looks like that." Keir wiped his mouth with the back of his hand.

"I wish there was something to help you with the seasickness." Tierney reached out a hand to keep him steady.

"I'm afraid nothing will help except maybe a knife to the gut." He closed his eyes and leaned into her. "I pray the Iskalt shores are closer than we think."

"I'm on duty soon." Gulliver gave Tierney a worried look. "We should get him back inside."

"I'll make my way below deck in a moment." Keir opened his eyes, lifting them to the heavens.

"Just be careful. Both of you." Gulliver left them for his short morning shift among the rigging.

"I've never seen such a strange sky." Keir took in another deep breath, a hint of color returning to his cheeks.

"The air is thick, and the salt burns your lungs." Tierney looked up into the angry green clouds churning overhead. "It's an eerie sight." She gave a shiver that had nothing to do with the chill in the air.

"It's better here at the center of the ship." Keir rested back against a stack of barrels containing a good portion of their fresh water. "I can almost feel normal right here."

The ship dipped over a big wave, and Keir groaned. "That didn't last long."

"Your color is fading again." Tierney took him by the arm. "Let's get you back down to your room. You need a cup of strong hot ginger root tea. It will help ease the nausea."

"I don't like your ginger root." Keir scowled, putting some of his weight on her as they made their way across the deck.

"Have you tried the pressure points I told you about?"

"What I need is a totem with magic I can use to find my equilibrium."

"Stubborn man." Tierney helped him move down the steep steps into the berth he shared with Veren and Gulliver. Both were working their shifts with the crew. "It will be nice and quiet in your room. Maybe you can finally get some rest."

"I don't want to rest. I want to do my part."

"Well, get some rest and give your body time to adjust, and maybe you can." She shoved through the narrow door into the larger room. "Sit." She pushed him down onto the edge of the bed. "Press here." She lifted his left hand and showed him how to press down on his wrist in just the right spot to relieve nausea. "Do that until I get back with your tea."

"Fine." He sat sulking.

Tierney pulled her woolen shawl close around her shoulders as she made her way to the galley, where the cook kept a pot of boiling water on when he was able. Tea was the one thing they had plenty of. It warmed the body and filled the belly.

"How's his Majesty this morning?" Darby shuffled around his small galley kitchen, stirring a pot of porridge and reaching for a wooden mug from his cabinet.

"Still struggling with nausea." Tierney pulled down the tin of freshly grated ginger root mixed with shaved citrus rind and a dried flower she couldn't identify. It smelled wonderful. Mild and calming.

"Make him drink this tea." Darby filled the mug with hot water. "And give him these to gnaw on." He set a tin of dry biscuits on a tray. "If he can keep them down, we'll get him some porridge with a bit of honey."

"Thank you." Tierney lifted the tray.

"Well, now, wait just a minute." He pulled down another mug. "You look like you could use a good cuppa too." He gathered several tins and added a pinch from each to a linen tea bag. "Good strong black tea with some lavender and lemon verbena and a smidge of honey. That will calm you right up and give you some energy for the rest of the day." He poured hot water over the little bag of tea leaves. "And a spot of porridge for you too. We all need to eat to keep our strength on this voyage." He winked.

The weathered old man set her to rights and sent her on her way.

She balanced the tray as she made her way carefully to Keir's room. He lay back on his bed, his fingers still pressed to his wrist, fast asleep.

She set the food on the bedside table, and his eyes snapped open. "I don't know what kind of witchery this is," he lifted his hands, "but it's working."

"I asked around and the old sailors swear by it." Tierney pressed the mug of tea into his hands. "Drink that and try to eat at least two of these." She opened the tin of unappetizing lumps that looked more like rocks than any biscuit she'd ever seen.

"Darby says you get to eat porridge if you can keep that down."

Tierney sat in the only chair in the room and stirred her porridge.

Keir scrunched up his nose as she took a bite. "I don't know if I want that."

"It's rather like eating paste. It doesn't taste bad. Though it doesn't taste like anything, really."

"I've had worse." He sipped the tea. Taking a biscuit from the tin, he nibbled on the edge of it. "Way better than the hardtack soldiers eat on the trail."

The ship continued to roll beneath them, but for the moment, Keir seemed to be feeling better.

"I don't know if it's better or worse down here where I can't see the sky." He leaned back against his headboard, gripping the warm mug between his hands.

"It won't be long before we reach the maelstrom, and then we won't have time to think about our stomachs."

"How long do you think it will take to go around it?"

Tierney shrugged. "I hope it's quick and the swift currents take us where we want to go."

"Tell me about Iskalt. What will we see first?"

She smiled, sitting back and putting her feet up on the edge of his bed. "The first things you'll see are the ice floes. They will look like land, at first, from a distance. Then, as we approach, we'll see patches of snow-covered ice floating on the sea. Once we see that, it won't be long until we reach the fjords."

"I don't know what that is." Keir smiled. "But it sounds wonderfully exotic."

"Exotic is not the right word for Iskalt." Tierney laughed. "The fjords are these massive sheer cliffs that extend out into the sea like the fingers of a giant's hands. The sea flows between them like rivers heading inland."

"And do people live on these fjords?"

"No. It's far too cold, and there isn't much land that isn't steep and rocky and covered in ice. But it's so beautiful with the afternoon sun glinting against the cliffs."

Her heart ached with longing for her homeland. She would never again take it for granted. She might never reach home, but she would give anything for one last sight of Iskalt before she died trying to reach it.

"And after we see these fjords, what comes next?" Keir reached for another biscuit, breaking it apart to eat small bites.

"I don't know, actually. I believe we will reach the far eastern shores of Iskalt first. The Northeastern Vatlands should be there, though I've never seen them myself."

"What is a vatland?"

Tierney sipped her soothing tea, grateful to Darby for the aromatic blend. "It's what we call places like the fire plains. They're rural areas between the kingdoms where the terrain is harsh and the climate intolerable. In Iskalt, we have the Northern Vatlands to the west separating Iskalt from Myrkur. It's a rough journey through the wild mountain terrain there, but there is one mountain pass we use most frequently to reach the shores of Loch Villandi. The Northeastern Vatlands are also a mountain range, but they're impossible to navigate. The far reaches of eastern Iskalt are wild and uninhabited. From Lake Fryst to the Northeastern Vatlands, it is nothing but frozen tundra. Cold beyond the likes of anything you can imagine. Along the edge of the tundra, the vast mountain range of the vatlands rises to impossible heights. It is said the mountains are so high one can't even breathe the air at the top. Beyond those mountains, there is nothing. Nothing but the maelstrom and Lenya."

"And where do you think we will make landfall?" Keir leaned forward, hanging on her every word, his seasickness all but forgotten.

"I hope we will make it to the other side of the storm to find the seas that flow between Iskalt and Eldur. One side borders the fire plains and the other the impenetrable mountains of the Northeastern Vatlands. If we can sail through those waters, then we are home free. We can then make our way across land."

"We are pinning everything on this voyage. I hope you are right about what we can expect on the other side."

"It's a gamble for sure, but it's all we had left."

Keri nodded. "What kind of reception will we receive when we arrive?"

Tierney couldn't help the smile that spread across her face. "When we reach Iskalt, I'll arrange for a messenger to travel ahead to give my parents the news of our arrival. I imagine they will ride out to meet us. Mother will be beside herself after all these months. She won't be able to sit still. Neither will Father for that matter. Then, they'll ride the rest of the way home with us and there will be chaos when my brothers and sisters realize I'm home.

"Father will want to hear every last detail of what happened ... twice. He will have many questions for you and Bronagh. It might feel like he's interrogating you, but he means well. He'll be on edge when he realizes he's hosting two unknown monarchs from kingdoms he's never heard of."

"Your father sounds ... stern."

"He is. They call him the ice king for a reason, but he's very sweet and loving to those who know him best."

"What will he think of me?" Keir drained the last of his tea and eased back onto his bed.

"He will wait to form an opinion of you until after he's questioned you. He'll want to know all about Vondur and Grima."

"You must have had a terrible time with your suitors and such a protective father."

"Oh, you have no idea." Tierney laughed. "When I was fourteen, I went with Father to one of his noble's estates. We were there to tour their land and discuss a potential contract between the crown and the duke who lived there. They produced the finest leather and furs in all of Iskalt. The duke's son was just a year or two younger than me. He was a brat." Her face fell. "It was hard for me then, before I came into the full use of my magic. I was the Iskalt heir, but I had Fargelsian magic. Others my age had no magic to speak of. Not until they were older. I hardly remember a time when I didn't have magic thrumming through my veins." Her fingertips rubbed together.

"Other children thought me strange. The duke's son made fun of me. I can't even remember what he said, but my father heard it. I ran to my rooms in tears. Father came to find me and told me I was perfect just the way I was. I dried my eyes, and we returned to the main hall for the evening meal.

"The duke was horrified and insisted he would punish his son for his insolence, but Father told him he would handle the punishment. He made the boy approach each nobleman in attendance that night—my father right there beside him the whole time—and confess to what he had done. He had to ask each nobleman to absolve him for his transgressions, and at the end of the night, my father made him publicly apologize to me. I've never seen him since." Tierney shook her head with a frown. "It is odd that he wasn't on Father's list of suitors."

She sat forward suddenly and laughed. "Oh my goodness! I've never seen that boy at court. Ever." She smacked a palm over her face. "My father banned him from court that day. I don't know why I never thought of it before. He never said a word to me about it, but it's something he would do."

"You are not making me eager to meet your father." Keir yawned, his eyes drooping with fatigue. "Maybe I should ingratiate myself to your mother instead."

"She's a tough one too. But she will like you." Tierney sat on the side of the bed, tucking the blankets around Keir. "You should get some rest while you can."

The ship gave another heave, and Tierney held onto the bedpost with an iron grip. A gust of wind rushed through the lower deck, snuffing out the candles in the room, leaving them in the darkness of the eerie day under the cold green skies.

Keir was fast asleep.

Her hand froze, hovering just over the dim crystal he wore around his neck.

It felt different. She couldn't resist touching it, running a pale finger over the smooth surface. The magic flickered inside the crystal. Just a flutter, gentle like the touch of a feather, but it was there. And it was different. There was not enough power left inside the crystal to be useful, but she could still feel it deep within the totem.

Keir said it was useless. He felt nothing from the empty vessel. The magic of Lenya was a strange thing Tierney wasn't sure she would ever understand.

But how might the two types of magic interact? They were vastly different sources of power, and she wondered if they would come together to entwine, or if they would repel each other.

Tia.

A bolt of energy shot through her, and she leaped to her feet, running down the hall and up the steps into a torrential downpour. "Toby!" she screamed into the wind. "I'm coming!" She clutched a hand over the heart thumping in her chest. She could feel him. It was faint, but it was there. Her brother, her twin, was still right there with her. And he knew she was trying to find her way home.

CHAPTER SEVEN
KEIR

If Keir had to stay down here breathing this foul air for one moment longer, he was going to march right up those stairs and jump off the side of the ship, hoping to swim all the way to Iskalt.

Who would willingly subject themselves to a ship's constant turmoil when they didn't have a kingdom to save?

"Keir." Imogen rushed toward him as soon as she saw him in the hall. "Are you sure you should be out of bed?"

With such cramped quarters, those on the ship had gotten to know each other quite well, and all formality had flown right over the side of the wretched vessel. Even Bronagh's soldiers had taken to calling her by her given name. It was as if, out here, they were all equals.

"I'm fine, just ..." He drew in a struggling breath. "Need sky." To see it, to smell it. The rains had finally stopped, the drumming against his skull coming to a blissful halt.

Imogen pursed her lips. "Tia was clear. You aren't allowed to leave your quarters."

Of course she'd given that command. She was the most stubborn, irritating, capable, beautiful fae he'd ever known. Wow, the sickness had addled his brain. "Tia is not your king."

Imogen crossed her arms, her young face twisting into a

smirk. "And neither are you. I am Grimian. I recognize no king of Vondur."

Keir let out a groan. "Are you going to help me or watch as I try to climb those steps, tumble back down, and break my neck?"

She cast a dubious glance from him to the steps before sighing. "Fine. But if Tia asks, you threatened me."

His lips twitched. The girl was scared of Tierney. He knew the feeling.

Imogen ushered him toward the stairs, one arm around his waist. "I hope you don't mind me saying, Keir, but you reek."

"You don't exactly smell pleasant yourself." They'd all been stuck on this boat for days, sweating in the damp, muggy air. It made him long for the cold of the Grima mountains or the ice he knew was coming for them in Iskalt.

At the top of the stairs, Imogen opened the door and blessed sunlight poured in, a welcome change from the past few dark and stormy days. Keir gulped fresh air, his feet stumbling as Imogen released him.

"Imogen," Captain Michel called. "I need you up fixing the sails."

Not wanting to slow down as they approached the maelstrom, they hadn't lowered the sails for repairs. It was only during the worst of the storms they'd drawn them in. But now, to fix any damage caused by the howling winds, it meant climbing into the highest reaches.

Keir's gaze followed Imogen as she made her way up the ropes, her agility astounding.

"She's incredible, isn't she?" Bronagh asked from beside him.

The two royals hadn't spoken much since boarding the ship. The truce still sat uneasily between them, the trust fragile.

Their entire lives, they'd been taught to hate each other, to only view the other as an enemy to be destroyed.

"When did the storm end?" Keir asked, still not looking at her.

"In the night. It was the strangest thing. The storm raged over the seas. I was watching it with Tierney from a doorway. And then, suddenly, it stopped."

"Like someone had turned off a switch." Tierney joined them, her eyes roving the calm waters before them. When Keir and Bronagh shot each other confused looks, Tierney groaned. "Oh, for magic's sake. A switch is how the humans turn electricity on and off."

"Electricity ..." Keir never understood what she was talking about, but her knowledge of the human world always intrigued him.

She rolled her eyes. "They don't use torches and candles and oil lamps for light. It's this ... okay, let's just say it's like magic. Imagine you had a glass ball and you put a crystal in it and told the crystal to provide light to read a boring document or something. Then, the light shone through that glass."

Bronagh clasped her hands together. "But why do we need the glass when the crystal could provide enough light on its own?"

Tierney scrubbed a hand across her face. "You know what, sometimes I just have to remember fae won't believe in human magic unless they see it for themselves."

"I wasn't aware humans had magic." Keir had pictured them as docile creatures without true power.

"Well, they don't call it that. It's technology. Anyway, what I was saying is, the storm just suddenly stopped, and the waters calmed in an instant. It was unnatural."

Keir leaned against the rail, trying to keep himself upright. He was no longer nauseated, but the weakness remained. And that's when he noticed it. It wasn't just the water that barely even showed the ripples in the boat's wake. The sounds ... "Do you hear that?"

Bronagh cocked her head. "Just the wind."

There was enough of a wind to keep them moving, but that was it. "Where are all the birds?" Before the storm, they'd seen many of them.

"We're probably too far from land for birds." Not even Tierney sounded sure of her words.

"That's true," Captain Michel said from behind them. "But it is not the only truth."

The three of them turned, taking in the man who'd gotten them here. He held his cap in his hands, wringing it between his fingers. Nerves flitted across his face.

"Everything okay, Captain?" Tierney glanced at Keir in concern.

She was right. The man looked stressed, almost scared.

Captain Michel looked out at the horizon. "I think we've reached the sea of glass."

When none of them spoke, he explained, "It's called that because all turmoil disappears here, all waves, storms. The water looks smooth as glass, the winds calm, and the sky a bright reflection. It was just a rumor ... I've never heard of anyone making it so far beyond the Vale of Storms."

This was it. They'd gone farther than any other. "And what comes after this sea of glass?" Keir met the man's gaze.

The captain swallowed, his face darkening. "The maelstrom."

Bronagh sucked in a breath. Tierney stilled completely. The sea of glass was the calm before the storm, the last bit of peace any of them might see.

He didn't want to ask his next question, but it couldn't be helped. "When do you expect to reach the maelstrom?"

"We can't know for sure, as our maps and calculations are mere guesses."

"Captain."

"Tomorrow."

Tomorrow. One day. One day left to play cards with the men who'd only just become his friends in a way, one day left to drink tea with common fae he'd never imagined getting to know.

One more day to feel the energy crackling between him and Tierney.

"Captain, may I have a word?" Keir mustered all his strength to stand up straight, to not let his weakness show.

The old man nodded and led Keir farther along the bow of the ship. When they stopped a far enough distance not to be overheard, Keir turned to him. "What do we need to do to secure the ship?"

Captain Michel trained experienced eyes on him. "Young man, my seamen have been preparing for this since the day we left port. Every bit of the hull has been repaired and reinforced. Anything on deck is strapped down to avoid projectiles damaging the mast."

"Or killing us."

"You will weather the maelstrom down below and allow my crew to keep you safe."

"If there are tasks to be done—"

"I will have my fae do them. This mission you embark on cannot be carried out by just any fae. If my kingdom is to have any chance at surviving what is to come, we need you and our queen to reach these foreign shores intact. I don't need you decapitated by a severed rope."

Could a rope really do that?

As if reading his mind, Captain Michel went on, "We're going to have ropes snap in the kinds of winds we've never imagined. If you don't think they'll be flying through the air fast enough to cleave your head right from your body, then you're dumber than you look."

"I get your point." Keir's jaw clenched. "We have to stay safe."

"There is no safe in the maelstrom. If the winds up top don't kill you, you'll probably drown when the hull splits. If luck is on our side, and that's a giant if, a few of us might make it out. But I don't have time to coddle anyone's pride. When I tell you to stay below, you will."

Keir wasn't stupid. He saw the sense in the captain's words, even if he didn't like feeling useless with a battle coming. But this wasn't a battle he could fight with sword and shield.

Only luck.

By the time night descended, an air of apprehension settled over the entire crew and passengers of the Wind Runner. No one knew exactly what kind of monster headed straight for them.

It was too dark down below, too full of worry and fear. One by one, they filed onto the deck and sat with their backs resting against a stack of crates that had been strapped and triple strapped to the deck.

Keir sat in the center with Tierney on his left, their shoulders pressed together. Gulliver sat on her other side, his hand entwined in Tierney's. To his right, Bronagh and Veren leaned on each other, neither seeming to notice the intimacy of the position. Maybe it didn't matter any longer. None of the proprieties, the expectations of society.

Tomorrow would be bigger than any of them, bigger than

the role they played within their kingdoms. Here, under a clear sky full of false hope and distant stars, there were two royal leaders from warring lands, the heir to a fabled kingdom's throne, a nobleman turned soldier, and the adopted son of a prince. They weren't ordinary fae, and this wasn't an ordinary task, yet their titles wouldn't help them now.

This night, everyone was powerless.

They sat silently together, soaking in the remaining moments of stillness.

Gulliver leaned closer to Tierney. "I love you," he whispered. The words tore at Keir's heart because they were so close to everything he hadn't been able to say to the fae in his life, everything he wanted to say now.

Tierney's lips curved into a smile, the fear leaving her eyes for a beat. "I love you too." She leaned her head on his shoulder. "I'm sorry you're here."

Gulliver smoothed a hand over her hair. "I've told you before it isn't your fault. Whatever happens, never blame yourself. Even if we die tomorrow, I'm glad I ended up in Lenya with you, that you weren't alone."

"Not me," Veren put in. "I could be back in my bed in Iskalt right now."

They all chuckled because if it wasn't for this journey, even Keir knew Veren wouldn't have regretted anything. He barely knew the man, and yet, he'd watched him change, just as Tierney had.

His father used to say suffering made one stronger, but he had it wrong. It wasn't the suffering that made a fae stronger, better. It was the desire to end suffering, to fight for something greater than one's self.

Keir settled his head back against the edge of the wooden crate, but he froze when Tierney jerked up.

"Toby," she said.

Gulliver reached for her. "What's wrong?"

She lurched to her feet. "I can ... I ... Toby? Are you there?" She walked toward the afterdeck.

Gulliver moved to stand, but Keir yanked him back down. "I'll go." He pushed to his feet and followed Tierney to the rail. She looked off into the darkness, her mind in another place. "What happened back there?"

She jumped at the sound of his voice and turned. Moonlight bathed her face, reflecting off her dark irises as she drew in a deep breath. "My brother ... I felt him."

"Felt him?"

"I've told you about how he's connected to my magic. I lost that connection in Lenya. That's why my magic doesn't work. I'm too far away from Toby." She shook her head, her eyes still holding a faraway look as she clenched her fists in frustration. "It's never made any sense. There have been so many times when Toby has gone to the human realm with Father and it never affected my magic. But somehow it seems as though whatever separates Lenya from the Four Kingdoms is much greater ... or more powerful than the veil between the human and fae realms. The closer we sail to Iskalt, the stronger the feeling becomes. It's not all there, but there are moments when I can sense him with me, feel his hand in mine. You probably think I'm losing my mind."

Keir shook his head. He'd seen enough unexplainable things recently that he believed in every possibility. A princess appearing out of the sky from a mythical kingdom. Stagnant fire plains moving and growing like they were alive.

"Your totem," she said. "Do you still have it?"

Keir drew it out from beneath his shirt. "It's useless." Without magic, it had no power, but he'd kept it anyway for the sheer comfort wearing it brought him.

Tierney reached for it, her fingers grazing his chest right

over his heart. The vessel kicked up a notch, reacting to her nearness.

"It's stronger."

"What?"

"The connection with my brother. When I'm near the crystal, I can feel him more intensely. It's like the power inside it touches mine."

"But there is no more power."

"That's not true." How was this possible? "It's just a flicker, not enough for you to draw out, but it's still there. I think you've been wrong all along. No crystal ever completely loses its magic; you just lose the ability to use it."

Studying her for a moment, Keir slipped the leather strap over his head. His chest instantly felt naked without it, somehow more vulnerable. "If it makes you feel closer to your brother, you should wear it."

It might not help her magic, but maybe it could give her some peace if tomorrow happened to be their end.

Tierney took it, tears filling her eyes. "Keir," she whispered. "I can't. It's yours."

He closed her fist around the totem, not wanting her to realize what it meant to him to go into tomorrow without it. Even if it couldn't protect him, it provided him with an inner strength to get through anything. "Yes, you can."

"Thank you." She slipped it over her neck, closing her eyes. "If I never make it back, at least I can sense him with me when it ends." When she opened her eyes, tears spilled over her perfect cheeks. She stepped forward, wrapping her arms around him and burying her face in his chest. "You're not the horrid man you try to appear, Keir Dagnan."

It took him a moment to make himself move, but he wrapped his arms around her, closing his eyes and soaking in her nearness, the way his body thrummed with energy.

He wasn't sure how long they embraced or why neither of them pulled back, but a slight rocking of the boat jostled them apart. Tierney leaned over the side. "It seems we've reached the end of the sea of glass."

The eerie stillness was gone, and the wind picked up. The water underneath the ship undulated slowly, just small waves. By morning, there'd be nothing small about them. This was only the beginning.

Tierney's hand slid into Keir's, her grip tightening. "When we get through this, I'll be almost home."

Home. Her kingdom, not his. Yet, the truth of the last thing he'd done before leaving Lenya sat heavily on his heart. He hadn't yet told Tierney of those final conversations.

"I should have helped you return from the moment my men found you on the battlefield." Instead, he'd tied her up and taken her to his father. "Tierney—"

She turned so quickly her chest bumped his. And then, she kissed him. This wasn't like the kisses back in Vondur, frantic and needy. This time, they were slow, methodical, memorizing every moment. Kissing Tierney had never been about getting something or even giving it; it was about living, about being.

For so long, he'd obeyed orders, done his duty, and failed to consider what life could truly be like. Like a kiss, feather-soft and so calming he could forget the storm coming for them, forget that soon they might be torn apart.

Forget that they'd been trained as royals never expecting choices, true decisions in their lives.

Tierney gripped the hem of his shirt, yanking him closer. The totem she now wore around her neck brushed his chest, sending adrenaline racing through his veins.

By the time Tierney pulled away, they were both breathing heavily.

Keir touched his lips. "What was that for?"

A sad smile tilted the edges of her mouth. "Tonight may be our last, Keir. For once, I didn't want to deny myself what I needed."

"And that was to kiss me?"

She brushed up against him again, her breath whispering over his lips. "If you wish, I can stop."

"Tierney, I could live a thousand lives and never wish for your kiss to end. Even if tomorrow is the end of our world, you broke mine long ago."

That brought a grin to her lips that threatened to stop his heart completely. "Well, my family has always said I'm trouble. Breaking worlds is in my nature."

"Do you ever stop talking?"

"Not when I'm annoying you. It's my job to—"

He swallowed her words in a kiss so bright it stole the stars from the sky. And all at once, that broken world started to look a lot more whole.

"Promise me," he whispered against her lips, desperate to have some kind of hope.

"Anything."

"Promise me you'll still be here to irritate me after tomorrow. That we'll make it through this. No heroics, no added dangers. We stay below and survive the maelstrom."

Tierney didn't answer him as she pressed her face into his shoulder, hiding the knowledge in her eyes. But he knew what they'd say.

She was a hero, someone who would always risk her life and walk right into danger. There was no promise she could make beyond tomorrow that wouldn't be a lie.

Chapter Eight
Keir

She won again. Keir tossed his cards down. "I'm out. I know when I'm beat." He reached for the wineskin at his belt. It was full of water. Staying hydrated seemed to help his seasickness almost as much as Tierney's wrist trick had.

That and the smooth sailing they'd had for most of the day crossing the sea of glass. They'd left the calm waters behind, and the ship rocked gently in the rising swells as they continued on their northeast heading.

"I told you not to let her play." Gulliver shuffled the cards and stuffed them back in the box he'd carved for them. He was a talented fae, and not just because he was a brilliant craftsman. He had a myriad of other skills. Some not exactly above board for the adopted son of a prince.

"I can't help it if I have good luck, boys." Tierney scooped up her winnings—a handful of coppers and a few trinkets she'd collected off them throughout the evening.

"If only her luck would see us through the maelstrom." Veren lifted his own wineskin and drank deeply.

"I'll drink to that." Gulliver reached for Veren's, but

"Right, right." He shoved his hands into his pockets. "But when we get home, I'm nicking the biggest bottle of wine in the Iskalt palace, and you can't stop me." He shot her a glare.

"Steal two, and I'll join you." Tierney grinned. "But I won't be the one to put you to bed when you're too drunk to walk in a straight line."

"It's a date."

"Just think of it, Gullie. A few days from now, we could be at the palace in our old rooms with all of our family and all our things."

"I thought Gullie lived in Myrkur," Bronagh said, leaning back against the crates, where they sat in the fresh air, soaking up their last moments of peace.

"I do, but my father is an O'Shea. He can create portals like Tia is ... supposed to be able to do, but she's rather awful at it." Gulliver shrugged. "I spent a lot of time at the Iskalt palace growing up."

"You have your own rooms there?" Keir asked, astonished. He supposed it was normal in their world for the ward of an Iskalt prince to have the rights of a natural-born son, but it was not so in Vondur. A man like Gulliver would be lucky if his adopted father was able to give him a name, much less a fortune and status.

"Why? Is that weird?" Gulliver shared a look with Tierney. "My best friend is the princess, and she's sort of my ... sister-cousin."

"Wait, she's what?" Bronagh snorted a laugh.

"Was I not supposed to say that?" Gulliver glanced at Tierney, his brow lifting.

"What he means is, his adopted father is actually my natural father. Mine and Toby's, of course. It's a really ... really long story." Tierney laughed. "But a good one with a great ending. If we make it through tomorrow, I'll tell you all about it."

"Is it ... not something your people know?" Keir asked, though Veren seemed to know all about this shocking revelation.

"Oh, everyone knows." Tierney waved a hand as if it was nothing. "Uncle Griff and my mom were married for a time, but she was really in love with my dad. And he's been my true father. We're just alike, though he likes to insist that I'm exactly like my mother."

"Tia's a perfect blend of Loch and Brea." Gulliver smiled. "The only thing she got from Griff is her strawberry blond hair. He has auburn hair and Loch has white-blond hair. She has her mother's face and eyes, so really, she's a bit like all three of them rolled into one troublesome package."

"And it worked out well for Gullie to get a father all to himself." Tierney leaned against him. "At least until Griff married Aunt Riona and they had Gullie's little sisters."

"I miss the little beasts, flying around like a couple of winged pests." Gulliver shook his head.

"Your sisters ... have wings?" Bronagh asked, a note of uncertainty in her voice.

"Their mom's Dark Fae like me. A slyph—a rare one too. They both inherited her wings and tattoos."

"I would like to visit your land one day, Gullie." Keir clapped him on the back. "It sounds fascinating."

"Myrkur isn't much, but it's got one thing going for it Lenya does not." Gulliver stretched his legs out in front of him. "No bloody fire plains."

"I'll drink to that." Keir threw his head back and laughed. "We'll raise a glass of this fancy Iskalt wine I keep hearing so much about and toast to the death of the fire plains."

"Here, here." Veren laughed. "I never thought I would miss

the snow and ice of Iskalt, but if I never feel the heat of the burning lands again, it will be too soon."

For a brief moment, they were all smiles. Just a group of friends who had nothing in common but the circumstance that had brought them together. Keir had never seen anything more beautiful than Tierney's face under the light of the stars as she laughed and joked with Gulliver about his sisters. Keir joined in their laughter at the look on Bronagh's face when Veren described what ogres were. He wasn't so sure he believed there were actual sentient creatures that looked more like talking, mossy boulders than fae, but he really hoped they would survive this journey so he could find out for himself.

"It is time, your Majesties." Captain Michel came to break up their gathering. "We've entered the currents of the maelstrom. We will reach the edge of the storm within the hour, and we'll be in the thick of it by dawn. Best get below deck now."

"The wind will pick up soon." Imogen bounced along the ship railing, peering into the darkness like she could already see the great maelstrom waiting to devour them. "We'll get our first look at her just before the sun comes up. I bet she's a magnificent sight."

Keir wished he could look at what they faced the way Imogen did. Like it was a great adventure just waiting around the corner, and not the cause of their imminent deaths.

Bronagh was the first to her feet. "May the magic be with you and your crew, Captain." She pulled him into an awkward hug. The weathered old man flushed with pleasure, patting her shoulder gently. "It has been my greatest honor to serve you, your Majesty." He stooped into a courtly bow.

"May this be the first of many ways you will serve the people of Lenya." Bronagh squeezed his hand and made her way below deck with Veren.

"I am happy to help if you need an extra pair of hands and

a mighty quick tail." Gulliver stood before the captain. "I know your crew is all seasoned sailors, but if you need me, I'll come."

"Thank you, Lord Gulliver. You're a fine lad and a good sailor." The captain clapped him on the shoulder. "But I think your princess is going to need you more."

Gulliver nodded, taking Tierney's hand.

"You have no idea, Captain Michel, what it means that you were willing to make this journey with us." Tierney choked back tears. "Please don't die." She flung her arms around the old captain, giving him a fierce hug before she turned and ran from the upper deck with Gulliver on her heels.

"Captain." Keir nodded. "The fate of all of Lenya rests in your capable hands, sir. All of our families are counting on this voyage to reach its destination."

Michel nodded, his hands shaking as he reached to wipe the beads of sweat from his brow. "I will do my best, your Majesty." He gave a proper bow, something no Grimian would ever give a Vondurian royal.

"You have my gratitude and my deepest respect, sir." Keir returned the bow. "May the winds be in our favor this day." He turned and left the old captain standing alone on deck. It was going to be a very long night ... for all of them.

Keir wished something—or someone—would knock him over the head so it would all be over when he woke up. It didn't take long for the seas to turn violent as they neared the massive storm. And along with the dips and rolling of the ship, Keir's seasickness returned in full force.

They'd all agreed to stay together in the berth Tierney shared with Bronagh. It was the smallest of the cabins, but it rested closer to the center of the ship than the one he shared with Veren and Gulliver. Still, they could hear the roar of the waves, the torrential downpour, and the shouts of the crew. Thunder crashed overhead so loud it drowned everything out for a moment before sound came flooding back in.

Keir pressed the sensitive point on his wrist, begging for the room to stop spinning. There was nothing left in his stomach to heave up, but it didn't seem to know that.

They all sat on the floor between the two small beds. Bronagh and Tierney clutched each other, and Gulliver's tail wound around Tierney's waist, anchoring her to his side. Truth be told, Keir wished he could hold on to her like that.

"How far into it do you think we are?" Veren asked. He'd asked the same question at least a dozen times already.

"The tug of the current is strong." Tierney chewed her bottom lip. "I can feel it in my bones. I think we must be right on the edge of the storm." The ship trembled beneath them, and the crash of thunder sounded like cannon fire, making them all wince.

"And if the boat starts to tilt hard one way or the other, it likely means we've lost control." Bronagh rested her head against the bunk behind her. "Do you think we'll fall into the center of the maelstrom, or will the ship just break apart?"

"Don't dwell on such things, Bron," Veren whispered. "We will be all right." But from the look on Veren's face, he didn't believe his own words.

"Why is it so bloody hot in here?" Gulliver wiped the sweat running down his face. "It must be a thousand degrees."

"We're nearing the fire plains." Tierney's face brightened.

"Why do you look so happy about that?" Bronagh groaned, fanning her face with her hand.

"Not your fire plains. Mine." Tierney beamed. "Don't you see? We're nearing the Four Kingdoms!"

"I hope we are, otherwise we're going to be cooked alive right here in this room." Keir ran a hand through his sweaty hair. The temperature had risen steadily since they sought their safety below deck. It was that putrid kind of hot that couldn't be anything but the fire plains.

Keir pulled his knees toward his chest. He was a soldier. It was unnatural to sit where it was safe, waiting for the storm to pass while others saw to the danger. It went against everything inside him.

"I feel it too." Veren nodded at him. "The maddening uselessness, but there is nothing out there to swing a sword at, Keir."

"Nothing but the wind." He sighed. "I still feel like I'm sitting out the biggest battle of my life."

"It's not our battle to fight. Not today." Veren turned his attention back to Bronagh sitting directly across from him, as if staring at her would keep her safe from the storm raging just beyond the ship's hull. One wrong move and it could break apart, sending them all to the bottom of the sea.

"Drowning is supposed to be a peaceful way to go." Gulliver laid his head on Tierney's shoulder.

"Hush, Gullie. We have to stay positive." Tierney bit down on her thumbnail, worrying it between her teeth.

The ship chose that moment to let loose a groan like the aged beams might splinter and crack any second.

Bronagh cried out as the boat listed sharply to the side, tossing them around the room like they weighed nothing. Keir rolled toward the door, landing on his back as something crashed and the light from the lantern guttered out leaving them in darkness.

"Ouch." Tierney cried. "Gullie your tail—"

The room tilted again, and Keir feared they were about to capsize.

He landed hard on his shoulder, and something soft and warm tumbled on top of him.

"Oh, sorry." Tierney's breath was hot in his face. "Who have I landed on?" she whispered, her hands braced against his chest.

Keir wasn't sure what came over him. Maybe it was the thought of dying, but he needed to taste her lips one more time. He found her mouth in the darkness, her lips soft and inviting against his.

"Oh." Tierney pulled back for a moment. "Keir," she breathed his name, and her lips claimed his again. "I think we must be dying." A salty tear splashed his cheek.

"Just a bit of a rough patch." Keir wiped the tears from her face. "We'll see it through."

"Well, the lantern's useless." Gulliver's tail made a swishing sound. "Everyone okay?"

"Fine." Bronagh sounded breathless as she sat up.

"Felt like we nearly lost it there for a minute." Veren sounded a bit breathless himself, and Keir wasn't so sure it was from the circumstances.

"We must be nearly through." Tierney sat beside Keir where they had landed near the door. She crept closer to him, and he wrapped his arm around her. If they tumbled again, he would be ready.

"Tia, you okay?" Gulliver sank down beside them. "I lost you." He groped for her hand in the darkness.

Keir lifted his hand from Tierney's shoulders as Gulliver's tail wrapped around her again. "I'll keep a better hold on you next time."

"I'm okay, Gullie." She tucked herself against Keir, grasping her best friend's hand. "We're all okay." She rocked side to side slowly, muttering to herself.

Just as Keir's heart finally found a regular rhythm again,

cries rang out along the deck and the ship began to groan and creak loudly. Tierney grasped his arm, her grip like a vise.

"Toby," she whimpered, clutching the totem Keir had given her. "I'm not going to make it home."

Keir gripped her on one side as Gulliver held her tightly on the other.

"You tell him we're going to be fine, Tia." Gulliver's voice was firm. "We will get through this."

"Does it feel cold to anyone else?" Bronagh asked. "Or am I in shock?"

"It's cold." Tierney shivered. "That can't be a natural shift in temperature."

"Are we on the other side?" Gulliver asked. "It almost feels like Iskalt cold."

"How can it be hotter than an inferno one moment and cold as ice the next?" Veren's voice shook.

Even Keir felt it. The sweat from earlier had soaked his clothes, and now his back was like a sheet of ice. He couldn't imagine what it must be like on deck.

The wind howled, and the ship trembled. Keir resisted the urge to fling open the door and run up the steps to the open deck to demand a progress report.

Really, he just wanted to see the stars one last time. To meet his death head-on rather than cowering below deck, waiting for death to find him.

A loud snap echoed in the silence, and the ship roiled.

Ice cold water flooded into the room. Tierney and Bronagh shrieked as they all scrambled to move away from the rising water.

"We're sinking!" Veren shouted. "We have to do something, Keir."

Clutching for the totem he always wore at his neck, he cursed himself when it wasn't there.

"We've failed everyone." Bronagh sobbed, turning to Veren for comfort.

The water flooded in quickly.

Another great shudder ran through the ship, and the hull split right before their eyes. Water rushed into the room just as lightning streaked across the strip of sky he could now see past splintered wood.

It seemed he would get to see the stars one last time after all.

Veren shoved Bronagh behind him, his eyes wild with fright and indecision. There was nothing they could do. The sea would have them soon.

The gap in the hull widened.

"Toby!" Tierney screamed as chunks of ice and snow streamed into the room. Keir could see more heading their way. Larger chunks of ice. Tierney had mentioned them before. The icy floes. The first signs of Iskalt.

"Tia." Keir slipped, nearly losing his grip on her. "I'm sorry, Tia. I'm so sorry for everything." But she didn't hear him. She was somewhere else, trying to reach her twin in her last moments.

Keir positioned her behind him. "Keep your grip on her, Gullie." He blocked them with his body and held onto the carved post of the bed, bracing himself for the inevitable. Tierney's fingers clawed at his arm, searching for a hand. He gripped hers, giving it a reassuring squeeze.

A massive wave crashed through the gap in the hull, bathing them in icy seawater. Something cold and hard crashed into Keir's head, and his grip slipped. The current pulled him toward the open sea. His head throbbed, and his stomach churned.

"Keir!" Tierney screamed. Her hand slid out of his.

The ship tilted at a sharp angle, and Keir stared into the maw of the maelstrom.

He caught sight of Tierney before he was swept overboard. Her eyes lit with fire and ice. Something warm and familiar shot right through him, but the waves crashed over his head and darkness took him.

CHAPTER NINE
TIERNEY

It started with a bone deep chill that soaked into Tierney's skin. It gave way to a scorching heat that flooded her veins.

And then, she felt him again, seeking, searching. Toby knew she was here. The cries of her friends faded away, and all she could feel was power, pure and familiar.

Just off the barren shores of Iskalt, Tierney's magic had returned.

The blinding pain snaking up her leg shocked her back to the present, to the chaos erupting all around her. Bronagh and Gulliver clutched each other as they clung to the bed that had started to shift, groaning as it moved toward the gaping hole in the side of the ship.

Veren held onto the wall as water poured into the room, shouting into the dark abyss. It took Tierney a moment to realize what he was looking for. Keir was gone, swept away with the raging sea.

The door splintered inward as another rush of water entered from the hallway moments before Imogen ran in. "Is everyone okay?" she yelled above the roaring of the storm.

Tierney didn't have an answer. She was frozen in place, her magic taking hold of her, warming her, controlling her. *Save yourself*, it seemed to whisper. She couldn't save everyone. Not Keir. Not Gulliver or Bron.

"Keir is in the water," Veren hollered.

Panic crossed Imogen's face. "He isn't the only one. We lost most of our sailors when the boat capsized. By the time it righted itself, it was just me and Da. You have to get up top. It isn't safe down here anymore."

Nowhere was safe.

Tierney wrestled frantically with her power, out of practice and weak. She tore its restraints from her limbs, propelling herself into motion. Gulliver yelled after her, but she didn't turn back before diving through the rift and plunging into the icy sea.

Saltwater stung her eyes, but she kept them open, using all her strength to draw power into every corner of her body, warming her limbs in the freezing ocean depths. Keir would have no such protection. She kicked deeper, her lungs crying out for oxygen.

If only her magic had the power to help her breathe.

The darkness of the water stole her sight, forcing Tierney to shoot up, gasping as her head breached the surface. A giant wave headed for her, and she looked up just in time for it to crest over her head, sending her tumbling underwater. For a moment, she didn't know which way was up, and then she saw the moonlight reflecting on the surface.

Swimming for the light, she reached it and caught sight of the ship, broken and sinking. It tilted on its side. The mast had long since snapped off and now floated among the waves. Someone clung to it, and she didn't know if it was one of the sailors or the man she searched desperately for.

Maybe it didn't matter. She could save someone.

Her arms ached but she forced them to cut through the water as waves tried to drag her under. Tierney had never been a strong swimmer, but this time, she had her magic to bolster her, lending her the kind of will she hadn't felt in months.

The thought that Toby was close enough for her magic to return kept her going, kept her from giving in to the pain and exhaustion eager to drag her into the depths. She refused to stop now.

Tierney reached the floating mast. It had broken in half, and the longer of the two pieces blocked her from her destination. She hauled herself over it on her belly and flopped back into the water.

Keir didn't move from where his body draped across the second wooden pole, his face in the water.

No, he had to be okay.

Tierney lifted his face, placing one hand on each cheek and instructing her magic to warm him. Color returned to his skin almost instantly, but still, he didn't move. She had to get him back to the ship. It might be sinking, but it was the only choice.

Drawing in a fortifying breath, Tierney slid him from the mast, doing her best to keep his head above water.

"I know you're stronger than this," she screamed, the words meant for the power inside her that still seemed hesitant to heed her command. "Please help me!" It had been so long since she used magic she'd forgotten how difficult she'd once found it to control.

But it wasn't working. Tierney treaded water, sinking lower and lower as her legs tired and her sodden clothes weighed her down. Keir slipped from her grasp, but she reached down and pulled him up again, not willing to concede the futility of it all.

"We are not going to die out here," she said, knowing Keir couldn't hear her. "I promise you that." Before, she'd refused to make promises, but right now, it was all she had. That and a magic with untold power that wouldn't cooperate.

It had to do more than warm her.

A wave dragged her under, and she tightened her hold on Keir, wrapping her arms around his middle.

She broke the surface with a roar. "I am Tierney O'Shea, and we are partners. When I call, you come."

Power flooded her veins, a power that didn't completely belong to her. She felt her brother lending his strength as he'd done so many times as her amplifier.

Someone threw a net over the side of the tilting ship, and then Veren and Gulliver were there, peering out at the sea, their eyes searching. Tierney only had to get to them.

The pain faded from her limbs, the ache disappeared from her lungs, and she shot toward the net with a series of giant kicks, not letting another wave take hold.

Reaching up desperately, her fingers found the thick net, and she didn't wait for them to pull her up. Using her magic for strength, she started to climb, dragging Keir with her.

She reached the halfway point, and the net moved, the boys pulling it in the rest of the way with the help of the few remaining soldiers. Keir's body tumbled through the gap made by a broken rail, and Tierney threw herself onto the deck beside him, her chest heaving.

When Keir still didn't move, she rolled toward him. "Not today, your Majesty." Lifting one hand, she curled her fingers into a fist, bringing it down with force to try to push the water from his lungs.

It didn't work.

The deck pitched, and she slid, her feet finding purchase on a trunk that had wedged itself into the second gap in the rail. Others held on to whatever they could find, but Keir ... his body hit hers like a sack of grain.

"Tia, you still there?" Gulliver yelled.

"Yeah, you okay?" There was no room for fear, not when the world around them had disintegrated into madness.

"As good as a human who's just been hit by one of their metal monsters."

"Cars, Gullie. You should know that by now." She pushed Keir onto his back again.

"Really not the time."

Biting her lip, Tierney searched Keir's face for any sign of life. She couldn't tell the tears from the rain on her face as a new wave crashed over the side of the ship and it righted itself, the bow still sinking lower in the water.

"Keir," she cried, brushing the sopping hair back from his face. "Please wake up." She'd heard stories of her mother saving her father long ago using her magic unknowingly. The power flooded into his heart and jolted his body into healing.

Determined to try, she placed both hands on his chest.

"What are you doing?" Bronagh crawled toward her.

"Whatever I have to." She closed her eyes against the rain and howling wind, against the imminent death and hopelessness. *Toby, I need you.* Searching inside herself, she felt her Iskaltian magic rise, strengthened by the moon. It was soon joined by her brother's presence, which in itself lent her more power.

It flooded down her arms into her hands, and she let it free to snake through Keir, to do what no natural thing could.

In the distance, she heard her friends calling to her, telling her to take hold of something. She felt the boat move beneath her with a resounding crack. And still, she focused.

Nothing.

Keir didn't wake; he didn't move. Even as she pushed water from his lungs, warming him from the inside out, he remained still. Her chest ached where that knowledge lived, and she started to pull back, letting the scene around her rush in.

Gulliver now clung to the rail, his body hanging over the

side as he screamed for help. Imogen had a hold of one of his arms and Veren the other.

The captain continued steering the broken ship, yelling into the wind.

And Bronagh tugged on Tierney's arm. "We're all going to need to jump."

She couldn't be serious. "What?"

"The ship is sinking. We need to get away from it before it pulls us under."

Tierney caught sight of a guard dressed in his golden Grima armor—a bad choice for a storm—as his grip slipped and was lost to the sea.

She scrambled to her feet and ran to help Imogen and Veren pull Gulliver onto the ship.

Peering into the water, she caught sight of a large broken piece of the hull floating atop the waves. Bronagh was right. They had to jump into the icy waters of the fjords and hope they made it to shore before the seas claimed them.

"Captain," she screamed. "We have to go."

He shook his head. "I won't leave my ship."

"Da." Imogen tried to run up to the bridge, but Veren held her back.

"Get her out of here." Captain Michel couldn't meet his daughter's eyes. "Please, majesties. Make the world a safe haven for my daughter."

Tierney looked from the sobbing Imogen to Veren who still held her. Her gaze slid to where Gulliver gasped on his knees beside a comatose Keir. And finally, it landed on Bronagh. They still had a chance to save Lenya, no matter how small. "We will."

Tierney shook off her fears and took actions. "Gulliver, help me with Keir." She couldn't leave him behind. Gulliver pushed wearily to his feet and helped her pull Keir up between them. "Everyone off this ship if you want to live." There was no time to soften her words, not now. Only time for the truth. The captain was right. Now wasn't about saving their own lives, but about salvaging their last chance to bring Lenya back from the brink of destruction.

Veren pulled Imogen to the gap in the rail. She'd stopped fighting him and cast one more desolate look at her father. He lifted a hand toward her, and then Veren pulled her with him as they jumped. Bronagh went next, disappearing over the side.

Tierney and Gulliver dragged Keir to the gap, but as they reached it, the deck tilted and they tumbled off the edge. A scream lodged in her throat seconds before she hit the water.

The blast of cold had her moving quickly to grab hold of Keir. Gulliver swam toward her, his tail working just as hard as his arms and legs. Together, they breached the surface and made their way to the floating side of the hull. The others reached it before them.

A crack rent the air, and they looked back just in time to see the deck split in two as the aft reared up.

"No," Imogen screamed for her father.

Tierney pulled half her body onto the wood. "Grab hold of me." No one moved. She tugged Keir up with her. "Now!" Hands reached for her, clutching her arms, her shoulders. She sent her magic into each of them, keeping them warm as freezing water crashed over their heads.

It was the only way she knew how to give them a chance.

Tierney's eyes fluttered open as she felt solid ground beneath her. The ground was cold, but it was land. The shocking memory of the previous night jolted her awake. She lay on a snow-covered beach, water and chunks of ice rushing in with the tide. Iskalt. It had to be.

And then, she remembered everything. "Keir." Her eyes searched the beach. Gulliver lay pressed against her, her magic keeping him warm. But the others were nowhere to be found.

Boots crunched in the snow, and Tierney shifted to look behind her where Veren walked toward her up the beach. "I was just returning to get you two. I helped the others into the cover of the forest. We have a fire going to keep us warm."

The woods. Tierney surveyed the landscape, her mind reeling with too much information at once. Behind them were dense forests leading to a range of majestic mountains, their peaks unreachable by even the strongest of Iskalt warriors. "We're ..."

"In Iskalt." Veren nodded with a grin. "We made it."

Not all of them. The agony of their losses lanced through her. Keir was gone. Had they lost his body to the sea? She wanted to cry, to give herself a moment to break down, but that wasn't her. Keir wouldn't want her to fall apart now, not when they were so close to saving his kingdom.

"I'm guessing we're not far from the Northeastern Vatlands."

Tierney tried to place them on a map in her mind. Her father had made her learn every inch of Iskalt during her studies. "We need to find a way through the mountains."

"Why don't you wake Gullie and come to the fire. You must be exhausted from keeping us warm all night."

"Is your ..."

He nodded, knowing what she wanted to ask. Veren now had full use of his magic too as long as the moon was in the sky. It was most likely how he'd started the fire.

Tierney pushed herself up onto her aching legs and nudged Gulliver with her foot.

He grumbled and rolled over, his body shaking from the cold without her there to warm him.

"Wake up."

Gulliver groaned as his eyes opened. "What happened?"

"We made it through an unsurvivable storm, lost our ship and way too many fae, but we're here. We're home."

"Home." He said the word like it was foreign to him and got to his feet.

Veren clapped them each on the shoulder. "Come on."

They trudged up the beach, crossing into the canopy of trees, a carpet of pine needles soft beneath their feet. Tierney's entire body ached like she'd just gone five rounds against the prison magic. But no amount of exhaustion could shake the triumph of her homecoming.

The first person she saw was Imogen. She'd curled in on herself near the fire, tears streaking her face. Tierney's heart broke for the girl who'd now lost both parents to tragic circumstances. She leaned down when she reached her. "Your father was a hero." Without him, they'd never have made it.

She didn't respond, didn't move.

Bronagh sat across the fire, her expression sad. They'd survived, but the cost of the journey was high.

And next to her, resting his back against a tree ... Tierney stopped, her breath stuttering in her chest. Keir's eyes were closed, but his chest rose and fell with slow breaths.

"How?" she whispered.

Veren shrugged. "We aren't sure. Maybe it was your magic or simply time. He woke up on the beach, same as us. He wanted me to get you to the fire first, but I knew you could stay warm on your own."

Her steps faltered, and she stared at him, taking in the way his hair stuck up in every direction, the cut on his cheek. He was still beautiful, even if a bit rough. His eyes slid open, latching onto hers.

Gulliver trudged past her to edge closer to the fire, his tail hanging limp and frosty.

Flames flickered in Keir's dark gaze, and she stepped toward him, each movement slow, tentative.

He lifted his chin to track her with his eyes. "I heard you jumped in after me." His voice was harsh, raspy, as if he'd injured some integral part of his throat.

Tierney lifted one corner of her mouth. "Someone had to save you."

He arched a brow. "Do I have to thank someone who speaks with their ego?"

She lowered herself to the ground beside him and nodded. "Yes. You very much have to thank me. And then, you have to do it again."

He tried to lean in, but when she noticed he didn't have the strength, she brushed her lips against his.

"Is that thank you enough?" he whispered.

"Absolutely not." This time, she let the kiss linger. He tasted of saltwater and life. Her forehead rested against his, and she breathed him in, unable to truly believe he was here in front of her. That they'd made it to Iskalt, even if they'd ended up in the far Eastern Vatlands, away from anything resembling civilization.

Veren sat down. "As nauseating as you two are, I think it's time we talk about what happens next."

He was right. They didn't have much time to linger. Tierney's stomach gave a fierce grumble. "We're going to need to find some food."

"That shouldn't be a problem now that we have our magic. Tierney, you and I will need to hunt."

Hunt. Her eyes widened. The mountains. She knew

exactly where they could go. "There's a hunting lodge near Lake Fryst, just beyond the vatlands. My father rarely uses it, but if we can make it there, we can take the time to recover before setting out for the long journey to the palace."

"It's still going to be a tough journey to reach Lake Fryst." Veren looked into the fire for a moment, lost in thought before he finally nodded. "But it's our best chance. None of us are fit for a long journey across the wilds of Iskalt. We need at least a day of rest here before we set out."

Several days on foot with clothes not fit for the Iskalt snows, and their trunks at the bottom of the sea. Just perfect.

At least she had her magic. With that, she was confident she'd get them all home safely to see their families again.

CHAPTER TEN
KEIR

Keir had never known such cold.

He would rather face the maelstrom a thousand times over if it meant he could get out of this frozen mountain pass with its drifting snow he could barely move through and the sheer cliffs that rose so high on either side of the trail they blocked out the sky.

They'd been climbing for days, huddled close to Tierney and Veren to absorb whatever warmth they could give them with their strange magic.

He still couldn't get over how easily magic came to her now. From within. Without the benefit of a totem to harness it. It wasn't natural.

They began their descent that morning, and already they were making much better time than they had on the upward climb.

"We may reach the valley tomorrow." Tierney shivered under the too thin layers of her shawl.

"I like the sound of a valley." Bronagh's teeth chattered.

"Don't get too excited. It's a frozen valley." Gulliver huddled beside her. "Nothing but snow and more snow."

"At least it will be flat." Tierney's eyes flickered with magic in a way Keir found fascinating.

That was a startling development Keir hadn't expected. It was a little unnerving to look into her eyes and see such power shining within their depths. It was astounding that she and Veren could use their magic to keep them all from freezing to death and still have enough energy left over to climb a mountain. Granted, they both slept like the dead whenever they made camp.

"We have to hunt tonight, Veren." Tierney trudged through the snow, her breath puffing out in white clouds. "We need a good meal if we're all going to make it to the hunting lodge in one piece. Do you think we'll reach the forests before nightfall?"

"I will hunt for something, no matter if we reach the forests or not," Veren said. "Then, you can rest."

"I can hunt." Keir kept his eyes on the ground, making sure his frozen foot had solid purchase before taking another labored step through the thigh-deep snow.

"We don't have proper weapons." Veren panted as he helped Bronagh through the snowdrifts. "The only things to hunt in these mountains are the rare small stag or mountain goat you can find down among the forests. They're hard to find and too fast for anything but magic to bring them down."

Imogen nearly toppled over, and Veren tried to catch her, but he was weak from using too much magic in the pre dawn hours. Keir managed to grab her around the waist and settled her back on her feet.

"Thank you." The captain's daughter had grown quiet on their journey through the mountain pass.

"It will be nice to have something more than shriveled berries and nuts for supper." The Grima queen's voice was muffled by the extra layer of fabric she wore draped around her neck and covering her mouth. All three women had created scarves and mittens from scraps of fabric they'd torn from their underthings.

"I will need help with the butchering." Veren sucked in a shallow breath. It was difficult to fill their lungs at this altitude. "I'm not sure I can manage that and the hunting without dropping wherever I stand."

"I'll go with you. We'll haul the kill back to camp between us." Keir rubbed his hands together to keep the blood flowing. "I'll do the butchering while you rest."

"Toby," Tierney muttered.

She said his name often.

"Can you sense where he is?" Gulliver asked.

"Toby?" She turned glassy eyes on Gulliver. "Oh, yes." She shook her head, something she did when returning from wherever she went when she searched for her twin. "We are out of practice. It's strange." She looked up at the cloudy sky that blocked out the sun and left them trembling in their frozen boots.

"He knows I am trying to make my way home, but I don't think he can tell where we are yet. We are still too far apart. It almost feels like ... he's not in Iskalt."

"Of course he's not." Gulliver snorted. He walked with his arms tucked inside his tunic and his tail wrapped around his waist. "Toby is more sensitive than Tia. He's probably known for a while now where we were. My guess is he's either in Eldur, searching for a way across the fire plains, or he's in Gelsi with Brandon, scouring the Aghadoon library for answers. The one thing I know for certain is Toby is ten steps ahead of everyone else, and considering he's the smartest of us all, he probably started heading right for us the moment he sensed our return."

"I think he just said you're thick-headed." Keir wanted to laugh, but it was too cold.

"Oh, no, he's right." Tierney suppressed a giggle. "Toby is the level-headed one with a sensitive spirit. If he'd been with us from the beginning, we would have been home ages ago—even without the benefit of his stronger O'Shea magic."

"I am anxious to meet this brother of yours." Keir measured his steps to Tierney's shorter stride. The day grew late, and she would be weary by the time they made camp. "Does he look like you?"

"He has darker hair and coloring, and he's much taller than me. He's gentle and kind." A beautiful smile played around her lips. She loved her brother very much. "Honestly, he's nothing like me. Or if he is, he is the best parts of me compounded a hundred times."

"Then, I shall like him immensely."

Keir sat by the fire, alone in the growing darkness. He'd never been so tired in his life. Weary to the bone, starving and freezing, he took it upon himself to see to their dinner while the others rested in their makeshift shelter.

They'd reached the shelter of the forests just before nightfall. It was a welcome change, where the snow wasn't quite knee-deep below the canopy of fir trees. Iskalt trees looked a little weak and stunted to Keir, but he was used to the massive ancient forests of Vondur.

While Keir and Veren hunted, the others had gathered bundles of fir branches they propped against a craggy cliff to create a lean-to structure large enough for all six of them. They would sleep easy tonight, gathered together in the warmth of Tierney and Veren's magic.

He could use a little of that right about now. He held his hands out to the fire.

"Smells wonderful." Tierney came to join him. "Is it done yet?"

"I think the strange creature might be ready." He turned the spit over the fire, checking the meat one last time.

"You don't have goats in Lenya?"

"We do, but they are small and annoying. Not much use for anything. This animal is huge in comparison."

"Mountain goats are a bit larger, but I'm hungry enough to eat this poor fella all by myself." Tierney tugged her shawl around her shoulders.

"We'll have to wait for it to cool off a bit."

"Let me handle that." She reached for the spit, pulling the creature from the fire with her bare hands.

"Watch out; it's hot." He lunged after her.

"Magic." She waved her fingertips at him, her eyes swirling.

Keir shook his head with a laugh. "I'll never get used to someone using their magic for trivial things. It seems like such a waste."

"Our magic comes from within. There is no limitation for us except for the time of day—for most, at least. So, I'm going to use mine to block the heat of this scalding hot meat so I can get it in my stomach." She tore off a big piece and passed it from hand to hand for a moment before she held it out to Keir.

"It's ready." She smiled, taking a big piece for herself. She made no hesitations, sinking her teeth into her dinner with a groan of pleasure.

"Yes, dinner is ready." Gulliver came to sit with them, helping himself to the basic fare. "Delicious." He nodded eagerly. "Oh, how I've missed you, dear succulent, juicy meat." He held up his haunch of goat. "Thanks for this, Keir." He turned to Tierney. "And thanks for the dome of heat. This is the first time I've been warm in days."

"I'm just harnessing the heat of the fire so it stays with us longer." Tierney shrugged. "We haven't had a fire big enough to do that with yet."

"Dome of heat?" Keir wasn't sure what that meant, but it had grown a lot warmer since Tierney came to sit with him.

"My magic pulls the heat in close to us, trapping it so we stay warm. If we keep the fire smoldering tonight, I should be able to pull the heat into the lean-to."

"Oh my goodness, it's so warm over here," Bronagh exclaimed as she entered the circle.

The others made their way over one at a time until they all sat around the blazing fire, stuffing their faces in silence.

It was the best thing Keir had ever eaten. Rich and flavorful, the roasted goat warmed his stomach and re-energized him.

"Did you do something extra with your magic?" He took another bite. Something about it seemed off. He'd eaten much of the roasted game on the trail, and it never fortified him quite like this.

"Maybe." Tierney gave him a mischievous smile. "I figured we could all use a little zing in our steps for tomorrow."

"You should conserve your energy. You're pushing yourself too hard."

"My magic?" She grinned, reaching for his hand. "I don't think you realize just how different my magic is from what you're used to in Lenya. I have done far more than keep a few people warm all day and night and make their food taste better. I'll be fine."

"Then, why do you collapse at the end of each day like you can't keep your eyes open?"

"Why?" She looked around at their surroundings. "Did you forget I'm a princess? I don't do hikes through snowy mountain passes. I do horses and sleigh rides with fur blankets and hot drinks. And for the last months, I've lived in a world where it's sweltering hot all the time. I'm just exhausted from all the physical stuff, Keir. My magic doesn't drain me like that, not unless I use way more than this. Please don't worry about me."

Veren came back from a trip into the woods, searching for some sort of plant he thought might grow near here.

"Look what I found!" He held up a fistful of an ugly-looking, shriveled green flower.

"Oh, is that what I think it is?" Tierney's eyes lit up with excitement.

"What is it?" Bronagh asked as Veren set a large nutshell packed with snow on the rocks closest to the fire.

"Mountain jasmine." As the snow melted, he crushed a handful of the leaves and added it to the water to steep.

Cupping his hands around the makeshift teacup, he heated the water with his magic. Taking a sip, he passed it to Bronagh.

"Oh, that smells lovely." She took a sip for herself and passed it to Imogen. "It's sweet and minty."

Veren went to work on the second cup of tea as they finished the first one. It felt good to drink something warm and sweet after days of drinking ice-cold water from melted snow.

"With a good night's rest, we'll be ready for the hike down to the valley in the morning." Tierney's eyes shone brightly in the firelight. "We'll be safe at my father's lodge soon if I don't get us lost. I think the hardest part of our journey is behind us now. Pretty soon, we'll be wrapped up in diplomatic meetings, and we'll have help heading to Lenya quicker than we can blink."

Something about that statement left Keir feeling almost sad. Out here on the trail, they were just a couple of weary travelers. Their needs were basic. Food. Shelter. Water. Fire. Companionship.

Once they reached the lodge, he was no longer just Keir. And she wouldn't be just Tierney. He would be representing Vondur, and Tierney would return to her role as the heir of Iskalt. Nothing would be simple for them anymore.

Keir wasn't sure Tierney knew what a valley was. This frozen wasteland, with its fierce winds and unforgiving, bitter cold, was like no valley he'd ever experienced before.

Nothing stood between them and the elements but Tierney's magical warmth. They made minimal progress across the frozen tundra. Huddled together, they moved slowly through what Keir could only describe as a howling blizzard.

He couldn't see anything but the person to his left and his right. They held hands so they wouldn't lose each other. But the wind made it impossible to speak.

Now and then, Veren brought them to a halt while he figured out which direction to follow. The first night on the open tundra, they had no fire, but Tierney created a bubble of warmth where they could rest without the snowfall and wind. They ate the rest of the roasted goat and slept fitfully before heading out at dawn for more of the same.

They were all running low on strength, and no matter what Tierney claimed, using her magic round the clock was taking its toll on her. If they didn't reach the hunting lodge soon, she was going to collapse.

Keir held onto her hand, her fingertips nearly fused to his in the icy temperatures.

Bronagh struggled to put one foot in front of the other as Veren coaxed her along. And poor Imogen clung to Gulliver's hand, shivering despite all Tierney did to keep them warm.

They were like sitting ducks out in the open like this. Keir wanted to ask if they should be worried about wolves when he heard barking and howling in the distance.

In their exhaustion, the last thing they could handle was a pack of wolves preying on the weak and injured. They wouldn't make it through the night.

Keir vowed he would keep watch all night if he had to. This close to their destination, they couldn't fail now.

"Toby!" Tierney cried, charging through the snow with renewed energy. "I'm here! I'm here!" She sobbed as she tumbled to the ground.

"Tia!" Keir rushed to her side, trying to pull her back to her feet. "We have to keep going." He tugged on her arm but didn't have the strength to pick her up. "Like you said, the hard part is behind us. This is just a walk across a field, right?"

She pointed into the white blur of the blizzard before them. "I'm here!" she cried out again.

Two bundled figures emerged from the snow.

"Who is that?" Was he seeing things?

"It's him." Tierney sank back down to her knees and fell into the snow.

CHAPTER ELEVEN
TIERNEY

S trong arms lifted Tierney out of the snow, and for a moment, she wondered if she was dreaming. She'd imagined this for so long it didn't seem real.

"Dad." Tears froze on her face as her magic slipped, letting the cold permeate her skin.

Lochlan O'Shea stared down at her with glassy eyes and pulled her closer to his chest. "I've got you. I'm here."

"We need to get them to the lodge." Her mom's voice was like a soft blanket settling over her. She ran a hand over Tierney's hair.

"Guys." Toby walked forward. "Stop staring at her and get moving. They're probably waiting anxiously."

They? Who else was here? Tierney couldn't get the words past her lips. If she tried, she'd start sobbing right here in front of all the people she'd just led through the frozen tundra.

"It's just a little farther," her mom said to the others. "Come, we'll do introductions once we reach shelter." She wrapped an arm around Gulliver and leaned in. "We've missed you, kiddo."

Her parents would never stop thinking of her, Toby, and Gulliver as kids, but right now, that knowledge warmed Tierney. They were kids, barely out of their childhood, not ready to traverse wild seas or unknown kingdoms. And yet, they had.

Her father didn't set her down, opting to carry her across deep drifts, bundled close to his snow-dusted coat, held safe in his strong arms. Her father, the man she'd run from. The one who'd tried to force her into a marriage she wasn't ready for. He was also the best man she knew.

He'd been wrong, but her actions weren't exactly the right ones either.

She felt pressure on her hand as a mitten slid over her frozen fingers. Lifting her head, she met Toby's gaze. Her brother, the one who'd led her home. She never wanted to be so far from him again. Not only because it meant going without her magic, but it wasn't until that moment as he walked beside her that she felt whole again.

A sigh of relief rushed through her when the hunting lodge came into view, a white-capped wooden monstrosity set along the rocky shores of Lake Fryst. She would never understand her father's and uncle's love for the cold of the far reaches of Iskalt. If she never traveled this far east again, it would be too soon.

The door of the lodge burst open, and there was Uncle Griff. Aunt Riona rushed out after him, her wings shooting her into the air as she crossed the snow.

Keir startled back with a curse as Bronagh gasped. Imogen just stared, her eyes wide.

Gulliver took off into a half-run, half-stumble. Riona collided with him, lifting him into the air in a hug and turning to reach for Griffin, who'd also started across the snow, though at a much slower pace.

The three of them clung to each other much the same way Tierney wanted to do with her family, but she couldn't make herself move, exhaustion weighing her down.

"Get him inside, Griff," Lochlan barked. "They started to freeze the moment Tia stopped using her magic to warm them."

Griffin scowled at him. "And Brea didn't step in?" He pulled Gulliver protectively closer.

"I'm kind of a mess right now, Griff." Brea sniffed and blubbered as she ushered them all toward the lodge.

Listening to her parents and uncle argue made Tierney smile. Toby caught sight of her and matched the expression. This was their family; this was home. The two brothers loved each other, but sometimes they also wanted to kill each other.

The moment they stepped into the lodge, Lochlan set Tierney down. She wobbled and righted herself before launching into her mom's arms.

Brea sniffled. "My girl," she cried. "I can't believe you're home."

"Mom, you're hogging her." Toby pulled Tierney away, wrapping long arms around her. She buried her face in his chest, finally letting a few sobs break through. Her power thrummed with approval, finally finding its other half. "See what happens when you go off to have a birthday party in the human realm without me," he muttered into her hair.

Tierney laughed, but it sounded more like a sob. "Never again." She looked up, meeting his glassy eyes. "You know it wasn't planned, right? It just sort of happened. I'd never leave you behind."

"Yeah." He squeezed her tighter. "I know." Leading her over to the fire roaring in the giant hearth, Toby sat Tierney down and wrapped her in a thick fur.

For a moment, she'd forgotten it wasn't just the two of them, but then Imogen sat beside her and burrowed under her fur, snuggling into her. "Oh, these are my friends." Tierney looked up at the two foreign royals then at Imogen. "I'll explain later, but for now, know they saved our lives."

"No one saved my life." Veren sat on the floor near the hearth, getting as close to the flames as possible.

Gulliver laughed, the sound musical after so many teeth-chattering days with nothing to smile about. "Except Bron." He gestured to Bronagh, the queen who'd allowed Veren to join her court.

Veren shared a smile with Bronagh but didn't respond.

Keir stood back from the others, watching silently, observing.

Uncle Griff walked out of the kitchen with a tray stacked high with bowls. "Who wants something hot to eat?"

"Oh, definitely me." Gulliver reached for a bowl. "What did you make, Dad?"

"What else would he make?" Her uncle wasn't exactly the best cook in the world, but there was one dish he excelled at, one she'd never imagined she'd eat again. "At least, I hope he didn't try anything else."

"Har har." Griffin rolled his eyes. "Yes, it's turkey soup."

"Turkey?" Keir stepped forward. "We have such an animal, but they'd never survive the cold of this place."

Veren dug into his soup with a sigh. "Are there any biscuits?"

"Yes." Riona carried out a plate. "And don't worry, Tia, I made these." She shot her a wink.

Tierney caught Keir's eye. "The wild northern turkeys adapt to their climate. They aren't plentiful here, but they are sometimes seen. My mother is the only one in the family who can ever catch them."

"Not true," her father said.

"Very true." Her mother laughed. "Though, I don't like to harm anything. I rarely go hunting, but if my hubby begs, I'll trap something for him. Just to get him to be quiet." She patted Lochlan's cheek.

"Hubby?" Imogen looked up at Tierney, confused.

"Our queen," Veren started, his mouth full, "was raised human. She says the oddest things."

Imogen's eyes went wide.

Tierney accepted a bowl of soup, not letting it cool or even using her power to do it before digging in. Soft noodles, thick chunks of turkey. It was heaven. Someone handed her a biscuit, and she dipped it in, moaning when she bit off the softened part. There was nothing better.

She watched Keir accept a bowl and sit with supreme satisfaction. He'd barely looked at her since her family found them, but that wasn't her concern at the moment. Not when Toby wedged in between her and the arm of the settee.

"Mom, stop staring at me." While Keir wouldn't look at her, her mother hadn't stopped. "You're being a creep."

Her mother laughed, her eyes tearing up again. "It's just ... I'd started to think I'd never be able to creep you out again."

She was so weird, but a weird Tierney hadn't wanted to live the rest of her life without. Tears gathered in her eyes once more, spilling down her cheeks. She'd thought none of these fae would ever stand before her again, would ever make her cry or laugh so hard it hurt.

Once she finished her soup, Griffin took her bowl, and she leaned her head on Toby's shoulder. "I'm surprised it's just you guys." The rest of her siblings would have clamored to come, no matter how young they were. Then, there were Uncle Myles and Aunt Neeve, Alona and Finn, Hector, the Myrkurian king who acted like another uncle, and every single one of her cousins.

"Trust me, it was a hard fight to get them all to back off. We didn't want to overwhelm you. Plus, we were going through a portal and didn't think bringing an army of fae to the human world was the best idea."

The mention of a portal made Tierney's insides clench, her stomach curdling.

Toby, reading her as always, took her hand. "Don't worry, we aren't making you travel home that way. We brought a sled and dogs."

Her face brightened. She'd only visited Lake Fryst a few times but she'd never had the opportunity to travel by dogsled. It wasn't needed when the O'Shea's had portals. Other Iskaltians used them to traverse the tundra all the time.

The chatter continued as the others finished eating, not touching on anything important. Tierney didn't tell her parents who Keir and Bronagh were, not yet. That time would come.

No one asked about Siobhan, and she knew they probably assumed something happened to her if she wasn't here with them. How would Tierney tell them she'd never found her friend? How would she face Siobhan's father?

"Okay," her mother said, sitting on the other side of Imogen. "It's time we learn who your friends are, Tierney."

Tierney wasn't ready for the truth. For them to know there was yet another kingdom to save, that the fire plains could endanger Eldur and eventually Iskalt.

So, she went with a version of the truth. "This is Imogen." She hugged the young girl to her side. "The bravest sailor I've ever met. Her father was the captain of the ship that got us here."

Her mother was astute enough not to ask what happened to him. "Well, Imogen, it is a pleasure to meet such a brave sea woman. I, myself, am quite accomplished on the water."

Tierney rolled her eyes. "You went on a ship once, Mom. And that was like a hundred years ago."

Her mother gave her a playful scowl. "It's nice to have you back, Tia, if only so none of us can have our egos inflate too large."

Tierney stuck out her tongue before continuing. "That's Bronagh. She's ... a good friend." She sent Bronagh a smile.

A laugh bubbled out of her when she caught her father scowling at Keir but not letting anyone see. "That's Keir Dagnan. He's ..." She didn't know what he was. "A good man."

Lochlan stood and extended a hand. "Thank you for bringing my daughter home safely."

Tierney met her mom's eyes, and they both rolled them simultaneously. Her dad was so predictable. Women fought in his army, yet when it came to his daughters, he was a big old fogey.

"Uh, Dad." Toby laughed. "Pretty sure Tierney didn't need anyone to get her here. Seriously, you're so dense."

Lochlan let go of Keir's hand and looked from his daughter to his wife. "I didn't mean ... sometimes, you O'Shea women ..." He shook his head.

To Tierney's surprise, Keir spoke up. "In my kingdom, our customs do not favor women. But your daughter opened my eyes to how wrong we have been, and how capable women truly are. She didn't need me to save her, sir. She saved all of us."

Tierney's cheeks warmed as she waited for her father to correct Keir. The king wasn't a sir, but Keir was also a king and wouldn't bow as her father probably expected.

Yet, to her surprise, her father let it go and looked at her with pride in his eyes instead.

Veren had inched closer to the fire, looking into the flickering flames. "Just so you know, your Majesty, I'm not marrying your daughter."

Tierney choked on a laugh. Keir sent Veren a dark glare.

Veren continued, "I thought we should get that cleared up first thing. I've spent enough time with her recently, and I'm not going to live with her for the rest of my life."

Toby and Tierney both burst out laughing.

"As if I'd marry you." Tierney shook her head, just glad to be home.

They weren't traveling home by portal. That news had been more welcome than any other. Griffin and Riona would go on ahead while the others stayed at the lodge for a day to recuperate. Her father argued they should wait longer so everyone regained their strength, but Tierney knew they didn't have time to wait when the people of Lenya were counting on them. Who knew how far the fire plains had expanded in their absence? Were Eavha and Declan okay?

They were leaving in only a few hours, but Tierney couldn't sleep. She sat in the sitting room alone in front of the fire, staring into it and remembering everyone left behind. She pulled the fur blanket up to her chin, her magic resting peacefully inside her.

Footsteps sounded on the wooden floor, and she looked up to find Toby approaching her. "Couldn't sleep?" he asked.

She shook her head.

"Me neither." He sat on the floor in front of the hearth, looking up at her. "My mind just wouldn't stop whirring, thinking about the fact that you're finally home."

"Aren't I usually the one who overthinks everything?"

A wry smile spread across his face. "Guess I needed to make up for your absence. I knew where you were. All this time, I've known you were across the fire plains, and I couldn't get to you. We're supposed to save each other, and you were out of my reach."

Tierney slid to the floor and pulled the blanket around

them both. "I was so scared without you." She'd tried to hide it, even from herself. A beat passed between them. "I didn't have my magic."

His eyes snapped to hers. "What?"

"There is something about the fire plains that kept us from our magic, but it was more for me. I was too far from Iskalt, from you. I could feel my magic just under the surface, but it couldn't come when I called. I couldn't feel you."

"I'm sorry you went through that." Toby had never had magic except for the connection between them that amplified her power. That and the portal magic he gained through their O'Shea heritage.

"Is that how you always feel? Powerless? Helpless? Like there's something inside you, some strength that you can't bring to the surface?"

"Not really." He shrugged. "But I've never known what it is to have power other than opening portals. This ... emptiness is the only thing I've ever felt."

Toby leaned his head against hers as they faced the flames.

"What was it like?" Toby asked. "Across the fire planes."

"Terrifying." It was the first word that came to mind. "At first, all I could think about was returning home. We were all separated coming out of the portal, and I didn't know where the others were. I was so alone and without magic."

He squeezed her tighter to his side.

"But then ... it got better. I found Gullie, and our circumstances changed." She wasn't yet ready to tell him about Keir holding her prisoner or his father almost killing her. "Eventually, it felt like this grand adventure. Lenya isn't like here. They're struggling. Their magic is dying, and they've been at war for generations. After a while, I knew I could make a difference. It's been so long since I felt ... useful in that way."

"Since the prison realm?"

She nodded.

He pushed out a breath. "Me too."

"I'm just glad to be back."

"And these fae who've returned with you?"

"They need us, Tobes." It was all she needed to say. He understood.

"Then, we'll do whatever it is we can to help them."

"I love you."

He sent her a knowing smile. "If you love me, you'll tell me what the deal is with this Keir dude."

"Dad wouldn't like you saying dude." He always joked his fae children were too human. Their mom had made sure of it.

"Don't change the subject."

"I really don't know what you're talking about."

"Really?" He nudged her. "That's what you're going with?"

"You're nosey."

"We never keep anything from each other. I mean, the first time I kissed Logan, you knew before Darra even did."

"Because Darra would have told Alona." Logan's sister was one of Tierney's best friends, but her favorite pastime was getting her older brother in trouble. It had taken their parents a little while to stop thinking of Logan and Toby as cousins. There was no blood relation, after all.

"No, it's because you would have guessed it anyway. Just like I know there's something about Keir you aren't saying. The way you two kept avoiding each other's gazes with Dad between you ... it was pretty epic."

"Shut up."

"Tell me."

"No."

"Tierney ..."

"Don't you dare." She knew what was coming.

He lunged sideways, his fingers digging into her sides to pin her to the ground. The blanket dropped away as the two of them wrestled. Tierney brought her knee up into his stomach and twisted.

Toby was daring but he'd never been able to beat her in a fight.

She scrambled away from him and reached for the iron fire poker next to the hearth. Toby ran for a broom leaning against the kitchen doorway. He returned and took up his stance.

"You can't keep anything from me." He jumped, bringing his broom down like a quarterstaff.

She blocked it with the poker-sword. "Try me." A grin spread across her face. Now, she felt like she was truly back where she belonged.

Toby ran at her, and she jumped away, leaping up onto the settee and over the back, landing in a crouch. Toby tried the same move, tumbling as he hit the floor.

Tierney was on him before he could catch his balance, sweeping his feet out from under him. He landed on his butt, and she pushed him back, arcing the poker. He blocked it with a grin.

"You've been practicing." She laughed.

"Can't have you beating me forever."

"What is the meaning of this?" Their dad's heavy footsteps crossed the room.

Tierney and Toby looked at each other, suppressing grins.

"You should probably let your brother up, honey." Their mom bit back a laugh, her cheeks puffed up with effort.

More entered the room, finding the twins still in their fighting stances with poker and broom.

Gulliver shrugged and went back to his room, used to their antics. Veren followed him, mumbling something about blasted royals waking him up.

Keir only stared, one eyebrow raised.

Someone gripped the back of Tierney's shirt, hauling her up.

"Let me go, Uncle Griff."

He clicked his tongue. "Tia, how many times have I told you that when you pull a dirty trick, don't let them get their weapon up in time to stop you?"

Lochlan groaned. "Letting you spend time with my daughter was the worst mistake I ever made."

"I don't know." Brea lifted one shoulder. "I quite enjoy watching her beat her brother."

"Mom," Toby groaned. "Thanks for playing favorites."

Her face turned serious. "I love all my children equally." She held a hand down. "But you know, girl power and all that. Plus, it's especially entertaining as long as you don't kill each other."

Lochlan turned with a grunt to return to bed.

Griffin scrubbed a hand over his face. "Please don't wake me up again. We have a long journey ahead of us."

"Griff." Brea shook her head. "You're traveling by portal. The rest of us don't have that luxury."

They returned to their rooms to sleep, and Tierney started toward the one she shared with Bronagh.

"I will get it out of you," Toby called.

"Go on. It's fun when you try, baby brother."

"Only by a few minutes!"

She sank into her bed, smiling at how normal the evening felt.

CHAPTER TWELVE
KEIR

They arrived back at the palace after five days on the sled, five nights of making camp, and staying warm with fires and magic. Keir couldn't take his eyes from the spires stretching toward the sky, the ornate balconies glittering with marble and some kind of dark gemstone.

It was grander than anything he'd ever seen in Lenya. The Vondurian palace was a fortress, meant to protect the people in a time of war. Nothing about this place said war, not the charming villages they passed by nor the cheerful peace of the snowy fields.

"It looks the same," Tierney whispered beside him. "Like time has just frozen in place."

"Time always marches on, Princess." Keir had taken on a more formal tone since Tierney decided not to tell her parents who he was. She had to have her reasons, and he would follow her lead. But it meant keeping his distance from her and from her brother's curious gaze.

They were twins who looked nothing alike at first glance. But the closer he studied them, the more he realized they had the same delicate cheekbones, the same curve of their eyes. And their smiles... while Toby's didn't hold nearly as much mirth in his, there was something secretive in the way he grinned that reminded Keir of Tierney.

Like he knew more than he revealed. It was as if he could see things that hadn't been said. The way Keir felt for Tierney, for one.

The guards near the front door snapped to attention. They didn't wear their battle armor for their post, and that told Keir they didn't have to be prepared to march against an enemy at any given moment.

Both of the guards smiled as the group approached on foot, having left the dogs in the village with their handler.

"Princess," the one on the right started, a young man with a too familiar look of genuine affection. "Welcome home."

"Caleb." Tierney ran toward them and hugged the guard, an improper gesture for a princess. She then hugged the other, a much older woman. "Clodagh."

"Princess." Clodagh had tears in her eyes. "We've been so worried about you."

Keir waited for someone to tell them it wasn't right to act so familiar with a member of the royal family. But he'd learned on the journey that few fae told Tierney what to do.

Caleb bowed to the king. "They're waiting for you, sire."

"Thank you, Caleb." King Lochlan patted the man's shoulder as he passed. "Tell Kala we're wishing her well with the pregnancy."

"I will. Thank you, your Majesty."

They walked under a grand archway into an even grander entryway. The moment they passed through the doors, the cold disappeared. Keir found an explanation in the hearth nearby, not wanting to think deeper about the immense magic these fae held.

Next to them, Lenya was little more than a cow pasture full

of fae who'd been killing each other for too long. Why would the kings and queens of these great realms want to help them?

As if she could sense his thoughts, Tierney's hand slid into his, squeezing before letting go. It was like she was telling him to trust her.

That was something, he'd come to realize, that had been inevitable.

Brea walked past them and turned to face the group. "I gave Griff instructions to have rooms made up for you all, but before we can be allowed to rest, I'm afraid there are fae waiting on us."

Tierney groaned. "Don't tell me you've called a council meeting right when I've returned. Can't I have a day before jumping back into heir duties?"

Brea wrapped an arm around her shoulders and pulled her along. "Do you have so little faith in me?" She leaned in, dropping her voice, but not low enough Keir couldn't hear. "Your father suggested it, but I wouldn't let him."

"It would have been protocol," Lochlan grumbled.

"Last time we were missing, they showed up without being summoned," Toby said.

Bronagh looked from Toby to Tierney. "Do royal children go missing quite frequently here?"

"You'd be surprised." Gulliver laughed.

Tierney scowled. "Toby and I just went to visit our cousins in Fargelsi. I left a note, so technically we weren't missing."

"Except, the note ended up getting lost underneath a bed." Brea shook her head. "And they were gone for two months that just happened to coincide with the Fargelsian Festival of Lights."

"Our aunt is the Queen of Fargelsi," Tierney explained. "It was all blown way out of proportion."

Keir barely followed the conversation as they walked

through the palace. What he wanted was a bath and a good night's rest in a soft bed. The latter being something he hadn't experienced since leaving Vondur.

All he knew was, it sounded like Tierney's life had been so different from his. He'd spent his youth training for battle and then fighting in them, not enjoying ceremonies or parties. There were no relatives to visit, no loving family except his sister.

Servants bowed as they passed, issuing well wishes to Tierney and Gulliver. The palace hummed with life at their return, as if everyone down to the lowliest servant had mourned their absence.

"Veren, your father has been summoned and should arrive shortly." Brea sent him a kind smile. "He has been beside himself."

"Losing one's heir does that." Veren didn't look particularly happy at the prospect of a reunion.

The halls quieted as they passed a pair of guards into a more secluded corridor. Tapestries adorned the walls, dressing them in bright colors that added to the warmth.

They stopped outside a set of ornate wooden doors.

"Why would the council be in the residence?" Gulliver asked.

A smile slipped across Tierney's face. "Because they didn't call the council." She shoved open the doors to reveal a massive sitting room brimming with fae.

Griff and Riona were there, but Tierney also seemed to recognize others.

A man ran for them first, sweeping Tierney into a tight hug. "My favorite O'Shea girl is back."

"After all our friendship," Brea shook her head, "you love my daughter more than me."

121

Tierney pulled back. "Mom, Uncle Myles is my friend now. I thought you'd gotten over that when I was like ten."

A tall woman with skin much darker than Tierney's joined them. "Myles, she won't disappear if you let her go."

"Aunt Neeve." Tierney hugged her.

It seemed everyone Tierney ever met was here. Her younger siblings circled her, clamoring for attention.

And then, she screamed.

A dark-skinned girl with long curly hair and bright eyes crossed the room, tears rolling down her cheeks. Tierney ran for her, joined soon by Gulliver. The three of them cried together, clutching each other like they couldn't bear letting go.

"You're alive," Tierney cried.

"You're back," the girl said.

Veren stepped up beside Keir. "Siobhan," he explained.

Relief flooded through him. For months, he'd watched Tierney disappear periodically into grief and guilt at her friend's disappearance, at the fact that she couldn't find her. This reunion meant everything to Tierney.

The door burst open behind them, and a guard ushered in a frazzled man with pale skin and a mop of blond hair. "Veren." He rushed forward and yanked Veren into a hug.

"Father." Veren's voice held a familiarity but also something more. When Keir glimpsed the tears on his face, he understood. Relief.

It wasn't until that moment he realized that no matter how much Keir had wanted Tierney to stay forever in Vondur, she'd never belonged there, and she never would.

None of them were meant to stay. He caught sight of Bronagh watching Veren, the same realization on her face. The three outsiders stood together, watching a family embrace their returned adventurers. Keir, Bronagh, and Imogen had a kingdom to save, a kingdom that belonged to them in a world very different from this one.

Keir stood in the room the queen had set aside for him, staring into the looking glass. A maid had left fresh clothes for him when she came to draw a bath—a fur-lined doublet and thick woolen trousers. Despite the always present hearths in every room, the place still chilled him, with its cold stone floors and marble-lined hallways.

Iskalt embraced its status as the ice kingdom, and he supposed those living here were quite used to it.

He was thankful he didn't have to share a room because it gave him time to think about what needed to be said to convince the fae of this kingdom to help his.

First, he had to admit who he truly was. Not a mere sailor or someone sent to protect Tierney. A king come to beg for the assistance his people needed.

He turned to survey the table in front of the settee, its dark top gleaming like amber in the light of the fire. He'd felt the power since the moment he set foot inside the room. It wasn't only here. This palace was rimmed in a power stronger than any he'd ever experienced. If he crossed the room and laid a hand on the table, he knew what he'd sense thrumming beneath the surface.

Magic. His kind of magic.

How was it possible?

A knock sounded on his door, and he tore his eyes from the table to open it. Tierney smiled at him from the other side, and he was so mesmerized he didn't see her brother with her.

Toby pushed past her into the room. "You can stop staring

at each other now." Another boy followed him in. "I know everything."

Tierney shot him an annoyed look as she closed the door behind him. Toby gestured to the boy with him. "This is Logan." He took Logan's hand, and the two made themselves comfortable on the settee.

"Like you and Logan don't constantly make eyes at each other." Tierney crossed her arms. "And you don't know anything."

"I know he's a king."

They all stopped.

Toby was the only one who kept speaking. "Gulliver told me."

Tierney groaned and flopped onto the settee, resting her feet across Logan's lap. "Of course he did. Gullie is a terrible secret keeper when it comes to you."

"Only because he assumed I already knew. But this time, you didn't tell me." He sounded hurt.

"It was my fault." Keir wanted to make him feel better. For Tierney. "I asked her not to tell anyone yet."

"Bull." Tierney shook her head.

"Where?" Keir searched the room for a bull's head or a painting, something that would explain anything that was going on and what it had to do with him.

Toby started laughing. "Oh, he's adorable."

"I know." Tierney giggled. "You should have seen when I explained electricity to him."

"I'm right here." Keir crossed his arms and leaned against the wall next to the hearth.

Tierney sent him a rebellious smile. "I meant, Keir didn't make the decision. I did. The truth is, he's come here for a reason, but there was no point in discussing it and having Dad distrust him even more before we were back at the palace where we could do something about it. You, Toby, have a little habit of telling Mom everything. And you know she can't keep secrets from Dad."

Toby huffed but didn't respond.

Keir had the distinct impression he'd walked into a dynamic more complicated than he could've imagined. In his family, Eavha and him only trusted each other. There were no other factors at play.

"What are you all doing in my rooms anyway? I could have been resting or bathing."

"Are you trying to tell me you haven't been ready for hours?" Tierney raised a brow.

Okay, fine, she had him. He'd gotten a bit of rest, but he couldn't just sit here when he needed to advocate for his kingdom. "When do I get to speak with your parents?"

She stood and crossed to him, taking his hand in both of hers. Her voice was soft when she spoke. "At dinner, I promise. We won't waste time now that we're here. We're supping in private with Bronagh and my parents. Not even Toby gets to be there."

Toby scowled at that, but Tierney ignored him. "They're going to help, Keir."

"I wish I could be as certain."

She looked up at him, so much sincerity in her eyes. "If you can't trust them, trust me. I know they will help, but should they not, I will. Believe in me, okay?"

He lifted a hand to her cheek, wondering how he'd gotten to this point, where he knew without a doubt that every one of her words was genuine, every one a promise she wouldn't break. Maybe it was when she'd saved him from the icy waters or even before that when she'd kissed him for the first time.

"I do," he whispered. "I believe in you."

The smile that graced her lips brought a light to her eyes he couldn't look away from. It was then, with her brother looking on and Tierney's words still ringing in his mind, he realized the truth.

He was in love with her.

And he still couldn't have her.

"Well, enjoy dinner." Toby stood. "We're going to go."

Logan lingered for a moment, watching them. "You look happy, Tierney. It's good to see."

When they were finally alone for the first time since the night before the storm let loose on the ship, Keir couldn't think of what else to say.

"Your palace is beautiful." He cringed at how bland the words were.

She chuckled and stepped away from him. "Thanks." Walking to the table near the looking glass, she lifted the crystal flagon and poured two cups of deep red wine.

Nearing him again, she held one out. "You'll never want Vondurian wine again."

He lifted it from her fingers and tilted it against his lips. It struck his throat, and he started sputtering as the strong, yet sweet liquid slid over his taste buds.

Tierney laughed. "It's much stronger than anything in your kingdom."

"Just a bit," he wheezed, catching his breath. Strong but also strangely delicious. The flavors burst across his tongue like nothing he'd ever experienced before. Suddenly, every other wine he'd ever tasted paled in comparison.

Tierney lifted on her toes and fit her lips to his. She tasted of sweet wine.

"Mmm," she murmured. "Delicious." With a smile, she stepped back and drank her wine. Keir wished she'd come close again, that she'd kiss him as she had in Grima or Vondur. But there'd been something hesitant in both of them since reaching the Iskalt shores.

They both knew their time was limited.

"So." Keir cleared his throat. "Your father ... tell me more about him." They'd been on the road for days, and he'd barely said two words to Keir.

Tierney hid a smile with her wine glass. "Well, he's ... difficult. He loves me very much, and he's a great king, truly the best, but we clash sometimes because we're both too stubborn."

"Oh no, don't tell me he's exactly like you." He wasn't sure if he could handle two of them.

"Sort of. I get my rebelliousness from Mom, but Dad and I share a ... profound belief in our own intelligence, as my mother says."

"Is that just a queenly way to say you both think you're always right?"

"Definitely not." By the way she turned away, he wasn't sure he believed her.

She stopped, still not facing him. "I am, though."

"You are what?"

She grinned over her shoulder. "Always right."

If she truly was like her father, he wasn't sure how he'd get through this night.

"Come on." She drained the rest of her wine. "We should get to dinner, but first, you'll need to finish that."

He lifted the wineglass. "I think I should have a clear head."

"Well, if you want to have supper with my parents on only a few sips of wine, it's your funeral. Me, I'd rather have a bit of courage in me."

He didn't want to ask what he needed courage for.

CHAPTER THIRTEEN
TIERNEY

Tierney and Keir were the first to arrive in the dining hall.

"Why such a big room for one table?" Keir moved to stand in front of the enormous fireplace at the front of the room. The poor man was always cold.

Tierney gazed around the familiar room, trying to see it for the first time through Keir's eyes. A long table sat on an ivory and blue rug under an enormous chandelier made of powerful crystals.

She cringed at the sight of so much power used for simple adornment. What must Keir think of them? She turned her back, moving to the buffet table to pour them each a glass of wine.

"It used to be a dining hall for the full court." Brea entered the room, dressed in her preferred tunic and trousers. She rarely wore queenly attire when it was just the family and a few guests. "When the twins were small, after I first came to Iskalt as queen, I couldn't handle the intensity of having the court present at every meal."

Brea stepped up beside Keir, admiring the family portraits that sat along the mantle. A human custom she insisted on

"I didn't want my kids to have to grow up behaving like perfect little princes and princesses all the time. I wanted them to enjoy the occasional food fight and laughter around the dinner table. So, I banned the court from the dining hall. We hold frequent dinners in a more formal setting where the court joins us."

"Food fights?" Keir turned toward the queen, his back straight as a rod and his hands clasped behind his back like a soldier.

Tierney lingered by the buffet table to watch them.

"Well, we had four kids under the age of ten, so tantrums often ended up with flinging mashed potatoes and vegetables they didn't want to eat." Brea shrugged. "When you have kids, you'll know what I mean." She clapped him on the shoulder and joined Tierney at the buffet.

Brea made a show of pouring her own glass of wine and muttered out the side of her mouth, "You're related to all the royals—or as close to related as you can get. So, what does my daughter do? She goes and finds herself a handsome king—don't be mad at Toby for telling me—from a fabled land and brings him home to dinner." She turned, leaning against the table. "And he is handsome, isn't he?" She elbowed her daughter.

"Mom," Tierney hissed, hoping Keir hadn't heard her. "He is a king. He has his own kingdom to rule. It's not like that."

"It looks like that." Brea gave her a knowing grin. "If you remember, I was supposed to be the heir of Eldur, and you see how that worked out."

"Stop it." Tierney's face flushed scarlet.

"Well, does he have a younger brother?" Brea raised her brows, all innocence.

"Why, are you leaving Dad for a younger model?"

"Of course not, but we're going to be right back here with

Kayleigh in a few years, and if the man has a brother, then they need to meet."

"Seriously?" Tierney rolled her eyes.

"Hey, I have a lot of royal children to marry off, and there's a serious lack of suitable candidates available. Excuse a mom for thinking ahead."

"He has a sister, Eavha. I would steal her here in a heart-beat, but she's head over heels for the commander of Keir's army." Tierney let her thoughts wander to how Eavha might be doing without Keir. The girl was brave and noble. She would inspire her people to stay together until help arrived.

"We have to send help to Lenya, Mom. As soon as possible."

"We will. After we hash it all out tonight. We have a lot to discuss." Brea's head tilted to the side. "Darling, why is that man staring at my chandelier like he wants to put it in his pocket and take it home? Gullie made that for me. And that makes it priceless."

"Oh." Tierney laughed. "We have so much to talk about."

She left her mother's side and went to join Keir at the fireplace.

"Drink this and stop staring at the priceless crystals." She shoved a wine glass in his hand.

"You know, this beautiful work of art contains enough power to restore my kingdom to what it once was. Between that and the table in my room, the entirety of Lenya could thrive for a generation."

"You don't need tables and chandeliers to do that." She took his hand, giving it a gentle squeeze. "We will send help soon."

Keir gazed around the opulent room. "I'm afraid I have nothing to offer in trade for the crystals we need to save my people."

"I don't know what you mean about crystals." Brea took her

seat near the head of the table. "But if your people are hurting and we can help, I am certain something can be arranged. It doesn't need to be an equal trade."

Love for her mother bloomed inside Tierney's chest. She didn't even know how dire the situation was in Lenya, yet she was already offering to help.

"I missed you so much." Tierney leaned over the back of Brea's chair and hugged her. "You have no idea how many times I needed my mother."

Brea took Tierney's hand and pulled her into the seat beside her, gesturing for Keir to take the chair opposite her. "Can we just call the time of death right now? Your jaunt to Lenya when you meant to come home has to be the final nail in the coffin of your O'Shea magic, Tia. I shudder to think where you might end up next time."

"I won't be using my portal magic without supervision ever again. I'm fully prepared to admit to anyone who will listen that I am no good at it."

"Do my ears deceive me or did the great Tierney O'Shea just admit she wasn't good at something involving magic?" Lochlan entered the room, a smile on his face. "Things have certainly changed during your time away." He dropped a kiss on her head and moved to his seat at the head of the table.

"Very funny." Tierney rolled her eyes. "You make it sound like I was on a holiday."

Lochlan's smile faded. "I can't imagine what you've been through. I'm just so glad to have you home safe."

"I hope we aren't late." Bronagh approached the table, every bit the queen she was. Veren followed her at a distance. Pausing to give his king and queen a proper greeting.

"Your Majesties, I hope I am not imposing. Queen Bronagh has asked me to join her in an advisory capacity this evening."

"Of course, please join us." Brea gave them a warm welcome.

"When we first arrived in Lenya, we were all separated," Tierney began. "I crossed paths with Keir almost immediately, but it wasn't until much later I discovered Veren had fallen in with the Grimian army and Queen Bronagh. Veren has become a close advisor to the queen."

"Well done, Veren." Lochlan gave him a nod of approval. "You've represented Iskalt with honor."

"Thank you, your Majesty." Veren took the vacant seat beside Tierney and across from Bronagh.

A host of servants came in to serve the first course, and Tierney laughed when she saw what was on the menu. Her absolute favorite human meal. "Spaghetti and meatballs!" She beamed a smile at Keir. "You're in for a treat, but you should know nothing will be spicy like the Lenyans prefer."

"Oh." Brea's face fell. "I didn't realize. I thought comfort food was the best way to go tonight."

"I'm sure this ... spaghetti dish will be delicious." Keir rushed to put her at ease.

"The food, you would love it, but Dad would starve. It's so spicy." Tierney laughed. It felt so good to be home again, but she already missed Lenya more than she thought she would.

After the servants left them for their meal, Lochlan lifted his wine glass. "I'd like to make a toast. To the safe return of my eldest daughter and the new friends she's brought with her."

"Here, here." Brea lifted her glass, and Tierney followed suit, not sure the Lenyans knew what a toast was.

"My people need help," Keir blurted, his stony soldier's face firmly in place. "I appreciate the warm welcome and the lovely dinner, but I worry for my people. My sister back home. My best friend. They are all in danger."

"We have a lot of ground to cover before we're all caught

up." Tierney caught his gaze. "Both Keir and Bronagh have made enormous sacrifices to be here. Without them, we would have never made it home. For that alone, I feel Iskalt owes them a debt of gratitude, and I would ask our king to provide them with the one thing they need more than any other. A small thing we have in great supply."

"And what is that?" Lochlan asked, taking a bite of his spaghetti and gesturing for the others to do the same.

"Magic." Tierney stabbed a cheese-slathered meatball with her fork. "Lots of it."

"Magic welders?" Brea frowned. "We do have plenty of those, but I thought your people had their own kind of magic." She turned to Keir in confusion.

"We do, madame," Bronagh began.

"Oh, please, call me Brea. Let's dispense with all the formalities this evening, shall we?"

"Of course, Brea." Bronagh nodded, examining her dish of noodles and red sauce. "In Lenya, we have great magic, but we must have a totem ... a vessel used to harness the magic from within. It's a certain kind of crystal of which we are in short supply." She lifted her eyes to the chandelier shining down on them. "Even as I sit here, I can feel the immense power of the crystal used to create this lovely light. It is enough to save my people—at least, it contains more power than any crystal I have ever seen in my lifetime." Her voice came out breathless and eager. "Such a vessel could change our lives."

"The mines once produced enough crystal for all Lenyans to access their magic," Keir continued. "But over the last many generations, the mines have failed, and there is little enough for the nobility and military officers to use for only the direst of circumstances."

"Our kingdoms have been at war for generations," Bronagh added. "We've fought for control of the last remaining mine and the reserves set aside by our grandparents." She shared a glance with Keir. "The Vondurian king and I have come to our roles only recently, and we have agreed the fighting must end."

"And no sooner had we signed a milestone peace treaty between our kingdoms than we were faced with an even bigger problem." Keir leaned back, uninterested in his meal.

"The expansion of the fire plains?" Lochlan sighed.

"You know?" Tierney gaped at her father. "How?"

"Much has happened here since you left, Tia," Brea said. "All the vatlands are expanding. On all sides. You must have noticed how much worse the northeastern mountains were than what has been recorded. The storms raging through the mountains and across the tundra have progressively expanded. The blizzard has reached the lodge. It won't be long before our home there is completely snowed in. And if it keeps moving at the same rate, all of Iskalt will drown in a sea of snow and ice.

"It's the same in the Northern Vatlands too, along the border with Myrkur. We've had reports of avalanches and earthquakes. That is why Siobhan and her father are here. Their estate has been destroyed. An earthquake shifted the lands where the manor house rested on the cliffside. Their home was dashed to rubble in a rockslide. Even the mountains themselves seem to be expanding, like they're growing right from the ground. Myrkur is experiencing the same from their side."

"And the Southern Vatlands between Eldur and Fargelsi have been expanding as well," Lochlan continued. "We don't know what started it, but we've been hard at work trying to find a solution. Half of southern Gelsi is gone. Almost the entirety of the Dragur Forest is marshland now.

"It's even worse in Eldur. It's coming at them from both sides. To the northeast, the fire plains drift across the desert, but to the southwest, the marshlands have engulfed the Teotann Oasis and nearly swallowed Loch Langt."

Tierney's eyes burned with unshed tears. "So, we're all in this together then." She took a deep breath, trying to wrap her mind around the enormity of the problem they now faced. It wasn't just a threat to Lenya anymore. It was a threat to all fae.

"Lenya is small." Bronagh picked at her meal. "I never truly realized just how small until Lochlan showed us a map of the four kingdoms this afternoon. I used to think Grima was huge, dwarfing the size of Vondur, but we are nothing compared to the might of Iskalt and your allies."

"Do not sell yourself short, Bronagh." Brea reached across the table to take her hand. "We owe our might to the lineage of Lenya. Your people once occupied all of the fae world in ancient times. Toby and my father, Brandon, have been researching in the Aghadoon library. They've recovered a great deal of lost history, but we still have not solved the problem. I fear if we don't soon, we will run out of time."

"Have you been able to slow the expansion at all?" Tierney asked.

"Some." Lochlan set his fork aside. "It's taken a great deal of magic to stall the spread, but we can teach you what we know."

"I think we should make that a priority and send someone to Lenya immediately through a portal with enough crystals to help them." Tierney turned toward her father, waiting expectantly.

"I'll check with the palace craftsmen to see what we have on hand. But you will need to be the one to open the portal. You're the only O'Shea who has been there. Are you prepared for the possibility that you might not be able to do it?"

Tierney shook her head. "No. I have to do it. But I will need Toby's guidance."

"Very well. We will put everything we have into that tomorrow. Who will return to Lenya with these crystals?"

"I would like to." Bronagh was the first to speak up. "I would very much like to return to my people to let them know what's happening."

"I will go with you, your Majesty," Veren volunteered.

Bronagh reached for his hand. "Stay. Your father and your family just got you back. I don't want to take you from them again so soon. We will see each other again."

"I don't like the idea of the queen traveling through a portal alone. Not when she isn't familiar with such magic."

"He means he's worried I'll send her to some other lost kingdom we know nothing about." Not that Tierney could blame him.

"Perhaps Imogen could accompany Bron back to Lenya," Keir suggested. "I should think she would like to tell her family about her father's brave sacrifice."

"I'm not sure she has any other family," Tierney said. "I believe she's very worried about what will become of her."

"I will see she has everything she could ever need." Bronagh lifted her chin. "It's the least we can do for the captain."

"Then, that matter is settled." Brea sipped her wine. "I will work with Bron in the morning to show her what little we've been able to accomplish to stall the spread, and then when night falls, Tierney and Toby will open a portal."

"Must it wait for night?" Bronagh asked. "I am very anxious to return."

"I am afraid in Iskalt, most matters of magic must wait for nightfall," Lochlan explained. "Where your magic is powered by these crystal vessels, ours is fueled by the moon. My wife has Eldurian magic, which is ruled by the sun. She will be able to assist you until a portal can be opened."

"I see." Bronagh nodded. "It seems we are not so different after all then."

"That's right." Tierney gave her a sad smile. "We are all fae."

"We are all fae." Bronagh reached for her glass. "That sounds like a wonderful toast."

"Here, here." Lochlan lifted his wine. "To the six kingdoms of the fae."

Smiling, they each drank their wine and returned to their meal.

"Once we have dealt with all immediate threats, Keir and Bron," Lochlan began, "we will have to draw up a treaty between our lands. Just something to note the assistance Iskalt and the other kingdoms will offer Lenya in the form of the crystals you need, and an agreement that your magic will never be turned against us."

"Dad!" Tierney couldn't believe him. "Is that necessary to discuss at the dinner table?"

"I don't know your friends, Tia. I must think of Iskalt." Lochlan refilled his plate. He seemed to be the only one with an appetite.

"You think I don't consider Iskalt? Of course, we need to settle an agreement in writing, but Keir and Bron have come a long way—a journey that should have gotten us all killed were it not for the courage of Captain Michel and his crew, who all died, by the way. Matters of diplomacy can wait."

"None of you would have been in such trouble if you hadn't run away from home."

"And what was I running away from?" Tierney crossed her arms over her chest. "You remember your stupid list?" She scowled at him.

"Iskalt must be secured for the next generation." Lochlan shot back.

"And I will secure it. In my own time. I'm not marrying anyone from that list, and I'm not having babies any time soon, so just go feed that list of yours to the goats because I don't want to see it again."

"It's okay," Keir tried to interject.

"Let them argue." Brea passed him the breadbasket. "It's their favorite pastime. You should try a spaghetti sandwich with garlic bread. It's my favorite." She pulled two pieces of garlic bread from the basket and piled spaghetti and meatballs onto one piece, smashing the second piece on top.

Keir helped himself to the breadbasket. His appetite seemed to have returned. "I expected as much," he interrupted, bringing Lochlan and Tierney's bickering to an end. "To be honest, I thought your king might demand a price we could not pay for access to the magic we so desperately need. If a peace treaty between our kingdoms is all he requires, I am more than happy to speak for Vondur that no fae of my kingdom will ever turn their magic on Iskalt or any of the four kingdoms unless it is a life-or-death situation in which they believe they are protecting themselves from harm."

"I have no qualms signing such a treaty," Bronagh echoed Keir's thoughts. "I know my council will fall over themselves to sign any treaty that might restore magic to our kingdom."

"We must speak to Queen Alona of Eldur and Queen Neeve of Fargelsi, as well as King Hector of Myrkur," Lochlan said, "but I see no reason why the four kingdoms couldn't all set up a system of trade for crystals."

"We have nothing of value to trade." Keir frowned.

"That's not exactly true." Tierney leaned forward. "The Queen of the Night blossoms would be a good trade. The ladies of the courts across the four kingdoms would pay a high price for such a lovely perfume."

"Well, I suppose we could also trade Gentian tea." Keir nodded.

"No. We don't want that stuff here." Tierney shook her head, thinking of the first time she'd tasted the bitter tea. "But your red peppers and Grima's hot chocolate drink would be perfect for trade."

"Chocolate?" Brea turned to Tierney. "Did I hear something about chocolate?"

"It's not exactly the same, Mom. But it's the closest thing to it I've ever tasted. It's sweet and creamy, and it smells like heaven in a cup."

"Iskalt will trade crystals for your chocolate drink." Brea beamed a smile at the Grima queen.

"I feel like all the chocoah in Grima couldn't equal what you propose to give us in return." Bronagh shook her head in wonder. "Chocoah for crystals." She threw her head back and laughed. "My brother will find that quite amusing."

"You have a brother?" Brea leaned forward. "Older or younger?"

"Younger." Bronagh smiled. "Donal is fourteen, though he thinks he's forty since he's been leading my army, fighting battles with enemy kings, and nearly getting himself killed."

"I have a daughter about his age. Maybe on your next visit, you can bring Donal with you."

"That would be wonderful; thank you for the invitation."

"Watch out, Bron. Mom is matchmaking," Tierney whisper-shouted across the table.

"I also have a nephew about your age." Brea ignored her daughter. "But I think Veren might have something to say about that." She winked at the young nobleman.

"You're so embarrassing." Tierney rolled her eyes, but she was so happy to be home she didn't care if her mother tried to set up marriages for all her children with the Vondurian and Grimian royals and nobles.

"Sue me. I'm a mother and I want my kids to be happy. Toby will marry Prince Logan someday, and I want all my babies, and my nieces and nephews, to experience that kind of love for themselves. You know, after we save the world again."

Tierney sighed. One of these days, she wanted a little peace and quiet where the world no longer needed saving every time she turned around.

CHAPTER FOURTEEN
KEIR

What a strange place. Keir stood on one of the upper balconies of the palace, gazing down at the snowy field stretching all the way to the nearest village. If he craned his neck, he could see a frozen lake, where a group of children pushed a black ball around with sticks, yelling at each other and falling all over the ice.

Other children ran through ankle-deep snow, chasing each other, their laughter reaching the balcony. He didn't understand what they were doing. It certainly wasn't the type of work children in Vondur performed. They typically worked with their parents in the fields or in the shops and many smithies, making items to provision the army. Once they reached an age, the boys left their homes behind to fight for their kingdom.

It had been the way of things for as long as he could remember.

"I was you once," a voice sounded behind him.

Keir turned to find the king in the doorway. There were no guards following him, and he wore no protection, having no obvious worries of someone aiming an arrow at him should he stand in the open too long.

Lochlan walked farther out onto the balcony. "My home was in danger, but the danger was within. I resided in a different kingdom, and all I could do was watch my people suffer."

"What did you do?" Keir asked.

Lochlan gave him a tight smile. "I fought. Now, my fae know peace." His eyes drifted to the yelling children. "They can play because we refused to give up on them. How long have you worn the crown?"

"Not long."

Lochlan nodded, as if he'd expected that answer. "Well, a good king always puts his kingdom before himself, always strives for peace."

"Peace. It's such a foreign concept. Lenya has been at war for so long no one alive remembers a time when the fighting didn't overwhelm our lands. Grima and Vondur have a tentative alliance now, but it is new."

"One thing I have learned in my many years upon the throne is that an army may fight, but if given the choice, they will trade their swords for plows, their horses for oxen. Give them that choice, Keir, and never take it away. They will love you for it."

Maybe they would have, but Keir would never get the chance to know. "And if fighting is the only option?"

"Ah." Lochlan nodded. "You wish you were able to return with Bronagh." He studied Keir for a moment. "Come, we have much to discuss."

Lochlan led him in out of the frigid temperatures, but the chill didn't leave him. It was a constant reminder that he was in this frozen kingdom while his fae suffered the effects of scorching heat.

They walked through the palace, across velvet carpets, to a sitting chamber with two settees facing each other in front of a roaring fire set back in the marble hearth.

A servant followed them in and bowed. "Sire, I have sent for tea."

"Thank you," Lochlan said absently. "I do not need anything further."

The man bowed again and backed out, shutting the doors and trapping Keir with Tierney's father, a man who'd intimidated him before they'd even met.

Tierney idolized the man. That much had been clear since she was Keir's prisoner in Vondur. But it was more than that. She loved him. Disappointing him hurt her. It was the kind of dynamic Keir never had with his own father. He couldn't imagine his father searching for him if he'd gone missing or worrying for him every day like it was clear Lochlan had done.

There were deep lines of exhaustion in the face of the Iskalt king. As if these last months still weighed him down.

"Please," he said, "sit."

Keir lowered himself to the settee, and Lochlan took the seat across from him. They didn't speak, the silence stretching between them. A knock sounded on the door before a young woman entered, carrying a silver tray laden with a pot of tea, two cups, and a plate of what looked like biscuits. Sort of.

She set the tray on the table between the settees and left.

Lochlan leaned forward, pouring tea into the two cups. "Milk?"

"Please." Keir picked up one of the biscuits and smelled it. There were dark spots across the top, and it reeked of sugar.

"Cookies," Lochlan explained. "My wife insists on making them herself with ingredients she gets from the human realm. I believe she calls them oatmeal. She tells me it's like porridge baked in the oven."

Keir set it down without taking a bite.

Lochlan chewed on one of his own. "They're actually quite

good. The dark bits are chewy and sweet. I forget what she told me they're called, but the children adore them."

"Is being wed to someone so connected to the human realm odd?" Keir asked, truly interested. Tierney was strange in her human sayings, but he'd sensed it was nothing compared to her mother.

"Young man, marriage itself is odd."

Keir laughed at that. "You seem to have a wonderful family."

A fond smile spread across the dour king's face. "They age me to no end, and sometimes I feel as if I will never be free of rebellious women and the boys who can't resist them, but then I remember I am one of those boys. My family is more than I ever imagined it could be. There was a time I didn't believe in much, not even in myself."

Keir had a hard time imagining that. This man, who seemed to know all, to wear his crown as if he was meant to. He was so sure of his actions. "You hide it well."

"The secret is to find one person who sees your vulnerabilities. If they allow you to have your doubts, to voice your questions, with the rest of the world, pretending becomes second nature. As long as that one person lets the act fall, it will not become who you are."

One person. Keir saw her so clearly in his head. Tierney saw who he really was, not the man raised by a cruel father or the one who kept her prisoner. She looked past everything he'd done, everything he tried to pretend he was.

"Ah," Lochlan said. "I thought so."

"Sir?"

"You've already found that person."

He had. The way Lochlan looked at him, a calculating gleam in his eyes, had Keir wanting to stand and run from the room. Instead, he sipped his tea and crossed one leg over the other.

Lochlan nodded, his face growing serious. A crease formed in his forehead, and blue sparked in his eyes. He blinked, and it was gone. "I am sorry. I don't know if anyone has explained our magic to you, but strong emotions draw it forth, and it isn't always easy to hide when it rises."

"Was there something I said that angered you?" The last thing he wanted was to get on this man's bad side. He needed him to help Lenya.

Lochlan sighed. "No. I was thinking of my daughter, and she always sparks such a reaction in me. Tierney is stubborn. I'm sure you've noticed."

Keir's lips twitched. "Maybe a time or two." What would Lochlan say if he knew Keir had held his daughter captive? Would he still be a welcome guest, a potential ally?

"But she is strong, stronger than any fae I have ever met. Ruling Iskalt is an honor, one Tierney earned when she was ten." He paused. "If I'd had crowned her then, the Iskaltians would have accepted her. At ten, I had never faced hardship. But she saved four kingdoms."

"Tierney is unlike anyone I've ever met."

"Keir, are you in love with my daughter?"

"Yes." He didn't hesitate. It was a conclusion he'd come to on the ship when they first sailed into the maelstrom. He hadn't wanted to love her, to need her. For so long, Tierney was a temptation, a fae he couldn't resist. He hadn't known it then, but they were connected.

"Hm." Lochlan stood and walked toward the hearth, staring into the flames. "I know what some think of me, but I have my reasons for wanting Tierney to marry. I'm not a cruel father, but if she is going to be queen, she needs someone to temper her, to calm her rash actions and weather her storm."

It was the perfect analogy. Tierney was a storm that had ripped through his life, wreaking havoc. But in the aftermath, there was peace.

Lochlan turned. "Do you wish to marry my daughter?"

Keir couldn't breathe. He couldn't summon words or pick out a single thought swirling through his mind.

"She refuses all the nobles of Iskalt," Lochlan went on, seemingly oblivious to the crisis inside Keir. "She needs a powerful ally, one who will always support her should anyone try to take her throne." He took his seat again. "My parents lost the Iskaltian throne when my father died, and it plunged our family into years of betrayal and took a war to win it back. My brother and I were raised in foreign courts. I do not want my people to ever go through such unrest again."

It made so much sense now why Lochlan was so desperate to secure the throne for generations to come. He was scared. History did not predict the future, but it could inform it.

"I would like to add a marriage to the treaty between our kingdoms." Lochlan steepled his fingers. "Lenya will receive access to all fire opal resources in the four kingdoms, but to secure our alliance, you will marry my daughter."

He didn't know. Keir held a giant secret, but if he was going to consider such a deal, if he truly wanted to marry Tierney, Lochlan had to know. He cleared his throat, coughing into his fist. "I ..." He drew in a breath. "There is something you must know before making such a deal, something no one knows other than my sister and my most trusted council member."

Lochlan waited, not saying a word.

Keir just had to get it out, to voice the very thing he'd been afraid of, the one act that made him a poor king. "I abdicated the throne."

Silence. It stretched like a violent sea preluding the storm.

Keir pictured Eavha's face when he'd told her what he

146

planned. She hadn't agreed with him, but she'd signed the documents as a witness in front of Lord Robert.

He'd never wished to be a king. Keir only wanted peace for his kingdom, and he achieved that. Once he stopped the fire plains, they needed someone who could rule out of duty, love. Not a man who'd gained his crown through his father's spilled blood.

Keir stared down at his hands, as if he could still feel the warm blood from not only his father but all the nobles who issued the King's Comhrac. Vondur deserved a fresh start.

Finally, Lochlan spoke. "Tell me, Keir, did you give up your crown out of a sense of fear or a true love for your fae?"

"I do not fear duty. I was not the ruler my fae deserved."

Understanding entered Lochlan's gaze. "Believe it or not, I do know what you speak of."

Keir didn't get how Lochlan could possibly understand, but he didn't question it. "Now that you know the truth, do you still wish for me to marry your daughter?"

Lochlan hesitated for a moment. "I do not care if you wear a crown, only that you're able to support hers."

"I will support her with everything I have. But you must know, whether Tierney and I marry is not up to you, and it is not up to me. She has a mind of her own, and she will make her own decisions."

A smile flashed across his face before it was gone. "Then, we have a deal."

"No." Hadn't he heard him? "Not yet."

Lochlan stood, extending a hand. "I am glad we could reach an agreement."

Keir didn't take the hand as he got to his feet. "There is no agreement."

Lochlan nodded. "You may leave now." He put a hand on his back and ushered him to the door.

Keir turned when he stepped into the corridor. "There's no deal."

The Iskaltian king only nodded and shut the door, leaving Keir to wonder what in the world just happened. Had he agreed to be married?

There was someone he needed to find. It took him the better part of an hour to seek Gulliver. He sat in a library with his father, a map spread out before them.

"So, Lenya is here?" Griff pointed to a blank part of the map across the fire plains, his eyes bright.

Gulliver leaned his chair back, balancing on two legs. His tail rose and flicked his father's hand. "I already told you that."

"Gullie, you've been to a land no one else even knew about. Forgive me for being curious."

Gulliver rolled his eyes to Keir. "Curious is an understatement. Obsessed is more accurate."

"King Keir." Griff shot to his feet. "You can help us. I want to know everything there is to know about Lenya."

Gulliver groaned. "You don't have to talk to him. He's just being obnoxious. I've already told him about Vondur and Grima."

"Yes, but their magic works from fire opals? It's fascinating."

"We do not call them opals," Keir explained. "But yes, they allow us to harness the power."

"Amazing."

"Ask me about the dungeons while you're at it, Dad." Gulliver scrubbed a hand across his face. "Would you like to know what I named the rats?"

Griff's mouth opened and shut, and guilt curled in Keir's gut. He waited for Gulliver to tell his father who'd kept him prisoner, but those words never came.

"Fair enough." Griffin sighed. "You don't want to talk about it. I'm sure Keir didn't seek you out to listen to you being mean to your old man."

Gulliver shook his head, a hint of a smile appearing on his lips. "Did you need me for something, Keir?"

Keir hesitated before walking forward and taking the empty seat at their table. "There's something I wanted to talk to you about."

Gulliver lifted a brow.

"Oh, do go on." Griff grinned. "This sounds interesting."

Keir swallowed heavily. He had to force the words out. Here went nothing. "The king has asked me to marry Tia."

Gulliver and his father stared at each other before bursting out in laughter.

"Lochlan will never learn." Griffin laughed.

Gulliver wiped away fake tears. "I hope for magic's sake you said no."

"I did ... but he didn't seem to hear me."

"Classic Loch." Griff lifted his eyes to the ceiling. "Everyone is either in agreement with him or simply wrong. Does he not realize his daughter ran away the last time he tried to marry her off?"

"I'm not going with her this time." Gulliver crossed his arms, still laughing.

"There is a difference now though." Griffin's laughter died away. "Tierney might say yes."

Keir's chest inflated with hope, but it slowly faded when Gulliver shook his head. "You have no idea. Keir and Tierney had this weird toxic thing going on, but they hate each other most of the time."

"So did your mother and I."

"Ew, gross. I don't want to imagine you two being as sickening as Keir and Tierney have been, even if I was around for a lot of it. I blocked it out."

"When hate turns to love, son, it can be the most wonderful, passionate—"

"Don't say passionate."

"—relationship."

Gulliver rested his face in his hands, his palms muffling his voice. "Why did you come to me, Keir? Was it for my blessing?"

Keir wasn't really sure. "I ..."

"The only blessing that matters is Tierney's, and if she finds out her father is playing with her life again, I guarantee it won't be pretty."

"I'm in love with her." There was desperation in his voice. Ever since Lochlan asked the question, all Keir could think about was spending the rest of his life fighting with Tierney, loving her.

"And that's great, but she won't play a part in any scheme. For the record, I believe you love her, and yet you still don't get it. You were raised in a kingdom where women had no control over their lives, no respect. You have come a long way, but the next lesson you must learn is that Tierney won't marry you just because she loves you—if she does. That isn't enough. You need to prove you respect her as much as you love her."

"And if I do that?"

"Well, she'll still probably say no."

CHAPTER FIFTEEN
TIERNEY

"There you are." Tierney wandered into the library, where Keir poured over a map of the four kingdoms.

"Your world is so vast I can hardly fathom it." Keir didn't look up from his scrutiny of the fire plains along the Eldur border. "Did you know there's an active volcano in Eldur that wasn't part of the fire plains until recently?"

"Yes. It's called Eldfal, and my mother was about my age last time it erupted, but it wasn't a natural event, so I'm not sure it counts." She moved to stand beside him. Hanging over his shoulder, she blew a warm breath in his ear to catch his attention.

"What?" Keir reached for his ear. "Oh, hi." He grinned up at her ruefully. "I was doing it again, wasn't I?"

"Fangirling over the four kingdoms? Yes." He was obsessed. And even if he wouldn't admit it, he idolized her father. The two men had become fast friends.

"I don't know what that means. But your world is so exciting."

"And the most you have seen of it since we arrived is this library and the palace." She grabbed his hand, tugging him

"You're up to something." He resisted for only a moment before he followed her from the library.

"I wouldn't be Tia O'Shea if I wasn't up to something."

"Where are we going?"

"You want to see Iskalt while you have the chance, don't you?" She turned, walking backward down the hall as she pulled him along. "Or would you rather pour over books about Iskalt instead of visiting the nearest village with me?"

"Let's go." He laid a hand at her back, and they hurried down the hall.

Gathering their cloaks, they ventured out into the stable yard across the palace grounds.

"Is it always this cold?" Keir tucked his face into the warm woolen scarf he wore around his face and neck.

Tierney laughed, her eyes bright in the clear afternoon sunshine. "It's a bit colder than normal but hardly noticeable for most of us used to the weather here." She waved at the stable hand when he emerged with two fine geldings. A chestnut and a dark roan.

"Thank you, Stephan." Tierney took the reins. "How is your mother doing? She was ill before I left, wasn't she?"

"Aye, your Majesty." The boy beamed a worshipful smile for the princess. "She is doing much better, thank you."

"Tell your mother I'll be along to visit as soon as I can." Tierney mounted her horse.

"I will. It's wonderful to have you home again, Princess." Stephan bowed, turning to hand the reins of the other horse to Keir before he trotted off back to the stables.

"You visit your stable hands' mothers often?" Keir arched a brow at her.

"As often as I can." Tierney made a soothing sound to her horse to ease his nervous shifting. "You coming?" She glanced over her shoulder at him.

"Shouldn't we wait for the others?" Keir climbed atop a horse.

"What others? It's just you and me today."

He trotted up beside her, giving his horse a gentle pat. "We're going into the village; you'll need a guard at least."

"I've never taken a guard with me into the village." She nudged her mount into a trot. "It's perfectly safe. You'll see."

They rode along the winding path that led from the rear of the palace down to the lake, where children played on the ice.

"I've watched them from the windows and balconies, and I still can't fathom what they are playing." Keir watched them battle across the ice for possession of the puck.

"It's only the best game in the entire world." Tierney's eyes sparkled in the sunlight as she watched the children. "It's called hockey. It's a human sport, but I grew up playing it with Gullie and Toby and all our friends in the village.

"Once my mother introduced the sport, Iskaltians took to it like they invented it themselves. I haven't played in ages, but I'll teach you before you leave for Vondur." A pang of something she didn't want to identify shot through her, and she rushed on. "There's almost always a game happening here at the palace. Father gave his permission ages ago for the village children to use the lake whenever they liked." Tierney missed those days sometimes. She had some of her fondest memories right here.

"Does the snow ever melt away?"

"Never. There are times of the year when the snows are infrequent, but there is always a blanket of crisp white dust covering the world." She waved to a group of girls walking along the wide path.

"Your Majesty." They all smiled, dipping into awkward curtsies.

"The village school is just over there." Tierney pointed across the expanse of snow-covered fields to a stone building that looked like it had been there for centuries. "I used to beg my father to let me go to school with the other children, but I had magic as a young child. Erratic magic, and I was prone to using it when I wasn't supposed to."

"Why does that not surprise me?" Keir chuckled. "Your children don't have magic?"

"In Eldur and Iskalt, we inherit the use of our magic when we come of age. I've only had my Eldurian and Iskaltian magic for a little more than four years, but I've had Gelsi magic my whole life."

"And it's unusual for a fae to have all three types of magic?" Keir asked.

"I'm the only one." She shrugged. "My mother has Gelsi and Eldurian magic. For a long time, it wasn't common for fae of one kingdom to interact with those of another, much less join in marriage. It's much more common now. My mother thinks in a few more generations, everyone will be like me but with Dark Fae features, and we'll all just be fae without any differences at all."

"Princess Tierney! Welcome home!" A cheery woman crossed the street into the village proper, waving frantically.

"Mrs. Fintan, how are you?" Tierney called. "Is Eloise in town today?"

"She's working at the general store; she would love it if you popped in to say hello."

"I'll do that." Tierney led them along a cobblestone street lined with fir trees and people coming and going about their business. It was a prosperous village, but most of Iskalt was like that under King Lochlan's rule.

"Do you know everyone by name?" Keir asked after she nodded to another passerby.

"I've lived here all my life, and I'm positive I spent more time in the village than at home."

Keir glanced around the town square, a slight frown on his face.

"What's the matter?" She rode close beside him.

"You have ... everything here. There's a mill and a smithy. You have stores and pubs, and I don't even know what most of these businesses are. It's ... wonderful. Eavha would fall in love with your village if she could be here."

"I hope she will come for a visit someday soon." Tierney turned them down a side street, pointing out the various businesses. "That's a bookstore. And there's an apothecary at the end of the street. They have everything you could ever need and then some. Then, there's a tea shop and something my mom calls a restaurant, where they serve the best beef strudel you have ever tasted."

"Is it like a tavern?" he asked.

"No, the tavern and the best pub is back the way we came. Gallagher's only serves food and watered wine. No ale, and he doesn't put up travelers for the night. Mom says that's a lot like human restaurants, where people go for a meal."

"And where are we going?" Keir leaned forward, all eyes for the cooper's yard, where all sorts of wares were for sale and in various stages of construction. "Surely you have somewhere you're taking me?"

"Sweeny's Pub. It's just down this street."

"But you said the best pub is back the way we came. Are you taking me to a substandard place?"

"Sweeny's is my favorite because they have good cider and plenty of snacks, but they also have more privacy. And we have things to discuss, you and I."

"We do?" The color faded from Keir's bright red face.

"You haven't forgotten that pesky little problem we nearly shipwrecked ourselves trying to get here to solve." Tierney narrowed her eyes at him. He was staring and acting odder than usual.

A smile quirked his lips, and he laughed. "We did shipwreck ourselves if you remember correctly."

"I've blocked it out. That was not a fun time." Tierney tried to bite back her laughter. She was so grateful to be here with Keir right now after all they overcame to reach Iskalt. She guided them down a narrow alley until they reached an unassuming stone structure with a simple wooden sign overhead proclaiming it as Sweeny's Pub.

"Does your father know you frequent the local pubs?" Keir slipped from his mount, looping the reins over the hitching post.

"Oh, he gave up trying to keep me away from Sweeny's a long time ago." She dismounted and headed for the carved wooden door. A bell rang overhead when she walked inside, blinking in the dim light until her eyes adjusted.

"There's my favorite princess." A big burly man with a balding head charged out from behind the bar, sweeping Tierney up in a bear hug. He whirled her around before he set her on her feet. "You can't be leaving for unexpected trips to lands unknown without telling me first." He stood back with his hands on his hips. "It near broke my heart to see your mother, our dear queen herself, so heartbroken at your absence."

"I'm sorry, Sweeny. It won't happen again. I'm swearing off the O'Shea magic for good. I'll leave portals to my brother." Tierney shrugged out of her cloak, leaving it to hang on the hook by the fire to dry with the others.

Keir followed her lead, his jaw dropping when yet another commoner cried out her pleasure that their favorite princess had come home at last. "Dear child!" A plump woman in a long woolen skirt scurried out of the kitchen, wiping her hands on her apron. "Poor old Sweeny was crushed when we found out you were lost. I prayed for your soul every morning and here you are, safely returned." She took Tierney in her arms.

"And I'm so happy to be back." Tierney let the woman mother her, returning her embrace like she wasn't the heir to the throne but just another villager.

"Your poor father." She clucked, fussing over Tierney's cold hands, leading her to warm up beside the fire. "Our king just wasn't the same without you by his side." She turned to Keir. "Ever since she were a little girl, she was always right beside him. Two peas in a pod those two." She left Tierney by the fire, turning her attention on Keir.

"Come, come. Any friend of our Princess Tia is a friend of ours. Come warm yourself by the fire. Frank, get them some hot cider." She turned back to Tierney. "You'll be wanting your favorites then? Cheese curds and freshly baked pretzels?"

Tierney groaned. "Mrs. Sweeny, you have no idea how many nights I dreamed of your pretzels and cheese curds with a hot cider to warm my belly."

"Have a seat, lassie." Mr. Sweeny shooed his wife off to the kitchens. "She'll be flapping her jaws at you till tomorrow morning if you're not careful."

"I missed you." Tierney lunged at the old man, wrapping her arms around his barrel-sized chest. "Now, it feels like my homecoming is complete." Tierney grabbed Keir's hand and led him to a corner table, where two hot ciders waited for them.

"You come here often?" Keir sat across from her.

"The Sweeneys are like my adoptive Iskaltian grandparents." Tierney took a sip of her drink and exhaled, a dreamy smile on her face. "My grandfather Brandon lives in Gelsi, and my grandmother Faolan lives in Myrkur with her wife, Shauna. They've only been married for a few years though. My grandmother Tierney was killed in a war before I was born, and my father's father was killed when he was just a child—and we don't talk about Dad's mother much—so the Sweenys are my surrogate grandparents."

"Here you go." Mrs. Sweeny set two baskets on the table. "You just let me know if you need anything else."

"Thanks, Mrs. S, you always have the best snacks." Tierney picked up a twisted piece of brown bread and broke it in half.

Mrs. Sweeny chuckled as she walked away. "Just like her mother."

"This will hit the spot." Tierney passed half of the bread to Keir.

"What is it?" He gave it a sniff and frowned. "Is this salt?" He flicked a piece of the rock salt off the bread.

"That's the best part." Tierney dipped the twist into a brownish yellow substance and took a big bite. "Just try it." She rolled her eyes at him.

Keir dipped his twist and took a bite. His eyebrows shot up as he chewed. "That's delicious. It's not like our bread at all."

"It's a pretzel. It's not bread like you're thinking. It's more of a snack that pairs well with ale or cider. We wouldn't serve it with a meal."

"You have spicy things." He pointed at the mustard. "It's more tangy than hot, but it's flavorful."

"Because we don't have to singe our mouths to taste our food." Tierney reached for the basket of cheese curds. "Try these. You'll thank me later."

Keir took a lump from the basket and dipped it in the brown substance served with it. Taking a bite, something gooey rushed out and juices ran down his fingers.

"Yeah, you kind of just need to go for it and eat the whole thing." She giggled, popping one of the curds into her mouth.

He grinned, cleaning his fingers. "I see why you were never a fan of our hard cheese."

"It's just wrong."

"See, I told you they would be here." Toby dropped into the seat beside his sister, and Logan pulled out the last chair.

"Do you mind if we join you?"

"Of course not." Tierney slapped her brother's hand away from the basket of pretzels. "Order your own. I've been deprived for months and months."

"No worries, dearies," Mrs. Sweeny called from the bar. "I'll have another round headed your way in a moment."

"Thanks, Mrs. S!" Toby called back.

"What are you doing here?" Tierney nudged her brother playfully.

"We have things to talk about." Toby pulled a map from his bag, spreading it across the table. "I sketched this from a map Grandfather found in the library."

Tierney leaned in, scrunching her nose up at the map. "It looks like the four kingdoms but bigger."

"It predates the Vatlands. This is a map of the original Lenya."

Keir leaned in to get a better look.

"Your people once ruled over all of the fae world long before our people even existed."

"What do you know?" Tierney turned to her brother.

"The Lenya of ancient times was destroyed by the formation of the vatlands. Your people managed to survive, but you were sealed off by the fire plains. There is a record we found that speculates your ancestors found a way to stop the spread of the fire plains.

"Over time, they receded. Grandfather believes the vatlands have expanded and receded at least one other time after that first instance. We have to find a way to destroy them, or it will happen all over again. Except, this time, it's possible none of us will survive."

Tierney reached for Keir's hand. "We have to find a solution. You need your magic. We have to get you a crystal so you can practice. It's been too long since any of you have been able to wield more than the simplest of magic."

"I thought of that." Logan rummaged through his pockets. "I went to the palace carpenter this morning and asked if he had any fire opals lying around. He gave me this one. I don't know if it's big enough for what you need, but it's a place to start until we can get more." Logan set the fire opal on the table. It was shaped like an icicle.

Keir just stared at it. "Your crystals are different from ours. The color is strange."

"Is it not the right kind?" Logan asked. "I can ask for another."

"No, it's powerful," Keir whispered, still not touching the crystal. "Ours are milky white, with streaks of clear blue and orange. I think they're weaker stones. We've been scraping the mines for what's left for generations. I think your fire opals must be purer."

"Can you sense how much power this holds?" Tierney ran a fingertip down the length of the fire opal.

Keir swallowed, his throat bobbing with the motion. "I think this totem is stronger than anything of its size I've ever seen in Lenya. I'm afraid to touch it."

"We're going to need all hands on deck to drive the fire plains back." Toby gave him a gentle nudge. "That means we're going to need everyone performing their best. You need practice, Keir."

"You're right. I ... don't even know what I'm capable of with this much magic. It feels ... wrong to use such a thing for practice. Like a waste."

"You need to get over that because there are a million more where this one came from." Logan slid it closer to Keir. "This is the first of many. As we speak, King Loch is ordering a second trunk of crystals just for your use during your time here in the four kingdoms."

"Start with something small." Tierney squeezed his hand, and she blew out the candle at the center of the table. "Just light the candle."

Keir nodded, wrapping his fingers around the fire opal. He sucked in a breath, his eyes closing. A look of wonder fell across his face, and Tierney wanted to kiss him. To feel for herself all that he was feeling right now.

Keir lifted the opal. Opening his eyes, he muttered under his breath, and the candle flickered to life again. A storm blazed in his eyes as he took another breath and dropped the crystal.

"How did it feel?" Tierney whispered.

"Like I could lay waste to the entire world with just this one totem. It's like nothing I've ever known."

Toby grinned. "The vatlands don't stand a chance against all of us together."

Chapter Sixteen
Keir

"I should be going with her." Keir paced the length of the throne room, waiting.

"We've been over this." Tierney lounged on her father's throne, and he couldn't help remembering the way she'd sat on the throne of Vondur the same way. Back then, it annoyed him. Now, she looked like she belonged there. "You can't both return to Lenya when we still need to figure out how to drive the vatlands back."

Keir stopped walking and turned to her. "What if all it takes is magic?"

Throwing one leg over the ornate golden arm of the throne, Tierney sighed. "Nothing is ever as simple as just needing magic. It isn't a cure-all for the world."

"But—"

"No, Keir. Stop. Bronagh will be fine. We'll figure out how to help her from here, and then you can return home for good and forget about all of us."

He didn't understand the bitterness in her tone, but when she mentioned him going home for good, something clenched inside him. Her father hadn't told her of their conversation, and it was clear both Gulliver and Griffin had kept silent as well.

"Tierney, I—" The double doors opening interrupted him.

Lochlan walked in with Toby, stopping when he caught sight of his daughter. He pointed one long finger at her. "Up."

She heaved herself off of his throne, muttering "It's just a chair."

Lochlan rubbed his eyes, as if the mere sight of her exhausted him. He took his seat as the queen breezed into the room with Bronagh, Imogen, and Veren. "Oh, good. You're all here. Let's get this started, shall we?"

Tierney hugged her arms across her chest, not meeting anyone's eyes. She hadn't spoken to him of her portals, but he knew fear when he saw it. The last time she opened one, she'd ended up a prisoner.

"Oh, and Tierney?" Her mom wrapped an arm around her shoulders. "You will also be going through."

"What?" Her eyes rounded, and Keir wanted to drag her away from this place, from anything that could hurt her.

"Told you she wouldn't like it, Mom." Toby rolled his eyes.

Lochlan leaned back on his throne. "Eldur and Fargelsi are trying to push back the swamplands. If we are to overcome the fire plains, attempting a less dangerous path first is wise. You and I will observe what they are doing and try to find a solution."

It was wise. Keir didn't relish the idea of stepping through one of the O'Shea portals either, but he'd do just about anything to help his kingdom.

The doors opened again, and two guards walked in, a giant wooden trunk between them. "Everything is aboard, your Majesty," one of them said.

Lochlan nodded to them. "Thank you. You may leave that here."

"Are those the crystals?" Bronagh asked, fiddling with the latch on the trunk. She managed to get the top open and revealed what must have been hundreds of small, fiery stones with colorful veins of magic running through them. It was ... Keir had no words.

The room thrummed with power, and he soaked it in, letting it set every nerve ending on high alert. It wasn't until Lochlan stood and clapped his hands that he snapped out of it. "All right, dusk has fallen, and there is no use waiting now. Toby will open the portal to the human realm as he is best at bringing fae with him. Once we are there, we must hurry before dawn breaks. Then, Tia will help Toby open a portal to Lenya, but she won't go into it with them. After that is open, we can leave for Fargelsi."

It sounded complicated; most things in this kingdom seemed overly complex to Keir. But he'd learned in his short time that the king was trustworthy, and he'd never do anything to put his children in jeopardy.

Lochlan walked toward them, pressing a kiss to the side of his wife's head before turning to his daughter. "Are you ready for this?"

Tierney hesitated for a moment before dragging her eyes up. Her jaw clenched. "Yeah. Yes. I'm ready."

"That's my girl. Okay, everyone needs to have a hand on Tobias. Veren, Brea, you should both stand back."

Veren was already across the room, staying as far from the portal as physically possible.

Stepping up beside Tierney, Keir put a hand on Toby's arm next to hers, their pinkies brushing together. Lochlan, Bronagh, and Imogen joined them, and Toby closed his eyes, resting a hand on the trunk.

Keir didn't see it coming. A burst of light erupted in front of his face. Someone pulled him forward, and his stomach dropped as he fell through open sky, landing on the soft earth, his arm bent in an awkward angle. Pain twisted through him, and groaning surrounded him.

"Thanks for that landing, Tobes." Tierney scowled as she pushed herself to her feet.

"Everyone hurry." Lochlan looked to the sky.

They'd left Iskalt at dusk, but here, in what Keir presumed was the human realm, the early light of dawn peeked over the horizon. He barely got a chance to glance around before Lochlan started issuing orders.

"We probably only have a few more minutes before the Iskalt power rests. Tierney, take your brother's hand. Picture Lenya; hold it in your heart. He will direct the magic."

Tierney shook her head and took a step back. "We've never done it this way before."

"Yeah, Dad, how do we know it'll work?" Toby looked more skeptical than scared, unlike his sister.

"It's a theory, but you need to try before we lose the moon altogether."

A breeze rustled the grass at Keir's feet, and he had no time to take in the human realm, to see anything other than Toby reaching out a hand to Tierney. They could do this. He knew it, but Tierney didn't.

Tears danced in her eyes. "I can't."

"You have to." Her father softened his voice. "Do we let our fears determine what we accomplish?"

She drew in a long breath. "But what if—"

"We have no use for what-ifs, Tia." He put a hand on her shoulder. "Only what is."

As hard as the Iskaltian king could be, Keir wanted to be a man like him, one who believed in the fae around him, who inspired them to greatness. A good leader didn't only help his fae; they motivated their fae to help each other.

After what felt like an eternity of waiting, Tierney nodded. "No what-ifs." She set her hand in Toby's, reaching the other out for Bronagh, who had Imogen on her other side. Toby gripped the handle of the wooden box of crystals. One moment they stood before him, and the next, it was only Tierney, a look of shock on her face.

"Did they get through?" Lochlan asked.

"I-I think so."

They wouldn't know until Toby returned, but there wasn't time to wait.

"Okay," the king said, holding out his hands. "Now, it's our turn."

In stunned silence, Keir grabbed hold of him and waited for the stomach-churning feeling he'd experienced only minutes before.

And then, he was falling again. This time, he landed in a thick patch of mossy forest. Tierney collided with him as she hit the ground, her knee digging into his gut.

But the warmth. It thawed out the chill—a persistent presence since the moment they washed up on the Iskaltian shore. Instead, a wave of heat enveloped them.

Tierney shrugged out of her fur-lined cloak. "I hate Eldur," she grumbled. "Always so dang hot."

Lochlan's lips hooked into a smile. "Try growing up here."

There was a story there, but no time to ask it because the snap of a stick told them someone was near. Keir immediately rose into a crouch, hand on the dagger at his waist. In Vondur, one must always prepare for an attack.

"What's he doing?" Lochlan asked.

Tierney shrugged. "Being weird."

A man stepped into view, a long sword hanging off his belt. He rested a hand on the hilt lazily. The intruder had an opposing frame, with a full beard and flashing eyes.

He stopped when he saw them. "Thought I heard trespassers back here. What's your business in Eldur?"

Keir would protect Tierney with his life. Today had been such a strange day, a fight would only cap it off.

Lochlan rose to his full height. "I speak of my business only to the queen. Do you realize to whom you speak?"

"Someone who thinks too highly of their own influence." Tierney smirked. "I've been telling him that my entire life, so you're a little late."

The man approached Tierney, and Keir moved to stand between them.

"Boy," their attacker growled. "If you know what's good for you, you'll step out of the way." He looked over Keir's shoulder. "Really, Tia? I thought you'd have better sense than to travel in the company of someone who'd try to start a fight he can't win."

Keir's spine stiffened when Tierney laughed.

"For the record, Uncle Finn, the only person who can best Keir in a duel is me." She ducked around Keir and wrapped the man—Finn—in a hug.

Shame washed over Keir. This man was the King of Eldur, and he'd wanted to fight him right here in his own forest.

"This is Keir," Lochlan said, walking past the man. "Don't scare him off, Finn. I like this one."

Finn turned to follow him. "Of the two of us, I think I'm less likely to send one of Tia's suitors running in the opposite direction."

Lochlan only grunted in response.

"He's not a suitor," Tierney said. "He's a king." Neither of those statements were true, but she didn't yet know.

Lochlan caught his eye, giving an encouraging nod. He just had to keep going, to figure out how to save Lenya, and then he could figure everything else out after.

They entered a clearing where sand and dirt mixed on the forest floor, as if the area couldn't decide whether it was a desert or a woodland. An army of fae occupied the space, some using their magic to push at an invisible foe.

"We're waiting for Neeve to arrive," Finn explained. "She sent word that she was a day's ride out. That was two days ago."

"The swamplands can be unpredictable." Lochlan rubbed the back of his neck. "If they had to travel around a bog or fight one of the creatures residing here, a small delay isn't something to worry over."

"Uncle Finn?" Tierney stared at the ground before surveying the surrounding area. "These aren't the vatlands. Dad would never have brought us so close."

"They are now. Until a few weeks ago, the ground we walk on was desert. It becomes more unstable by the day. We must be vigilant and on guard for quicksand as it changes."

"Tia!" A girl who couldn't have been more than a few years younger than Tierney ran toward them, giving Tierney a tight hug. "When my mom told me you'd returned, I wanted to go to Iskalt right away, but they needed me here."

"This is more important than me, but it's good to see you, Darra." Tierney released her. "What progress have you made?"

"Very little." As the girl reported to Tierney, Keir walked farther into the clearing. The ground underneath his feet was soft, saturated. Water seeped up through the grass and sand with each step he took.

For a moment, he watched the magic wielders work. They'd all been right. He may have wanted to go to Lenya, but being here would provide more aid than he could there.

The sound of many hooves pounding the dirt preceded horses thundering into the clearing. Keir turned to watch an impossibly tall woman jump from her saddle. She moved with the grace of someone who'd spent their entire life trying not to be seen. That must mean this was Neeve, the maid turned queen.

There were no excited greetings or introductions, only mild hellos before she got down to business. "The marsh is almost to the palace grounds." She gave a weary sigh. "If we do not stop its further movement, I do not know what will happen."

A hand slipped into Keir's, and he squeezed, knowing Tierney needed the strength as much as he did.

Finn scrubbed a hand over his beard. "We've been at this for the last two months now, and it's only grown. I don't know what more we can attempt."

"There's always more," Tierney put in.

"Our fae are tired." Darra sighed. "We cannot keep operating as we have been. When nothing works, we must change our tactics."

"What did you have in mind?" Lochlan looked willing to take the young woman's advice, and it reminded Keir of Eavha and how often he'd brushed her aside. He vowed never to do that again.

"Tia is here now. No one has a power like hers. Maybe she should try."

Tierney shook her head. "This isn't the prison magic, Darra. It's ancient and more powerful than we could ever imagine. The magic of the vatlands has created swamps, frozen mountains, fiery wastelands, and even a maelstrom in the center of the ocean. They're designed to keep us all apart, every kingdom."

"Yes, but you have the magic of three kingdoms in your blood." Even her father was looking at her like this idea might work.

"It's not that easy. I have the three, but that does not mean they are equal within me. My Fargelsian training has been in depth and I have the most experience with it. My Iskaltian magic is nearly equal, but my Eldurian magic is a distant third—and I've been without all of it for many months now. I can only attempt the simplest acts and this is not simple."

Neeve rubbed her forehead. "She's right. But we can't stop trying. It has been a long day and evening is nearly upon us. I'll have my fae begin shortly with some of the more complex Fargelsian spells and Tia can join with the other Iskaltians as best she can. We need all sides of magic working together in this."

Finn, Lochlan, and Darra followed her to where the other fae gathered near a fire that lit up the night.

Tierney didn't move to join them, her voice soft in the dark. "I feel like I'm letting them down."

"Tierney, look at me," Keir said.

She lifted her eyes, locking them on his.

"You aren't letting anyone down. No one knows your magic better than you."

"That's the thing, Keir. Ever since we've returned, I feel like I don't know it at all. I worked for years to control the power and never fully grasped that control in the way others do. But being without it for all those months ..." She shrugged helplessly. "It's like a muscle memory has been lost."

"You'll get it back."

"I hope so."

He pulled her into a hug, and she rested her head against his chest.

"I want to do whatever is necessary to help your kingdom."

"I know you do."

"But I'm afraid of unleashing multiple sides of my power at once. What if I make it worse?"

"Can it be worse than threatening to destroy all fae life?"

She let loose a muffled laugh. "Probably not. Maybe we should just all evacuate to the human realm."

His nose scrunched. "I've heard your stories, your weird sayings. I think I'll take my chances with the fire plains."

She pressed a kiss to the side of his chin. "And if we can't stop them?"

"We never stop fighting."

They stood that way for a while, watching the Fargelsians work under the light of the moon. The Eldurians retreated to their tents to await the return of their magic with the sun.

Keir didn't sleep that night. Instead, he lay awake imagining a different world in which the vatlands never separated the kingdoms, never left Lenya on their own to become a warring land split in two. He could have grown up with prosperous villages, a father who loved him, the ability to keep his family safe.

In that world, there were no Comhracs, no battles with gold-clad warriors. Children didn't die of starvation. Mothers didn't live in fear.

Maybe, just maybe, it was the kind of world they could create one day. But first, they had to figure out how to have a future at all.

He crept from his tent as the sun rose to find the Eldurian contingent preparing to get back to work. Finn and Darra argued over something while Neeve looked on.

Lochlan sat on his own, a tin cup of tea in one hand.

Tierney wandered into the clearing, her mind clearly occupied.

"Everything okay?" Keir fell into step beside her.

"No."

"Care to tell me what's wrong?"

"Quicksand." She pointed through the trees. "Almost fell in it. The vatlands moved last night. They got too close to camp."

Something had to be done. If they couldn't solve the

problem of the swampland, Lenya had no hope of holding off the fire plains.

Tierney joined the others and explained what she'd found. They jumped into action.

There wasn't much Keir could do but watch the efficient way the two kingdoms worked together now that the sun was out. He'd never seen such an alliance, but the Queen of Fargelsi and the King of Eldur stood side by side, their magic pooling in their fingertips as they tried to push the powerful vatlands back to where they belonged.

But where was that? The vatlands existed long before any of them were born, but they weren't natural to this world. For the first time, Keir wondered if simply stopping the spread wasn't enough.

Could they destroy them altogether?

"Lochlan," Finn yelled, "get your kingly butt over here."

Keir followed Lochlan and Tierney to where Finn was bent over, examining something on the ground. He pressed a hand to the soil, where only a few blades of grass poked through.

"Keep going," Finn yelled as his magic soaked into the ground. "I think it's working."

Neeve lowered herself to her knees to imitate Finn's actions, her eyes widening. The movement was small, slow, a tiny trickle of water pulling back through the ground. They all saw it.

Whatever they'd done, however this happened, Keir needed to learn everything.

Because for the first time, he saw the faint lines of hope in the form of receding water, drying land emerging from the murk of the swamp.

CHAPTER SEVENTEEN
BRONAGH

Bronagh's stomach sank to her toes as a light erupted around her. She clutched the trunk handle as if her life depended on it. Because it did. And not just her life. The lives of all her fae rested on this one chance to return to Lenya with enough magic to protect them from the immediate threat of the fire plains.

Without warning, the ground rushed up to greet them, but a small tug somewhere around her navel slowed her descent, and her feet touched the ground gently.

"That wasn't so bad." Toby glanced around, as if he magically transported himself to new lands every day. "It's rather hot here, isn't it?" He fanned his face with his free hand. The other held the trunk suspended between them.

"I don't think she's breathing." Imogen lunged for Bronagh. "Your Majesty, are you all right?"

Bronagh couldn't seem to remember how her lungs worked, and it took her a moment to suck in a breath.

"There it is; she's fine." Toby patted her shoulder in a soothing gesture. "It's never a fun way to travel if you're not used to it." He eyed the bleak countryside. "Any idea if we're where we're supposed to be?"

"We aren't in Grima, that's for sure." Imogen wrinkled her nose. "It don't smell right, does it, your Majesty?"

Bronagh shook her head. "Vondur." She pointed across the dry, cracked ground, where a well-traveled road stretched into the distance. Turning, she squinted into the bright afternoon sunlight. It was disconcerting to leave one place at dawn and arrive at another in the blink of an eye to find it nearly dusk with a blazing hot sun. "That way." She pointed to a hillside, where the road disappeared. "The palace is just beyond the crossroads."

"Do you think they'll receive us, Majesty?" Imogen bounded beside her queen, eager to help carry the trunk, but Bronagh wouldn't let it out of her sight.

"We have a peace treaty with Vondur now." Bronagh picked up her pace. "They will honor it." At least, she hoped. They had much bigger worries than an age-old war no one wanted to fight anymore.

Dust kicked up just beyond the hill. "Let's hurry." Toby matched Bronagh's pace. "Maybe we can hitch a ride."

Bronagh smiled at the strange saying. "You're not at all like your sister in so many ways, but in others, you're the same."

"Mom says I'm her quiet, even-tempered child." Toby shrugged. "I think that's Mom talk for I'm her favorite."

A troop of scouts trotted along the road, kicking up more dust. Bronagh was sweating and eager to get out of the baking hot sun. The ground crunched beneath her feet, and she swore the bottoms of her shoes were melting.

"Hail there!" a soldier called out to them. "Do you seek refuge from the burning lands?"

Bronagh shielded her eyes from the sun as she looked up to see a mixture of Vondurian and Grimian uniforms. She smiled at the sight. "I am Bronagh Agnew, Queen of Grima. I have returned from Iskalt with Prince Tobias O'Shea. We must speak with Princess Eavha Dagnan right away."

"Your Majesty, you made it!" A young officer slid from his mount. "We've been worried sick for your return." He led his horse across the hard ground to her side. "Please, take my mount. I will carry your trunk."

"I would keep it with me if you please." She passed the trunk off to Toby and pulled herself up into the saddle. "I'll tie the trunk to the back of my saddle, but could my companions also have a horse?"

"I'll ride with Imogen." Toby smiled and thanked a soldier for lending him his horse.

He pulled Imogen up to sit behind him, and Bronagh led the way down the worn road to the crumbling castle, where she hoped they could all work together to defeat the fire plains before it was too late.

"Bron? Is that you?" A shriek of excitement echoed from the ramparts, where a leather-clad Eavha leaned over the parapet to get a better look. Her pet rested on her haunches beside her.

"We have returned." Bronagh beamed at the young girl. "And what a tale I have to tell you!"

"Who is that with you? Is it Tia?" Eavha gasped and ran across the wall to the tower steps that led to the courtyard.

"Well, I can't wait to tell my sister someone thinks she looks like me." Toby ran a soothing hand over his horse's mane and urged her into a trot.

"Eavha is more exuberant than observant." Bronagh laughed. "But she grows on you. She also adores your sister."

"And she has a very large cat chasing her." Toby's eyes shot up as they entered the courtyard and the princess came darting down the stairs to meet them.

"Sheba, don't freak out our guests." Eavha made the big cat sit before she came to greet them.

"I have so much to tell you." Bronagh slipped from her mount, reaching back to release the trunk from its binding.

"Did you find it? Is my brother okay?"

"Iskalt? Yes. And it's beautiful. Keir is still there with Tierney and the rest of her family."

"They'll be in Fargelsi by now." Toby dismounted and turned to greet Eavha. "Hi there, I'm Tia's twin brother."

"Toby?" Eavha's jaw dropped open, and she lunged at him, wrapping her arms around him. "I didn't think I'd ever get to meet you."

"It's a pleasure, Princess Eavha." He released her and gave her a small bow. "I won't be with you long. I'll need to return to my family once the moon rises."

"The moon?" She turned questioning eyes on Bronagh.

Bronagh just shrugged. "Let's go inside, and I'll tell you everything."

"We don't have the luxury of time, I'm afraid." Eavha looped her arm through Toby's and the other through Bronagh's. Imogen followed them with the chest of priceless crystals. "The fire plains are upon us, and we're losing the battle. Most of Lenya is lost, and we're surrounded now.

"How many have we lost?" Bronagh was afraid to hear the answer.

"Too many to count." Eavha guided them into the palace and straight to the throne room, where most of the Vondurian court were in attendance.

"Leave us," Eavha called to the room. "I will be in the council chambers with Queen Bronagh and Prince Tobias." She marched across the room, careless of the whispering.

Bronagh sent Imogen with a maid to get settled comfortably and have a proper meal. She was clear that the girl must be cared for as if she were a princess herself. As far as Bronagh was concerned, the girl would never want for anything the rest of her life ... however long that might be.

When they were alone in the small hall behind the throne room, Eavha threw her hands up in the air. "I hope you have the answers to all our problems in that powerful trunk of yours because just the feel of it is terrifying."

Bronagh flipped the latch and opened the trunk filled with the most potently powerful crystals anyone in Lenya had ever seen.

"Oh my." Eavha sank into the nearest chair. "I've never felt so much power from one little box." She clutched the totem around her neck. "I wouldn't even know what to do with them."

"We're going to have to figure it out. It isn't just about Lenya and the fire plains anymore. It's happening on the other side too. They call places like the fire plains vatlands. And they're all expanding."

"My family and the royals from each of the four kingdoms are hard at work searching for a solution." Toby reached for a crystal from the trunk. "Our magic is different. We don't need such vessels to reach it, but none of that matters. Iskalt, Fargelsi, Eldur, and Myrkur are all your allies now." He handed Eavha the crystal, but she shrank back from it.

"I couldn't ... it's too much. I wouldn't know what to do with it."

Toby smiled, placing the crystal back into the box. "We will work together to find a solution. But I must leave you tonight. Now that I have visited Lenya for myself, I will return once we have more news."

"I have some news myself. I fear you'll never believe me." Eavha eyed the crystals, moving to sit at the large wooden table near the windows. "You'll want to sit down for this." She set a key on the table. It was an old-fashioned kind of key made of silver and set with blue sapphires.

"Keir gave me this key before he left. It unlocks a small chamber in the king's rooms. It contains all the knowledge of ancient Lenya."

"Like a library?" Toby leaned forward. "We have lots of experience with ancient libraries."

"Not a library. A book. A journal really." Eavha's brow furrowed. "A journal of all the kings of Vondur, all the way back to the very first one. But it goes back even further than Vondur. It has histories of every ruler of ancient Lenya. I've studied the book night and day, looking for answers, and I thought I found it. This has all happened before. I think it's how our kingdoms came to be isolated from yours."

Toby nodded. "We've found similar histories."

"There was one line I read." Eavha leaned forward. "It spoke of how the fire plains came to be and how they were controlled. When our people retreated to this side of the plains, they were fleeing in much the same way we are now. But they were able to stop the spread."

"How?" Toby and Bronagh both hung on her every word.

"There was a spell of some sort, but it was in a language I didn't recognize."

"May I see this book?" Toby asked.

"That's just it." Eavha shook her head. "It disappeared."

"Someone stole it?" Bronagh asked.

"No. It vanished. Right from my hands, like magic. Like real, honest-to-goodness magic. One moment it was there, and the next it was gone. I know I can't expect you to believe such a thing, but—"

Bronagh held her hand up to stop her. "I've seen enough strange things since I left Lenya. I believe you."

"What are we going to do, Bron?"

"We're going to use these crystals and put our best soldiers and magic wielders to the test. We'll do the best we can with what we've got."

"And I will be in touch with more news as soon as I'm able." Toby took Bronagh's and Eavha's hands in his. "We are all in this together."

CHAPTER EIGHTEEN
TIERNEY

I t took nearly two days to leave Fargelsi and portal back to
the human realm, wait for night, and return to Eldur,
where the sun was just setting when they made camp
along the banks of Sol Loch. Normally one of Tierney's favorite
places to visit, with its warm sulfur springs and hot mud baths,
it was now in danger of being consumed by the fire plains.
Already, the vast lake was evaporating in the intense heat.

They waited impatiently for the sun to rise so they could
get to work. Neeve accompanied them to Eldur to help push
the fire plains back in the same way her people were doing
along the Gelsi-Eldur border dealing with the marshlands. It
was slow going, but it was working.

Uncle Finn and his Eldurian magic wielders were well-
rested and ready to get to work. Tierney was anxious to do her
part, bringing as much Gelsi magic as she could contribute
alongside her aunt and the handful of fae she'd brought with
her. Even Brea was prepared to aid with either side of her
magic wherever it was needed.

"This is exhausting." Keir paced across the cracked desert
clearing. They were camped as close as they could get to the
plains without risking their tents to fires. "Does it not drive you
mad to wait for the sun and the moon to use your magic?"

"Not any more than it would drive me mad to need a vessel to use my magic. Just think of it like the sun acts as a totem for all of Eldur. They have to await its arrival to be able to reach their power."

"I'm just anxious to see this work."

"It started working for Gelsi, it will work here." Tierney pointed to the horizon. "Look, they're gathering already. Come on."

Sweat poured down Tierney's face as they crossed the desert sands, trying to ignore the way her shoes felt like tiny ovens strapped to her feet.

Dozens of Eldurians knelt in the sand, waiting for their magic to rise with the sun. The Gelsi fae were already at work, their hands reaching into the hot desert earth, letting their magic trickle into the ground, soon to meet with Eldurian power. Together, the two kingdoms would heal the fire plains, pushing them back within their borders.

Part of Tierney wished they could push them all the way to Lenya. She wanted a world where her friends weren't so isolated.

"Ready for this?" Tierney's mother said as she and aunt Alona came to join them.

"We've got this." She squeezed her aunt's hand. Alona would wait with Keir, Uncle Myles, and Lochlan while everyone else went to work.

Sinking her fingers into the hot sand, Tierney called on her Fargelsi magic, murmuring the words Aunt Neeve taught her.

Laekena pao sem brennte hefur verio.

The ground heated as Eldurian fire magic poured in to join the Gelsi magic. Tierney held her breath, waiting for some sign that the plains were receding. For the sand to cool and moisture to return to the air. Something.

"It's not working," she whispered to her mother.

"Keep trying." Brea pushed her hands deeper into the ground, the Gelsi spell falling from her lips.

An hour later and nothing had changed. Neeve sat back on her heels. "I am afraid we are wasting our energy."

"Why would it work in Gelsi but not in Eldur?" Tierney frowned, dusting the sand from her blistered hands. "It doesn't make any sense."

"We will just have to try something else." Brea stood and brushed the sand from her leggings. "We have enough magic wielders here that we are bound to come up with a solution."

But Tierney didn't miss the shadow of worry that filled her mother's eyes. "We can't leave them trapped in Lenya much longer, Mom. If we can't find a solution ..." Her eyes filled with tears as she thought of the danger Eavha and all her people could be in right this moment.

"If all else fails, we will bring them here. We will not let them suffer. We just need more time." Brea ran a hand through her sweaty hair. "The one thing we don't have enough of."

The wind kicked up, and sand whirled around them.

"Something's happening." Tierney looked around, hoping for a miracle, but she knew what this was. "Keir! Over here!" she called, waving him frantically over to her side.

"Your grandfather really shouldn't be driving that thing. He's never been very good at it." Brea ducked her head and held on to Tierney.

"What's happening?" Keir reached her side, draping an arm around her as if to protect her from some strange foe.

"It's okay, Keir," Tierney shouted over the roar of the wind.

Golden light sparked above them, and the Library of Aghadoon appeared, settling into the landscape like it always belonged there.

"He must be out of sorts if he forgot to hide the village."

Brea shook her head with a smile. "I think you need to help Keir out. I'm not sure he's breathing."

Tierney reached for his arm. "It's fine; everything is fine. It's just my grandfather."

Keir gaped at the sight of the normally concealed village. He pointed at the buildings, blinking his eyes as if to clear the vision from his sight.

"Did that ... just drop out of the sky?"

"There's no place like home." Brea snickered, and Uncle Myles threw his head back and laughed. Everyone else just shook their heads at whatever human nonsense they were talking about.

"You know, sometimes I hate living among the fae." Brea shook her head. "No one ever gets my jokes."

"Begone, my pretty!" Myles cackled in a creepy voice as he advanced on Brea, hunched over with his hands raised like claws. "Before someone drops a house on you!"

It was Brea's turn to laugh.

"Just ignore them." Tierney sighed. "My guess is they're shouting movie quotes at each other. Let's just pretend whatever they're doing didn't just happen."

"What about that?" Keir pointed at the village. "How did that place just fall out of the sky?"

"It's a really long story." She linked her arm around Keir's. "The short version is this is the village of Aghadoon. It contains a very powerful library with all the histories of the fae. My grandfather Brandon—former King of Fargelsi—is the custodian of the library. If he's gone to the trouble of moving the village, then he's likely found something important."

"Okay, but I want the long version of this story at some point. Libraries don't just fly around, Tia."

"Here, they do." She tugged him toward the crumbling

columns that marked the entrance into the village. Brandon was already making his way down from the library.

"Hi, Dad, what have you found?" Brea walked to greet him. He carried a large leather-bound book, thick with handwritten pages. He held it open to a specific spot.

"It's not a solution, but it's important." Brandon paused to drop a kiss on Brea's forehead. "Sorry for the sloppy arrival. I was in a hurry." He thrust the book out in front of him. "The vatlands aren't natural."

Tierney had never seen her grandfather so rattled. "What do you mean?" She moved to stand behind her mother, peering over her shoulder to see the book.

"It seems there was an ancient war among the original Lenyans who ruled these lands before us. There were many kingdoms at that time, and they were at constant war with each other for one reason or another. They couldn't negotiate peace, so they agreed to live separately. They created the vatlands as physical boundaries to separate their kingdoms and bring an end to the conflict. For ages and ages, it worked and there were no more wars. But then, the vatlands began to expand as they are now."

"What did they do?" Tierney stepped closer, her heart in her throat as she hoped for some clue that would lead them to the answer.

"They died," Brandon said flatly. "Except for a small group, who somehow survived."

"Doesn't that book tell you how they survived?" Her voice cracked. They needed answers, not more dead ends.

"Not that I have found , but we're still looking."

"We are running out of time, Grandfather."

"May I ask where you found this book?" Keir's face had gone pale with shock.

"The library here is a mystical place. I'm not sure I can

explain where it came from, but it showed up while I was searching for information on your homeland."

"That is my father's book. How could you possibly have a book that sits in my father's rooms in the palace of Vondur? I gave my sister access to that very book before I left, hoping she would find some source of information in it."

"Are you certain it's the same book?" Tierney sniffed back her tears.

"May I?" Keir reached for the book, and Brandon let him take it. Flipping through the pages, Keir stopped on a page toward the back. "It's the same. This is my father's handwriting. I don't understand how you have it. Can your flying library reach Vondur?"

"The library houses all the knowledge of the fae worlds." Brandon scratched his head. "That doesn't mean every book and scroll is physically there at all times. The magic of the library shows us what we need based on the subjects we are searching for. It's possible the magic somehow acquired this book ... or perhaps an identical copy of it simply because we needed this information."

"That is a conversation for another time." Tierney pulled their attention back to the important discussion. "The fact is, we need to study this book. It has to be what Keir's father mentioned when he told me he had access to great knowledge of the histories of all the realms. At the time, it seemed like he knew a lot more than he was saying. This book might be the clue to what we're looking for."

"Why is it always a magic book we have to decipher to figure out how to save the world?" Brea muttered.

"There is one other thing." Brandon's voice grew soft. "There was a treaty the ancients created when they set the vatlands in place." He glanced at Brea, taking a deep breath before he continued. "The vatlands were meant to be stationary as long as the terms of the treaty were honored. It seems when Tierney crossed into Lenya, taking the magic of *three* kingdoms with her into a land that had no such magic, she broke the treaty. The magic saw her arrival as an invasion of three kingdoms against one, and it triggered the consequences the ancients set in place. They wanted the treaty to last, and so they made the consequences of breaking it so dire no one ever dared risk it."

"But how can that be?" Brea asked. "Tia has traveled across vatlands before. We all have."

Brandon shook his head. "When she was a child with Gelsi magic, yes, but since she came of age and inherited the magic of Eldur and Iskalt just a few short years ago, has she made such a journey?"

"Anytime we've visited Gelsi, Eldur, or Myrkur in recent years, we've traveled through portals." Brea's shoulders slumped.

"So, you're saying it's my fault." Tierney took a step back. "All of it." A vital piece of her soul shattered inside her, and she couldn't see past the veil of tears clouding her eyes. "The expanding fire plains that have killed thousands. It's because of me and my stupid, childish impulsive behavior."

"Tia." Brea took a step toward her daughter.

Tierney shook her head. "No." She turned and walked away from their sympathetic eyes.

CHAPTER NINETEEN
KEIR

"Any luck?" Keir asked Brea as she approached.

The queen gave a sad sigh and shook her head. "She won't talk to me. I'm the only one in this entire realm who could understand the power inside her, how it's shaping her reactions, her emotions, but I can't help her if she won't allow me to."

"You mean she's even more upset because of the magic?"

"In a way. If we do not control it, it amplifies our emotions. The news is horrible, but it is not her fault. She didn't know the consequences of such an action. Yet, there's so much turmoil inside her I'm not sure she'll be able to see that."

"Let me try, Mom." Toby walked toward them through the dark. He'd only arrived a few minutes before, returning from Lenya.

His mom placed a hand on his shoulder. "Honey, I think the best thing we can do for her right now is give her peace."

"But—"

"Come, let's get you fed. From what Tia tells me, I'm sure you didn't enjoy the food in Lenya with all of its spices." She looked at Keir. "He's always had a bit of a weak stomach when it comes to spice, like my husband."

"Mom." Toby groaned.

187

Keir was torn between following Toby to get a report on Lenya and seeking out Tierney. The latter won out. Once Toby and Brea were safely occupied and not watching, he walked off into the dark. Pulling a crystal from his pocket, he used it to light his path.

He found Tierney sitting on a sandstone boulder at the edges of Sol Loc, where the water had receded from the banks. She had her knees pulled up to her chest and her chin resting on them. For a moment, she didn't look like the version of Tierney he knew—the warrior, the fierce princess.

Instead, she was just a girl, one who'd received the worst news of her life.

"If you knew me at all, you'd know I want to be alone," she said without turning to look at him.

Keir stepped forward, stopping at her side. "It's a good thing I don't know you at all then." He lifted a brow and looked down at her. It was a lie. He'd started wondering if he knew Tierney O'Shea better than anyone else in her life. For one, when she said to leave her alone, he refused to allow her to wallow.

They both stared at the shrinking lake as the silence stretched between them. Finally, when Tierney spoke, her voice wavered like she was trying not to cry. "Do you hate me, Keir?"

"No," he answered quickly.

"You should. Your fae are dead because of me. Your lands ..." Her breath stuttered as it pushed past her lips.

Keir didn't move. "My fae are dead because our ancestors decided magic was the only way to peace."

"Isn't it?"

"Come on. I know you better than that. There's always another way." She'd spent months in Lenya with no magic and managed to bring peace to his kingdom for the first time in many years.

At first, he thought she might consider his words, but she shook her head. "Peace has no meaning if there isn't anyone left to enjoy it."

"Tierney O'Shea, are you giving up?"

Her head jerked up, and her eyes snapped to his. "No."

"Really? Because it sounds an awful lot like you are. We're still trying to pull back the fire plains, and I'm not ready to call it a failure yet. I refuse to believe we came this far only to be stopped by a little magic."

"A little magic." She snorted. "You mean all the power of our ancients? They were strong enough to divide the kingdoms, to place the vatlands between us."

"And you're stronger." He lowered himself to the boulder at her side. "*We're* stronger."

"You sound like my Uncle Myles with his undying hope. Stop it. It's not natural for you."

Keir bumped her shoulder. "Maybe I'm tired of fearing the worst. Maybe I'm tired of focusing on what's wrong and want to make things right."

Tierney glanced away into the dark. "That doesn't change what I did."

"No, what your magic did. Aren't you the one who says it's like its own being? That you can't always control it?"

"Yes, but—"

"No, listen. You made a giant mistake. I won't say you didn't. But you didn't set off to hurt anyone." He pictured his kingdom, how both Vondur and Grima now worked together. If they managed to succeed in fighting off the fire plains, a new day would dawn for all of Lenya.

Tears streaked down Tierney's cheeks, and she didn't wipe them away. "But I did. I hurt so many fae."

Every sob that echoed out of her further cracked his heart. He wasn't sure when her feelings had become his, but he couldn't stand how broken she looked. Wrapping both arms around her, he held her against him.

Tierney clutched his tunic, crying into it, her back shaking. "I don't know how to get past this."

"You keep fighting."

"What if I don't know how?"

Keir smoothed the hair back from her face and pressed a kiss to her forehead, closing his eyes. "You will." He had more faith in her than he'd ever had in anyone else. Trust didn't come easy to men like him, but he knew Tierney's heart. He knew every intention she'd had was of the purest sort.

They sat together for a while, neither of them feeling the need to speak. Tomorrow, they would go back to battling the fire plains, but tonight, it was just the two of them and the dark.

After a while, Tierney's breathing evened out into sleep. She leaned most of her weight on Keir, and he smiled into her hair. In sleep, she wasn't sad or fierce, irritating or stubborn. She was just Tierney, free from the masks she wore.

Keir gathered her into his arms and stood. Her head lolled onto his shoulder, her breath warming his neck. The night was hot, his skin sticky with sweat, and yet he didn't want to let her go. Not now, not ever.

Carrying her through camp, he greeted Brea and Toby with nods. Toby tried to follow him, but Brea held him back.

Keir ducked into Tierney's tent and lowered her slowly to the bedroll. She murmured something unintelligible, and he smiled. It was so rare he saw her with her defenses down. He could have watched her all night.

On his knees, Keir bent forward, pressing his nose, his lips to the spot right above the corner of her left eye. "I'm not giving up on you, Tierney," he whispered. "Please don't give up on yourself."

Most of the camp was quiet as Keir emerged from the tent. The Iskaltian magic wielders were working at the border of the fire plains while the Eldurians rested. Tierney would be vexed she fell asleep instead of helping, but he didn't have the heart to wake her.

A single figure sat by the fire, more for light than warmth in this hot climate. Keir had no desire to be close to anything that would add to the heat, but he found himself walking in that direction regardless.

Brandon O'Rourke looked up as he neared. "Ah, our Lenyan friend. I was wondering when I'd finally get to speak with you." He gestured to the space next to him. "It's a little crowded out here, but I've made room for you."

Keir glanced around the empty area before lowering himself to the ground. "You're the one who ... er ... flew the village here."

"Yes, yes. Normally, I would be among my books right about now." He gestured to where the village rose out of the dark. "But I came to speak with my daughter and then was hoping to speak with you."

"Me?"

"Oh, yes. Lenya is fascinating to me. We did not know of its true existence until the library decided to show us the right materials. You use fire opals as magical totems, correct?"

Keir only understood about half of what the man said. He pulled out his crystal. "We don't call them opals, but yes, they allow us to harness the power."

Brandon shook his head, his eyes wide. "Truly amazing. And here we thought the human realm was our most incredible discovery. You sailed here through the stormy seas, I'm told."

Keir nodded. "They call it the maelstrom and told us it was impassable. It probably would have been had it not been for Tia's magic returning."

"The maelstrom. Brilliant." He stared into the flames, and Keir could practically see his mind turning. "Where would you say this maelstrom was?"

"Far out at sea."

"Yes, I know that, but did it come upon you while you passed the fire plains?"

"Actually, it was after we got around them, but not long after."

He smiled, as if he'd known that would be the answer. "I have some theories, young king. I think the maelstrom occurs when the sea and the air around it shifts so suddenly from the extreme heat of the fire plains to the icy blasts of the mountain vatlands. It's an unnatural phenomenon."

"Wait, so you're saying it's all a part of this magic as well?"

"In an indirect way, yes."

That meant ... "If we succeed in pulling back the fire plains, the maelstrom—"

"Might disappear. But like I said, it is only a theory."

The implications of such a theory were endless. If Lenya was no longer limited in their use of the seas, it changed everything from fishing capabilities to trade.

A snore came from Tierney's tent, and Keir looked back over his shoulder.

Brandon followed his gaze. "Is my granddaughter well? I probably shouldn't have revealed what I'd found."

Keir couldn't fault the man for bringing them any and all information he found on the vatlands. "No, she would have wanted to know." He sighed. "She blames herself for all of this, you know."

Brandon was quiet for a moment. "Every action we take has consequences. The severity of those consequences comes down to luck." He paused. "The O'Shea portal magic is both the most powerful and most unknown magic in the fae realm. Tierney has never had much control over it, and her actions were rash and irresponsible."

Keir was about to defend her when Brandon continued.

"But that girl has done more for the four kingdoms than any other living fae. She was a child when she started correcting our mistakes from long ago, righting our wrongs. Now, it is time for us to do the same for her.

"No one is ever blameless. And no one is ever entirely at fault." He pushed to his feet. "I think I'll return to my bed in the village. When Tierney wakes up, tell her she is welcome to an actual room, though I doubt she'll take me up on it. Stubborn as her mother, that one." He smiled. "But stubbornness is what saves us all."

He walked off, leaving Keir alone with the night and his thoughts. For so long, he'd blamed his father for problems in Vondur, he'd blamed himself.

No one is ever blameless, young king. And no one is ever entirely at fault.

They would fix this mistake made by their ancestors long ago. They would defeat the vatlands. And then, maybe everything they'd done would be worth it.

Maybe there would be fae left to enjoy the well-earned peace.

CHAPTER TWENTY
BRONAGH

Bronagh stared across the wasteland at the remnants of the newest village to succumb to the fire plains. Where wooden houses once stood, only ashy ground remained. Stone pillars and fences bore the mark of fire, black scorching up their once smooth surfaces. In the center of the village was a well, now nothing more than a circle of stones, the ground beneath them sucked dry.

And it was so close. Too close.

The children and feeble of Grima were safely tucked into the mountain fortress, the network of caves that had hidden Grimians for generations.

As the fire plains expanded up into the mountains, though, even that wasn't safe.

The line between Grima and Vondur was blurred, the borders overtaken by bubbling geysers erupting from the ground, hot steam pouring into the atmosphere.

Now, there was no division, no two kingdoms against each other. Only one.

"We don't have long." Eavha stepped up beside Bronagh, Sheba shadowing her as always. The huge cat intimidated Bronagh, but there was also a strange comfort in the protection she provided, though not even her long teeth and razor claws could fight their enemy now.

"Are you afraid, Eavha?" For their fae, for their kingdom, and the future they wouldn't have.

Eavha lifted her chin. "You cannot have courage without first experiencing fear."

"And it's going to take every ounce of our courage to overcome this now."

Donal joined them, his arms crossed over his chest. He was too young for this, they both were, but circumstances forced them into roles they had to embrace. "When the Iskaltian prince returns, can't he just usher our fae to safety through that ... portal he opened?"

Bronagh shook her head. "We will succumb to the fire plains before they do, but they are not immune. Each of their vatlands is expanding, covering more ground and encroaching on their villages."

"Vatlands." Her uncle crossed his arms where he stood a few paces away. "Magic without totems. Are we sure we wish to put our faith in such notions?"

"Keir is there. He is of Lenya."

"He is of Vondur." A scowl flashed across her uncle's face. Old ideas were hard to overcome.

Eavha turned to face him, her cheeks flushing red. "And what is wrong with Vondur, Grimian?"

Uncle Cormac started to respond, but Bronagh cut him off. "Not now. There is no time for this." She turned and walked back to where their party gathered. Sweat dripped down the small of her back, and it would only get worse.

The air hung heavy with the scent of sulfur and the intense heat. "Declan, bring the crystals." She'd tasked the general with protecting them on the journey. Eavha trusted him, and that was enough for her.

Declan lugged the trunk forward and set it on the ground. He popped the latch, and when he opened it, a collective gasp wound through the group.

Here, on the edges of the fire plains, the best warriors of all of Vondur and Grima stood together, red and gold, friend and foe. These were the fae trained to use totems to their greatest potential. One day, she hoped the magic could be accessible to all Lenyans.

Imogen crouched next to the trunk and pulled out a crystal, lobbing it toward the nearest soldier. He plucked it out of the air, and she threw another one, never missing.

"What you hold are the fire opals of the kingdoms on the far side of the fire plains. They may be our only hope of holding them back. We must work in shifts to have totem wielders awake at all times. This will not be easy, and it may not be short. Our fae are counting on our ability to stop the spread." She had no delusions that they'd be able to push the fire plains back, but they may just be able to slow its progression until Keir learned of another solution.

"Is everyone ready?" When a few soldiers murmured in assent, she nodded to Declan. "Your men are up first."

"Yes, your Majesty." Declan was good at taking orders, at playing the role of king's general. In her case, at the moment, he was the queen's general. She hoped Keir wouldn't mind if she stole him.

Declan approached the place where the air seemed to shimmer and move. Sweat broke out across his face. Bronagh joined him, clenching her jaw against the intense heat.

As Declan's men lined up, they lifted their totems.

"Now," Bronagh yelled.

Light exploded from the opal, and Bronagh's feet lifted as the force of the power threw her backward. She hit the ground and stared up into dark skies. Despite the early hour, rain clouds blocked the sun from view. She couldn't help thinking how fitting it was as she tried to breathe.

"Bron." Eavha bent over her. "Are you alive?"

A laugh burst out of Bronagh, and she stopped when pain lanced through her. "Yes." She rolled onto her side and pushed herself up. "I'm fine." Around her, most of Declan's men picked themselves up off the ground.

Declan surveyed them with a dazed look. He was the only fae still standing.

"That was ..." Bronagh shook her head. She'd never felt such power. It called to her, wanting her to let its full force free. These fire opals were not the weak crystals the fae of Lenya were used to.

She stared at the opal lying in the grass beside her.

"It's moving," Declan yelled. "Everyone get back." He jumped just in time to see the ground where he'd been standing die, green grass going black before crumbling into dust.

The Lenyans scrambled away from the heat, urging their horses closer to the forest at their backs.

No, this wasn't happening. Bronagh stilled and focused on the crystal in her hand. "Eavha," she called. Eavha, Declan, and Donal ran toward her. "We have to slow it down."

Her uncle joined them, an opal clutched in his palm. "Let the magic inside you, let it filter through you. Gain control through your will."

Bronagh closed her eyes, slowing her heartbeat and sending all her energy into the stone. Magic curled around her fingertips, arcing up over her arm and engulfing her in a wave of power unlike anything she'd ever experienced. Was this how Tierney felt every day of her life?

It was exhilarating to be this strong.

She gripped the opal tighter in her fist, imagining she held the magic in the palm of her hand. This time, when she let it free, it had a leash around its neck.

A blast of golden power hit the hazy edges of the heat. A geyser of steam extinguished as the others joined her.

"I think it's slowing down," Declan yelled above the roaring in Bronagh's ears.

Energy leached out of Bronagh until it was all she could do to hold herself up. They'd done it. They'd slowed the spread. At least for the moment.

The crystals worked, but they weren't enough.

If they were going to reclaim Lenya's scorched plains, it was going to take a lot more power than they possessed.

CHAPTER TWENTY-ONE
TIERNEY

"I swear, all we're doing is making it angry." Tierney tucked her face under the scrap of fabric she'd wrapped around her head to shield herself from the sand storm. Each grain of sand felt like tiny hot needles stabbing into her flesh.

She mopped the sweat from her brow and searched the sea of dirty faces around her. "We're throwing everything we have at this, hoping something will stick. We need to work smarter."

"I think we're all tired and we might need a break." Brea stretched her back and groaned. "This old lady needs a glass of wine and a bath. A cold one." She wiped the sweat from her face with the back of her hand.

Tierney paced back to the campsite, flinging herself down on the ground in the shade of a lone tree. She saved the more comfortable seats for her parents, aunts, and uncles. They were old, after all.

"Aunt Neeve?" Tierney waited for her aunt to sit as the other royals made their way back into camp. "I don't understand how this is working in Fargelsi and not here."

"I don't either, love, but I received a report this morning that it continues to work. They've managed to push the marshlands back toward their borders. It will take time, but I believe we can eventually heal the entire marsh. We have fae working from both sides now. The Dragur Forest is nearly free of the effects already."

Tierney was thrilled for Gelsi and Eldur. It was a relief to know something was working somewhere. It was getting worse everywhere else. Ice storms were raging across Iskalt. If they didn't get results here in the fire plains soon, they were going to have to join the magic wielders back home to see if they could make progress there. For now, it was safe to say Iskaltians knew how to handle a blizzard.

"Tell me again how it worked."

"Darling, let your aunt Neeve have a rest." Brea fanned her face with a palm frond. "We need our wits about us if we're going to figure this out."

"That's just it, Mom. I feel like it's right there, just out of my reach. I can feel it, like my magic knows the answer and it's just waiting for me to catch up." Tierney worried her bottom lip, chapped from the hot desert winds racing across the plains.

"Is it something in your magic specifically?" Keir came to sit in the shade with them.

"No. Yes. Maybe? I don't know." She threw her hands up, wishing the answer would just fall out of the sky.

"Maybe your young man is onto something," Neeve said, and Tierney chose to ignore her aunt's nosey insinuations.

"Like what?"

"It wasn't exactly a specific Gelsi spell that worked. It was more a request to heal the land. But it didn't work until we joined with the Eldurians, like we needed the right blend of magic we just happened to stumble upon."

"Oh!" Tierney sat up straight, trying to force her mind down the right path to the answer that continued to elude her.

"What is it, Tia?" Her father was the one to catch on to her excitement.

"I need a map! Does anyone have one?"

"Yes, we all carry maps of the world in our pockets when we're on an emergency expedition to save Eldur and Lenya." Brea's dry humor rolled right off Tierney's back.

"I have one." Keir fished through his bag. "Well, a sketch of one I made from a map I found in the library at the palace. Not your magical flying library." He passed her a journal opened to the center page.

"Perfect, you already added Lenya." Tierney's eyes darted across the pages, her mind working faster than she could articulate her thoughts. "May I draw on this?" She glanced at Keir.

"Well, yes, but don't ruin it." He handed her a quill and ink. "I'd like to replicate it for our records once I return."

Tierney sketched a line where the original fire plains should be within their boundaries along Eldur and Lenya. "If you had to guess, where would you think the maelstrom would fall on this map?" She held it out for Keir to see.

"Somewhere in here." He pointed to the narrowest part of the sea separating Lenya from the far reaches of Iskalt. "Your grandfather and I were just talking about this the other day. He believes the maelstrom occurs because it resides between fierce opposing temperatures."

Tierney nodded. "That makes sense." She sketched a quick spiral shape where the sea narrowed. From there, she drew a line to represent the Northwestern Vatlands.

"Look at this, everyone." She held up the map, using the feathered quill to point to the fire plains. "What if all of this is one big vatland? The fire plains, the maelstrom, and the impenetrable mountains?"

"That is possible." Lochlan studied the map. "What are you thinking, Tia? If we can find the right magic, we can heal all three areas? That still doesn't solve our current dilemma."

"Look here." Tierney scrambled across the sand to sit at her father's side. "It's working in the marshlands." She pointed to the map. "With Gelsi and Eldurian magic." She pointed to either side of the marshlands.

Lochlan's eyes widened in surprise. "My daughter's a genius." He scanned the map.

"Sure, she's your daughter when she's a smarty pants, but she's mine when she opens portals to lands that shouldn't exist," Brea muttered.

"It's the borders." Lochlan dropped the journal, beaming at his daughter. "It takes the magic of the lands on either side of the vatlands."

"So, the fire plains need the magic of Eldur, Lenya, and Iskalt." Tierney returned her father's smile.

"Then, we have a lot of work to do because I'm the only Lenyan on this side of the world." Keir stuffed his journal and quill back into his bag.

"We have about an hour until dusk. This is only going to work for a short period, so we're going to have to make the most of the time we've got." Brea set off to tell the others. They would need all hands on deck to try this.

"It puts a damper on things when you've got to wait for the sun and moon to get things done." Keir shook his head as everyone scattered to deliver the good news.

"I think this is going to work, Keir." Tierney wrapped her arms around his waist and laid her head on his chest. "We're going to fix this so you and your people won't be so isolated. Think of what that will mean for Vondur and Grima."

"If it works." Keir let out a nervous breath. "Do you think I can do it? The part where I have to perform powerful magic for Lenya when the most complex thing I've ever done with magic is restore my energy during a long battle."

"We'll help you." She laid her hand over his, a crystal

clutched in his fist. "But the magic itself will guide you. You just have to listen and trust in it."

Keir nodded. "All we can do is try."

As dusk fell, every Eldurian, Iskaltian, and Keir lined up along the border of the fire plains, as close as they could get to it without burning. Even in the fading light, the air shimmered with heat.

"What do we do?" Keir whispered, leaning close to Tierney. "I mean, how do we know how to direct the magic?"

"Start by embracing your power. Let it flow from the crystal into you, and then direct it into the earth like the Gelsi magic wielders do."

Keir nodded. "I sure hope this works." He sank to his knees, waiting for the signal to start.

"Begin!" Lochlan's voice, magically amplified, echoed across the camp.

Streaks of every color of magic lit up the sky and ground as each person added their magic to the attempt.

"Now you, Keir." Tierney held her hands steady as her Iskaltian magic joined the others. It was a wonderous sight, and it reminded her of another time, long ago, when all fae had united as one to fight a common foe.

It brought tears to her eyes to think of how much she loved these people. All of them willing to help each other or die trying.

Keir's magic hummed like a live creature in his hands. It was beautiful, like a song in its musical quality. She watched as he clutched the powerful opal now pulsing with a fiery light.

Sinking his hands into the sand, he released his magic, guiding it into the land that needed healing.

Tierney held her breath, waiting for something to happen.

"It's not working." Keir groaned.

"Give it a little longer." Myles paced behind them, his human eyes on the shimmering wall of heat. "These things take time and patience."

"Myles, look!" Neeve pointed to the sky.

Tierney looked up, keeping her magic steady. The boundary of the fire plains shone with an iridescence, like a rainbow of colors reflected back at them. Gasps of surprise echoed around them as the wall began to collapse, shrinking from the magic of the united kingdoms.

"It's so beautiful," Tierney murmured, sniffing back her tears.

"The colors are pretty," Keir said, "but why the tears?"

Tierney shook her head. "It's not the colors. It's the people. The unity. It's the most amazing thing I've ever witnessed, and this is the second time in my life I've seen it. I feel so lucky to be part of it. Then and now."

"Forward!" Lochlan called. "Careful now, we don't want the boundary to snap back in place as we move. Keir, be very careful as you move forward. Don't break your connection with the magic."

Lochlan paced behind the row of magic wielders, barking orders. "Someone get the boy another crystal. He's going to need it as a backup."

"There has to be enough magic in this one crystal to get us all the way to Lenya." Keir lifted his hand from the sand, carefully moving forward a few steps at a time.

"This is powerful magic, Keir. It will go quickly." Tierney stepped forward, keeping her magic steady as she moved.

"What do we do when the Eldurian magic fades?" someone called out. "Will it bounce back?"

"We have no way of knowing." Lochlan paced, kicking up sand in his urgency now that they were making progress. "Eldurians, give us a shout when you're nearing the end of your power."

The dusk stayed with them long enough to move the boundary back at least a league. As the Eldurians pulled away when their magic faded, everyone held their breath, prepared to run if the boundary wasn't stable.

A cheer went down the line when Keir, as the last magic wielder, stepped away and the boundary settled exactly where they'd pushed it.

Exhaustion swept through Tierney, and her arms felt like dead weights, but she was happier than she could ever remember being. "It worked!" She cheered with the others. "Can you believe it, Keir?"

"I just wish we could keep working at it." He stared behind them. The fire plains shimmered and glowed in the darkness as they made their way back to camp. "It could take months of this to reach Lenya."

"We'll be ready at dawn." She took his hand. "And we'll keep working at it until there is nothing left but scorched earth."

Every fae that worked the boundary had blisters and burns from the blackened charred ground that now lay cooling in the evening breeze.

"Isn't it wonderful, Tia?" Toby and Logan joined them, strolling hand in hand in the moonlight.

"It's exhausting work, but look at how far we reached?" Logan beamed at them. "At this rate, we'll be walking to Lenya in a few days."

"We have no idea how far it is," Keir said.

205

"Think positive." Logan shrugged. "This was just the first day. We've figured out what we need to do now. I'll wager we reach twice as far at dawn."

"I'll take that wager." Keir grinned, slapping Logan on the back. "I bet we'll reach three leagues by the time Tia's moon magic wanes."

"Dude, she has Eldur magic too. She can't even tell when the switch happens." Toby's teasing voice made Tierney smile. She liked seeing them all get along so well.

"Then, we'll base it on your father's magic," Keir decided.

"You're on." Logan lifted a brow. "What are we betting?"

"Loser has to wake Tia up before dawn every day for a week." Toby snickered. "She's vicious in the mornings. She's been known to give a few magical black eyes and fat lips when she doesn't want to get up."

"Very funny, Tobes." Tierney stuck her tongue out at her brother.

"Oh, I don't know, I think she'd be nice if I were the one waking her up." Keir grinned down at her, taking her hand in his.

"So, what you're saying is, you're going to lose." Toby nudged Keir.

"Could be well worth it." Keir shrugged, and Tierney's cheeks flushed.

"Awe, they're so cute," Logan whisper-shouted. "Do you think they'll ever figure out they're nuts about each other?"

"Poor Keir is in for a long wait. Tierney's always been the stubborn one." Toby shook his head in mock sympathy.

CHAPTER TWENTY-TWO
KEIR

I t took them just two days to push the fire plains back to their original borders, moving their camp as they went. Everyone was hot, sweaty, and dirty, but in good spirits.

They received word that the blizzard had receded into the mountains in Iskalt, and Myrkurians and Iskaltians were working together to drive the snows from the Northwestern Vatlands back into the mountains. For the Myrkurians, it seemed to be the willing act of assisting their Iskaltian neighbors with the task that fulfilled their requirement. King Hector led a team of ogres carrying magic wielders into the mountains to places they couldn't have reached otherwise, and the Slyph took to the skies to survey the progress.

They were going to defeat the vatlands and the ancient magic that caused them in the first place. The magic was exhausting, but they worked during the short windows of dusk and dawn, leaving them the better parts of the day and night to rest.

Keir emerged from his tent, pulling the fresh tunic away from his body. Even as the sun began to set, it was hot, and the charred ground burned through the soles of his boots.

The shimmering wall of heat danced across the clearing of the blackened ground. He'd grown used to the temperatures but already reached for his wineskin filled with cool water. Tierney showed him how to protect his water supply so it wouldn't boil and evaporate while he worked.

Kneeling on the hot ground, he waited for the sting of it to leave him, using a bit of magic from his totem to protect his skin from blistering.

"I wonder what Lenya will be like when the fire plains are gone." Tierney approached him, knowing he was always the first to arrive at the border, and among the last to leave.

Keir stared at the horizon, trying to see what it might become in time. "I think it will be a lot like Eldur in Vondur, and a little more like Iskalt in Grima."

"Sounds like the best of both worlds." She sank to the ground beside him. "You ready?"

"Almost." He pulled on the magic of his second totem. He'd had a hard time accepting the second one when the first one went dark. He still felt like it was a reckless use of so much magic, and probably would always feel that way. Logically, he knew he could easily find another one from the supply they brought with them or even one of the rough natural fire opals littering the ground back at their original campsite. But Keir would always fear for the future of his people. They needed to be responsible with their magic so they never again faced a world where fae fought over a few scraps of power because their ancestors were greedy.

"Let's do this." It was a bit early to get started, but Tierney had both sun and moon magic, and Keir liked to call on his magic when no one was looking. He still struggled to harness such enormous power and liked to have a firm grasp of it before the others arrived. It wasn't vanity on his part so much as extreme performance anxiety. These people understood their magic in a way Keir didn't.

Tierney leaned forward, and together they pressed their

hands against the scorched ground. Little by little, as they had pushed the borders back, the scarred and broken ground began to heal. New grass and thorny shrubs were already peeking through the ground behind them. In a few short months from now, Keir wondered if any of them would be able to tell the fire plains ever existed.

He closed his eyes as both sides of Tierney's magic enveloped him. If he were honest with himself, this was the true reason he liked to begin early. When it was just the two of them, Tierney's magic filled him. He was in awe of her power.

He took a ragged breath as her power joined his. There was something intimate about the way they worked together this way. But if he thought a single pure fire opal held more magic than he'd ever sensed in one vessel, it was nothing on Tierney herself.

"It's okay." Tierney shifted away from him.

"What do you mean?"

"Lots of people get nervous around my magic." She shrugged, staring at her hands pressed against the ground. "But I promise there is nothing to fear from me. We're in this together, Keir."

She thought he was afraid of her? It struck him then, not only just how powerful Tierney O'Shea was but also how lonely it must have been for her.

Keir smiled. "Your magic is fierce, but I can't imagine you any other way." He bumped her shoulder. "I could never fear you. I trust you too much for that."

Tierney's smile rivaled the sunset, and Keir wanted to be the one to make her smile like that every single day.

"Let's take back the fire plains."

"You doubled down on your bet with Toby and Logan, didn't you?"

"They're determined to put me on wake-up Tia duty. I'm starting to think they have ulterior motives."

"Those two are always up to something."

As the others began to arrive and cast their magic against the fire plains, they moved forward until they were slowly walking toward their first major obstacle. A lava pool.

Up until now, they'd only recovered flat barren plains. The wall of heat moved in a straight line with them, from the Sea of Iskalt to Radur Bay to the south. Once they hit the lava pools and the active volcano, they were going to have to be more careful.

Lochlan and Toby strolled together behind the magic wielders, the king stepping in for anyone who grew tired and needed a break.

"Steady everyone, we're approaching the lava pool." Lochlan and Toby helped each fae position themselves far enough away from the small pool so they could easily continue on.

"Be careful, everyone," Keir called, eyeing the spotters he'd suggested Lochlan appoint. "I've seen these pools spew lava like geysers."

"Remember to test your footing," Lochlan called out. They weren't certain how steady the ground would be around the pools.

"Remember to breathe too, Tia." Keir put himself between her and the bubbling pool of angry lava.

He took a step forward, and his foot started to sink into the sand. He wasn't the only one who took several quick steps back. He waited for the spotters to tell him where to move before he proceeded.

Within a few moments, they uncovered more than half of the pool, giving it a wide berth on both sides.

"Something's happening," Tierney shouted. "The magic is wavering!"

"Hold steady, everyone." Lochlan joined his daughter, adding his magic to the mix.

Everyone held their breath as the lava pool bubbled and the wall of heat pushed against them.

"Be ready to run to me if this fails." Lochlan moved to join Finn and Brea to create a heat shield that would protect them if their magic failed.

"I think it's collapsing, Dad." Tierney pushed forward, letting both sides of her magic guide the others.

With a rush of blistering hot wind, the wall bulged and collapsed. Tierney ducked, and Keir covered her with his body as they all ran for Lochlan and the heat shield.

Keir waited for the fire plains to burn them to ash where they stood, but it never came.

"Look," Toby cried. "I think you did it! The fire plains are gone."

Keir stood up, releasing Tierney from his grip. Together, they all stared at the ruins before them. Lava pools were already cooling. The ground still trembled, but only smoke and steam billowed up into the sky from settling volcanoes. It was a valley. And it was clear as far as they could see.

"Have we reached Lenya?" Logan stood to his full height, craning his neck to see through the dissipating smoke.

"Not yet." Keir wished he could get a clear picture of what lay ahead of them. "I think there's another lava pool at the end of the valley." He shielded his eyes from the blazing sunset. "But I think we just took down a giant portion of the plains in one fell swoop."

Cheers went up as they continued forward. Crossing the now open valley took most of the little time they had left before dusk turned to night. They arrived at another lava pool with hardly an hour left to work before the Eldurians had to stop.

"How much farther do you think?" Tierney approached the fiery line of the new border. The land itself was burning here, but they just might make another big push tonight.

This time, when they pressed against the larger lava pool, they were prepared for the push back. It seemed the fire plains would not give up their hold without a fight.

"Press on, boys." Logan took a step forward, urging his Eldurian comrades to follow.

Keir wanted to caution him not to stray too close to the lava pool, but his words caught in his throat as the ground beneath him began to shake and the rancid hot winds broke free to crash over them once again. Everyone stopped to watch in awe as another huge section of the fire plains failed, collapsing farther this time.

Smoke belched from the lava pool, and a loud sound like cannon fire accompanied the tremors.

"Fall back! To me, to me!" Lochlan cried as billowing black smoke rushed across the field.

Tierney stumbled toward Keir, and he grabbed her hand, pulling her toward her father. "Logan," she shouted, coughing on the churning smoke.

"It's going to erupt, Tia. We have to move." Keir's feet sank into sand so hot it melted right through his boots to scorch his feet.

Flaming stones rained down like pieces of the sky falling from the heavens, and heat shields went up all around them.

"Logan!" Toby screamed, running toward the lava pool.

"No!" Tierney stopped him, wrapping her arms around him. "Help me, Keir!"

Keir grabbed onto Toby, refusing to let him go as Tierney flung a heat shield over them.

Logan stood just a few paces away, swaying on his feet. A streak of blood and soot ran down his face. Toby screamed, struggling against them as Logan stumbled to his knees.

"He's gone, Toby." Tierney clutched his head to her shoulder. "Don't look. Don't look." She shielded his eyes, her tears streaming down her face.

Logan slid forward, a hand stretched out toward Toby as he fell face-first into the charred sand. A molten red stone glowed against the back of his head where it had struck him and caved in his skull. Keir held onto Tierney and Toby as they all slid to the ground, their sobs breaking his own heart for the gentle young man he'd hardly known.

"Toby," Tierney whispered. "Shhh, Toby. I'm so sorry." She rocked him gently. "I'm so sorry."

"We need to move, Tia." Keir set his own heat shield in place, just in case hers slipped. Lava rocks still rained down around them, and any one of them could face the same end Logan just experienced.

"We have to get him." Toby pushed to his feet. "I have to bring his body back to camp. He is the heir of Eldur. I will not let him burn up out there. We will take him back to his people."

"We'll go together." Keir stood, helping Tierney up. Together, the three of them walked across the burning ground, safe for the moment under the protection of their combined magic.

Toby gathered Logan into his arms, struggling under his weight, but he refused help. Tierney and Keir walked silently beside the heartbroken prince of Iskalt.

"Logan!" A woman's blood-curdling scream met them as they left the burning lands behind.

"Aunt Alona, I'm so sorry!" Tierney stepped toward the Queen of Eldur, her husband just managing to hold her up.

Princess Darra knelt on the ground at her mother's feet, sobbing her brother's name.

Death was a part of Keir's life. But this grief? This raw, overwhelming grief was not something he'd ever witnessed before. In Vondur, the endless years of war had hardened them. Death was expected. Some even embraced it.

But this? This was something he couldn't watch. Their grief was so painful and personal. Keir shouldn't be here to witness it.

Toby laid Logan on the ground at his parents' feet. Tears streaked the soot covering his face. This was heartbreak in its rawest moments.

"Stay with Alona and Finn," Tierney whispered. "Stay and mourn your loss." She pressed a kiss to Toby's forehead.

"No. We need to keep moving." Toby stood, a wild look in his eye. "He will not die in vain."

"We've lost the daylight, brother." Tierney wrapped an arm around his shoulders. "Stay with Darra. She will need you."

"Darra," Finn whispered, sinking to his knees beside his daughter. "You must leave and return to the palace, sweetheart."

"No. I'm staying here with Toby and Logan."

"You are the only heir now." Alona's hands shook. "This place is too dangerous."

"Griffin!" Tierney shouted as her uncle came running from the fire plains. She grabbed his arm and pulled him in, whispering in his ear. "Take Darra and Toby to the farmhouse with Alona and Finn. They need a quiet place to mourn. I'll see to Logan's body."

"They won't go." Griffin gave her a heavy look. "You know what you're asking, right?"

Tierney nodded. "They can blame me for it later."

Griffin nodded, and in a flash of violet light, the grieving family vanished through a portal to the human world. Keir would never get used to seeing that.

"Can you help me with him?" Tierney sniffed back her tears. "We need to get his body to camp and send him with an escort home to the Radur City palace."

Keir lifted Logan into his arms, following Tierney to camp as she called out orders to fall back from the unstable border. They would be at it again at dawn. Hopefully, they would reach Lenya soon. Or whatever was left of it.

Chapter Twenty-Three

Bronagh

There was nowhere left to go except up.

The fire plains surrounded the fae of Lenya who'd come to fight, Vondur and Grima forces pushed together to become one. At their backs was the last remaining way into the mountains, little more than a goat path. Most of the fae from the villages hid in those passes, waiting for the fire plains to claim them.

Bronagh once thought she could save them all.

"Magic wielders, don't break formation," she yelled. "Next wave!"

Fresh totem wielders stepped to the front, if anyone could be called fresh at this point. She'd lost count of the days they'd spent losing ground, expending every last ounce of energy, of magic.

The store of crystals she'd brought from Iskalt was almost depleted.

Eavha bent over to catch her breath, getting her first break in hours. She looked as they all did: tired, weary, ready to see what they'd refused to recognize.

They'd lost.

"Bron, we should get everyone into the mountains."

Declan stood at her side, his shoulders wilting in defeat.

Yet, his words spoke of what they all wished was possible. "There's still a chance. We can keep fighting it."

"It's over, Deck."

Bronagh watched them glare at each other before crouching down to where her brother practically collapsed on the ground, his chest heaving.

"It isn't over until there's no more breath in our bodies." Declan was stubborn, and they'd needed that before. But now, Bronagh wasn't sure what they needed.

Eavha plopped herself on the ground with a weary sigh. "We've lost. At least if we escape into the mountains, we can stop fighting long enough to enjoy our final days."

"No."

"Declan."

He knelt beside her. Bronagh felt like an intruder hearing their private moment, but she was too tired to move, too tired to do much of anything.

"I won't stop trying to save us." Declan's jaw clenched.

Eavha looked up into his eyes. "Why? Why can't you just give in and come with me?"

"Because I love you too much to just let you die."

Love. It had never been a foreign concept to Bronagh. Her mother and sister, despite their faults, had loved the family. Donal was the most important fae in the world to her. Even their uncle loved them very much, though his actions might not always show it.

But the kind of love she witnessed between the Vondurian princess and the general ... there was only one man who'd ever made her feel an inkling of what they had. One man who came into her life such a short time ago, yet she could hardly remember a time without him.

If these fire plains overcame them, she'd never get to tell

Veren how she felt. She wouldn't get to ask him to give up his kingdom to help her put Lenya back together.

There would be no Lenya anymore.

"Bron." Donal lifted his head. "Eavha is right. We should get into the mountains."

She shifted her gaze to the sheer cliffs above her head, to the single narrow path winding around to the far side of the mountain. They wouldn't be able to reach the Grimian caves where her fae awaited word of their success, but if they made it up into the highest passes, it might give them an extra week, maybe two.

Sweat dripped down her back. The heat intensified with each day, each hour. Yesterday, two Vondurian soldiers were killed by steam erupting from the unstable ground.

"Sister." Donal pushed himself up. "You're the queen. It's your decision. Do we keep going until the remaining crystals empty of power?" There was no judgment in his tone, and she knew he'd accept whatever she decided.

She looked from Donal to Eavha and Declan, who were peering at her with more trust than any Vondurian should. Then, there was her uncle, yelling orders to the magic wielders, trying to keep the plains at bay. Her golden warriors, their armor shed in this heat. The Vondurians, who put aside their animosity and obeyed her command.

Something soft nudged her shoulder, and she lifted a hand to find Sheba beside her, the giant cat giving her an understanding look. She should be terrified down at eye level with a beast who could rip her throat out. Instead, it gave her clarity.

The fire plains were a predator like no other. They would give no quarter, had no master. Unlike Sheba, who did little more than intimidate Eavha's foes, they wanted to destroy.

And they'd get their wish.

"We have to make it into the mountains." It wouldn't save

them, but they'd have a week, maybe more, to say goodbye to each other, to Lenya.

Donal nodded and took off to talk to their uncle. A few moments later, the command rang out. "If you are not currently wielding a totem, make for the mountains."

Activity surrounded her, soldiers gathering their few remaining possessions, hurrying to be the first up to those ominous cliffs.

"You two should leave with the first wave." Declan gestured to Eavha and Bronagh.

Bronagh shook her head. "I stay until my last fae has made it."

Eavha linked her arm with Bronagh's, tears streaking down her dusty face. "I'm with her." Her voice didn't waver.

Declan rolled his eyes to the roiling red sky, where plumes of smoke and ash rose among the clouds. He muttered something Bronagh only heard parts of, the words "stubborn" and "cursed" reaching her ears.

Sheba growled, and Declan put his hands up in front of his chest. "Eavha, tell Sheba to back down."

"She has a will of her own. I'm not her boss." With that, Eavha dragged Bronagh to the line of magic wielders. Her uncle pressed crystals into their hands.

All they had to do was give their fae enough time to get away, then they'd make a run for it.

Magic bloomed in her, weaker than it had been before. "This crystal is almost dead." She reached out to her uncle. "Can you hand me another?"

He shot her a panicked look. "There are no more."

If there'd been any last shred of hope, it was gone now. "Well, then, I guess this is it."

"Your Majesty," Declan yelled, "look."

Bronagh peered into the fire plains, seeing only billowing

smoke and spewing lava. The air shimmered with heat. Then, it was there. Movement at the farthest point where the plains curved around a row of giant blackened boulders toward the volcano.

"What is that?" Eavha stepped closer, but Declan yanked her back.

A girl walked out into the open, looking like she'd stepped right through the burning heat. Behind her, a line of fae appeared, each directing magic down into the very earth.

"Is that ..." Eavha gasped. "It's Tia."

Bronagh peered closer, her broken heart melding together with a new hope. "They've done it," she whispered to herself.

The Lenyans who'd started toward the mountains stopped what they were doing, and a cheer rose up.

Tears stung Bronagh's eyes, drying as they sizzled on her cheeks. They really did it. She caught sight of Keir, of Toby.

And Veren.

A giant grin spread across his face, but he didn't lose focus on the magic.

The other fae were strangers, but they'd come to save Lenya, to save all their realms.

Shouting erupted among the newcomers, but Bronagh couldn't hear their words. Fae scrambled backward to where King Lochlan beckoned them. The ground shook, the fire plains moving once again.

"Everyone back!" Bronagh yelled, stumbling away from the wall of heat.

When she regained her footing and searched out the fae on the other side, her eyes caught on Veren still running to the protection of whatever his king offered.

His mouth opened in shock, and if Bronagh had been closer, she knew she'd have heard him scream. That look wasn't one she'd ever forget. He dodged a geyser of steam, but it wasn't enough. As the fire plains bounced toward him, he stumbled, reaching for someone to help him.

Tierney sprinted forward, gripping his hand and dragging him to her father, but even from this distance, Bronagh could see.

Veren Rhatigan wasn't moving.

"No," she whispered, blinking back tears. Moments ago she'd prepared for the fire plains to steal the lives of everyone in Lenya, but now when there was finally hope ... she couldn't comprehend what was happening.

"Sister." Donal's arms came around her, but she hardly noticed he was there.

Veren. She saw the day he'd appeared at court, already a trusted friend of her brother's. The way he'd embraced Grimian ways and never stopped searching for his missing friends.

Her entire body shook until a voice boomed through the light of dawn. "We need help." It was Tierney.

Bronagh pulled away from her brother. Despite the fissure straight down the center of her heart, she was the queen, and it was time to save her kingdom.

CHAPTER TWENTY-FOUR
TIERNEY

"We need help." It was the only thing Tierney knew to do. She couldn't stop staring at the charred remains of Veren's body, the bottom half completely black from being caught in the shifting fire plains.

But it wasn't time to mourn. Not yet. Keir's crystal had no more magic. As soon as they caught sight of the Lenyans, it brought them a renewed sense of purpose. None were so determined as Veren.

Ducking underneath her father's heat shield, she knew it couldn't last much longer as the fire plains grew closer again. Dawn was almost through, and if they didn't end this now, they might never succeed.

"Aimpliu," she whispered to herself so she could continue. The Fargelsian spell allowed her voice to carry. "Bronagh, listen to me. There's not much time. We must break through now or not at all. We need every bit of magic your fae have left, even just the smallest traces in the stones. Dig deep to bring it out. This will take all of us. Channel it into the earth. We're coming for you."

She had no way of knowing if Bronagh understood, only

that the Lenyans were backed up to the mountains making their final stand.

It would be a final stand for all of them.

"I need Eldurians and Iskaltians at the front, those not too exhausted to give everything they have left." She issued the commands like she was in charge here. Not her father, not King Keir. And her father didn't intercede. Instead, he ushered his fae to obey her.

Tierney lined up with them, waiting for her father to drop the remnants of his heat shield. "I know you're tired," she said to those around her. "I know Lenya is not your kingdom. We have lost friends over the last days." Her eyes flicked to Siobhan, who understood what Veren's loss meant. "But what we have not lost is our resolve.

"We have one more chance to right the wrongs of our ancestors, to become the alliance of kingdoms we were meant to be. Those fae across from us are no different from your neighbors, your friends, and your family. Seek out whatever you have left, let your magic guide you, and become a hero today."

Her father stepped up beside her, his hands raised. "I'm proud of you, Tia."

She glanced over her shoulder to where Keir paced, unable to help without his magic. He met her gaze, giving her a nod of thanks.

If the Lenyans had no more power, if they weren't prepared, all of them were doomed. Yet, she readied herself anyway. Not a single one of her fae, Eldurian or Iskaltian, gave up, gave in. She'd never been more proud.

A smile curved her lips. "Let's do this."

Heat rushed in as her father dropped the shield. Her Iskaltian magic weakened, telling her there wasn't much time left. She dug into her Eldurian side, channeling every bit of energy she could into the ground.

The fire plains seemed to shake and inch back. Tierney stepped forward, gritting her teeth against what felt like flames licking up her arms. "Geyser," Brea yelled. A handful of Eldurians scrambled out of the way.

Molten lava burped from the ground in front of them, but as soon as the plains receded past it, it hardened. Not much farther now.

It was working. Bronagh had heard her.

After days and days of this, pain and exhaustion wound through her limbs. Her body wilted, but she remained upright. When she stumbled, strong hands caught her from behind.

"Keep going, Tierney," Keir whispered.

For him, she would. For Lenya. She caught sight of Eavha, totem in her palm, and pushed harder. Beside the Vondurian princess, Declan directed power into the ground. They were both okay. That knowledge gave her a renewed energy.

The fire plains bent and wavered from the Lenyan side, and the magic wielders there advanced. Tierney could almost reach out and touch her friends now. Just one more push.

"For Logan," she gritted out. "For Veren." With one final heave of power, the sky cracked in a roaring thunder and rain exploded from the clouds. They stood there in shock for a moment, rain drenching their rapidly cooling skin, a balm to their scorched palms.

Tierney took off running, crossing the remaining feet to launch herself at Bronagh and Eavha, catching them both against her in a hug. Relief breathed new life into her, gave her the will to remain standing.

Keir joined them, sweeping his sister into his arms, tears dancing in his eyes.

Around them, Eldurians, Iskaltians, Vondurians, and Grimians celebrated. Some fell to their knees; others stared up into the sun breaking through the rain clouds.

Tierney opened her mouth, catching drops of water on her parched tongue. Nothing had ever tasted so good.

Keir caught her around the waist, and they fell against each other, holding each other up. He bent to kiss the side of her sweaty face as the rain washed the soot away.

Bronagh backed away from them, turning to walk toward the charred mess of ground that was once the fire plains.

"I have to go after her." Tierney patted Keir's chest. "Stay here with Eavha and celebrate."

She took off after the queen. Bronagh kept going, passing craters that once bubbled with lava, cracks widened by steam breaking free. She didn't stop until she reached where they'd left Veren's body, his top half still looking like the arrogant, charming boy Tierney hated and appreciated for most of her life. He'd challenged her, made her see truths she'd wanted to deny.

And when it came down to it, he'd fought to survive right alongside her, for her. Their experiences bonded them, made them—dare she say it—friends.

Bronagh kneeled beside him, a hand on his chest. Tierney approached slowly, her heart aching because a part of her still thought this was entirely her fault.

She lowered herself to the ground beside Bronagh, surprised at how cool it was. Rain gathered in her hair, dripping down her face, but she didn't shield her eyes. Instead, she looked down into Veren's face.

"I always thought he was handsome," she started, emotion clogging her throat. "When I was younger, I fancied myself in love with him."

Bronagh sniffled. "He told me the story. He hated how he'd used you, felt great shame for it."

That made Tierney smile. "He changed a lot when he came here." She brushed sopping hair out of his face. "I think it was your influence."

Bronagh shook her head. "No, that was all him. He changed me too. Before Veren arrived in Grima, my life had no color. Every part of me was a formal, bland girl who did what she was told. It wasn't who I wanted to be, but it was who I thought I was allowed to be since I was never supposed to be queen."

Her chin dropped to her chest. "But then, this warrior walks in, and it ... it's hard to explain. He brought me to life."

"You were in love with him." Tierney had suspected as much, but the confirmation speared through her in a jolt of pain.

Bronagh wiped her face before her tears were replaced with rain. "No. I am in love with him. Death does not cause it to cease."

She thought of Toby, how no news of this victory would soothe his grief. Of Finn and Alona, having lost their only son and heir. Imogen, now an orphan. There was too much loss in this battle, and the only foe had been magic itself. Magic had created the vatlands. It had separated the kingdoms and nearly destroyed them.

Tierney looked down at her hands, now washed clean by the rain. "And it saved them."

Bronagh's body shook with tears, and Tierney pulled her into a hug, letting her sink into her.

"Your Majesty," a small voice said.

Tierney looked up into the young face of Imogen, the girl with nothing left. Like so many others.

Imogen kneeled on the ground next to Bronagh, and the queen tilted into her embrace.

Tierney pushed to her feet, knowing the two of them likely needed each other more than they needed her. She walked back toward the joy that was hard to feel. Even in accomplishment, the costs seemed too high.

CHAPTER TWENTY-FIVE
KEIR

The palace of Vondur was scarred beyond measure. Not even the crystals infused in the walls had saved it from the fire plains. Keir picked through the blackened ruins, reminders of the life he'd lived before. He wasn't the only fae mourning what was lost. Most of the villages of Vondur and Grima would need to be rebuilt, brought back from destruction.

Friends were gone.

He hadn't known Logan well or even Veren, but their losses sat heavily on his mind, as did the losses of so many men, women, and children of his realm.

"We were here just days ago." Eavha walked up behind him, her voice wavering. "I was sitting right in this room."

They stood in the throne room, where marks of the fire stretched up the walls and the furniture had turned to ash. "We've lost everything."

"Not everything." Eavha slid her arm into his. "We saved our fae, and that's what truly matters."

She was right. Homes and possessions weren't the true value of Vondur. Those who occupied the homes were. In the two days since they'd destroyed the fire plains, fae trickled out of the mountains. In the weeks and months to come, more of them would return home to build new lives.

"We're going to have to rebuild." His mind worked through so many plans. The palace could be even grander than it was before now that they had a practically unlimited supply of magic. The war with Grima was through, meaning he could create more of a home than a fortress meant to withstand battle.

"Keir." Eavha stepped away from him as she sighed. "We need to talk."

"Nothing good ever begins with that phrase." He crouched down to brush ash from a painting that had somehow survived the heat. It was protected by glass made from crystal and depicted their father sitting atop his horse prepared to ride into battle.

"All the documents in the palace have been destroyed." She paused. "Including the ones only Lord Robert and I knew about."

Keir didn't have to ask what she meant, but he didn't have an answer for her unasked question.

"Talk to me, brother."

He closed his eyes for a brief moment and stood, turning away from his father's portrait, the image of the man he'd never wanted to be, the one he was scared of becoming. "I never wanted this." He gestured around the room, not exactly meaning the destruction.

"I know." She did. More than anything, more than anyone. Eavha had always known. "But I don't want it either. You left me in charge against my will, and that's not me. I don't want to be a leader. I want adventure, to explore this new world that has opened to us. The crown was never meant to fit my head."

"Nor mine." Both children of a king who wanted nothing but power, both wishing it hadn't fallen to them.

"Yes, but I'm not the one who called for the Comhrac."

"If I hadn't, we'd all be dead by now." His father never would have allowed a mission to seek Iskalt.

"I know. I didn't mean you were wrong." She touched his arm. "But the duty fell to you. Vondur needs you."

Did they?

Eavha gave him a tight smile. "Think carefully of your next decision. It will define our kingdom." With that, she turned and left him in the throne room that had never felt so empty, so forsaken.

He walked from the room, down the hall where tapestries once adorned the walls and now lay scattered along the floor, ashes under his feet. When he entered the courtyard, his eyes went past where the heavy wooden gate once stood to the top of the wall and the two figures sitting there.

Toby had returned the day after the final fight with the fire plains, but he'd barely spoken to anyone except Tierney. Even his parents couldn't get anything out of him. They would have to return to Iskalt soon, but for now, they camped outside the gates of the palace, offering any assistance to his fae they could.

He'd forever be grateful to them.

Declan walked toward him, a grim expression on his face. It had been there since they first discussed how much work there was to be done. "The King of Iskalt would like to speak with you."

"Are you his messenger boy now?" Keir attempted the joke, but they'd all found it hard to smile once their relief and celebration died down and reality set in. They may have succeeded in saving their fae, but the work had just begun.

Keir followed Declan from the palace to a sea of tents that housed what was left of Vondur and the contingents from Eldur, Iskalt, and Grima. Bronagh planned to leave within hours, but the rest would stay for a few days longer at least.

He found Lochlan seated next to his wife, along with

Finn and Alona of Eldur and Bronagh. Deep circles lined Finn's eyes, as if he hadn't slept since his son died. Alona's face was stoic, her jaw clenched, her brows drawn tightly together.

Lochlan nodded to Keir as he entered their circle around the fire. Since the destruction of the plains, a chill wound through Vondur for the first time. "Have a seat, Keir."

It would always strike him as odd, the familiarity the royals had with each other. If the Fargelsians were here, he knew they'd call everyone by their given names as well. Keir sat next to Bronagh on the ground. None of them seemed uncomfortable by the lack of accommodations. Another surprise. If anyone had asked his father to sit on the ground, even in an army camp, he'd have thrown a fit.

"We have suffered too many losses." Brea looked at Alona in sympathy and reached out to grip Finn's hand next to her. "Precious losses we can never get back, but each of us here also has a duty."

Finn swallowed heavily. "We will return to Eldur and begin mining for more opals. We'll send word to Hector in Myrkur to do the same. Lenya will need them for rebuilding."

Bronagh attempted to offer him a smile, but it never quite reached her eyes. "Thank you. Lenya will forever be in your debt."

"We do not do debts." Lochlan leaned forward, looking at them each in turn. "When our worlds are threatened, we come to the aid of our allies without expectation of payment. We are all fae, and fae take care of each other."

Brea sent her husband the most glorious smile.

Lochlan continued, "Iskalt may soon see a major change, one I've been waiting for, but whatever we look like, we will be your allies."

"That's ..." Keir cleared his throat. "We are eternally grateful." If Tierney had never accidentally portalled to Lenya, he never would have found the other fae kingdoms.

Bronagh lifted her chin to speak, her voice clear. "Grima and Vondur will no longer war with one another. We will be as one in Lenya, tied together by our common heritage." She looked to Keir. "We've never been different, after all. We're all of Lenya, all after the same thing. We want to survive, to thrive. And our fae finally get to experience peace with full bellies and safe homes. No more lost family to battle. No more grief."

Keir's eyes drifted to the walls, where he knew Tierney and Toby were hidden. No more grief. No more loss. Thrive.

He looked to Lochlan, one of the few fae aware of the documents that were destroyed in the palace by the fire plains, and the king gave him a subtle nod.

"Tradition in Vondur does not pass the crown from father to son. For so long, bloodshed and death won the throne. Cruelty and war kept it. If we are to enter peace, we cannot have a king who did not come to power through such peace."

No one seemed to understand, but only Bronagh spoke. "Keir, if you're talking about holding some kind of election for the throne, I'm not sure now is the time. Our fae are displaced. We have so much work to do."

Keir shook his head. He knew this was the right thing, but it was difficult to get the words out. "You said Lenya is to become one. I do not think we can accomplish such a feat as separate kingdoms."

"What—"

"You, Bron. You should rule the Vondurian fae." It seemed so simple now, such an obvious decision. He never should have expected Eavha to want the throne. "Vondur and Grima cannot thrive unless it is done together."

Lochlan gave him an approving smile, and he knew he'd said the right thing, the kingly thing.

"Only a true king gives up his power when he knows it will better serve his kingdom," Brea said the words to Keir, but her eyes flicked to her husband and softened.

Bronagh was silent for a moment before turning to Keir and meeting his gaze. "I, Bronagh Agnew, queen of Grima, promise to count all Lenyans as my own. There will be no more division under me, no more war. All of Lenya will prosper."

As Keir heard the sincerity in her words, he knew he'd done the right thing, the only thing.

Darkness enveloped the world by the time Keir walked toward the palace. He would never sleep within its walls again, but he couldn't find his bed without walking through one more time.

Movement across the courtyard caught his eye. He'd thought everyone was back at camp, but a small glow illuminated that perfect smile.

"Thought I'd see you here." Tierney walked toward him, the light emanating from her palm growing larger.

"Comes in handy." He gestured to her magic.

"Oh." She closed her palm, and the light winked out. "Just a Fargelsian spell. It draws starlight from the sky."

"You're incredible." The words tumbled past his lips before he realized it, but they were true. This woman was fascinating, stubborn, strong, and beautiful.

He could barely see her in the dark, but the soft smile that curved her lips was unmistakable. "Today has been a long day."

"How is Toby?"

Her shoulders sagged. "He loved Logan. The two of them ... I think they've been in love since before any of us knew what love truly was. I miss Logan too, but my heart is shattered for my brother. Through our connection, I can feel a part of his pain, but it's more than that. Looking at him ... I don't know if he'll ever recover from this."

"I'm sorry." It was the only thing he could think to say. He was sorry for what happened to Logan, sorry that her people had to sacrifice themselves for his.

To his surprise, she stepped closer and wound her arms around his waist, pressing the side of her head to his chest. Neither of them spoke as he held her to him, not wanting to let go.

He rested his chin on her head, closing his eyes. "I'm giving up my throne."

She stepped back so suddenly his arms reached for her. "You can't do that."

"It's my throne." He crossed his arms. "I can do whatever I want."

Her eyes narrowed, and he recognized it as her fighting stance. "Keir, Vondur needs you."

"No, Vondur needs a united Lenya. Bronagh is going to rule both kingdoms."

She opened her mouth to speak before shutting it, unable to refute his claim. Finally, her voice came out small. "Did you do this out of some misguided allegiance to me? Keir, just because I helped save Lenya doesn't mean you owe me anything. What we have is—"

"Love." He stepped toward her. "What we have is love." His hand lifted to caress her cheek, and she didn't pull away. He'd have sworn she wasn't breathing if he didn't feel a small puff of air leave her mouth. "I love you, Tierney, and I know you feel the same."

"You don't know anything," she whispered.

"I know I have no misguided allegiances because of what happened in the fire plains." His eyes met her gaze in challenge. "I abdicated before we boarded the ship bound for Iskalt."

Her mouth popped open, and he wrapped his hand around the back of her head, digging his fingers into her hair. "You ..."

"I fell in love with you the first time I kissed you." He leaned in. "I tried to stop it, to remind myself we were from different worlds and that one day we'd go our separate ways. But what if we didn't have to?"

"What are you saying?"

"I don't want to be apart from you, Tierney O'Shea." His lips were only a breath away from hers now. "I couldn't bear it."

Her kiss was soft at first, testing, tasting. His lips traveled from the corner of her mouth, arching over her cheek to the sensitive spot below her ear. "I love you," he whispered, trailing kisses down her neck. "I love it when you argue with me." He kissed the underside of her jaw. "I love it when you best me in sparring or with magic. You're so much more than I ever imagined, so much more than I deserve."

Tierney put a finger under his chin and brought his face up so their eyes met. "There is nothing you don't deserve, Keir." She pressed her lips to his, and this time, there was nothing soft about it. Her body molded to his in the dark, seeking out connection wherever it could find it.

"I love you too," she whispered against his lips.

In the coming days and weeks, he knew he'd wonder if it was right to leave Vondur, to make a new home in Iskalt. But he'd never question this, her. Tierney O'Shea saved his kingdom, saved his life, and she saved his soul.

CHAPTER TWENTY-SIX
TIERNEY

"It's good to see you back home and settled again." Siobhan reclined against the lumpy old sofa in the library. "I just wish Veren could have made it back." She played with the fringe on the pillow in her lap. "I can't shake this feeling of overwhelming guilt that I wasn't there for all of you. Maybe he would have made it if I'd done my part."

"His death was an accident." Tierney plopped onto the sofa beside Siobhan, weary down to her bones. "It's not anyone's fault, but I feel the same guilt."

"Must be a survivor's thing." Siobhan sighed. "I just wonder how different things might have gone if I'd ended up in Grima with him from the beginning. Having an extra Iskaltian there might have made the difference. With Logan and with Veren. We might have made that final push a bit faster."

Tierney choked on her tears. She'd shed too many in recent days. Instead, she reached for Siobhan's hand. "If it's anyone's fault, it's mine for screwing up the portal in the first place."

"Then the whole of Lenya would have suffered." Siobhan reminded her.

"How about we just blame fate for being cruel?"

"Deal." Siobhan squeezed her hand.

"Well, I for one, am glad we're back in Iskalt." Gulliver

rummaged around in his bag, placing several new figurines on the mantle over the enormous fireplace. He'd returned from Lenya with a bag full of new carvings and spent crystals he planned to turn into something beautiful. Tierney had no doubt they'd be just as stunning as the queen of the night blossom he'd carved for her. It lay next to her bed now. A constant reminder of her time on the other side of the fae world.

"But I can't wait to get home-home soon." Gulliver adjusted a series of fiery flames he'd carved from the brightest orange crystals he could find. A reminder of the fire plains that were no more. "I miss Myrkur."

"You can't go home yet." Tierney glanced out the window and caught sight of three odd specks of white in the sky. "There's too much work to do between Lenya and the four kingdoms."

"I guess we're the five kingdoms now, aren't we?" Siobhan said softy, staring out the window as the bird-like specks drew closer to the palace.

"Exactly. And we will have so much work to do to bring Lenya up to speed with the rest of us. Trade agreements and the like. Father will need you and I to act as liaisons since we know the Lenyans so well. I imagine we will be needed for a delegation trip soon"

Gulliver turned to face her, hands on hips and his tail lashing behind him. "I am not going back to that awful place, and you can't make me! And I will not think of Vondur or that crappy dungeon ever again."

"Relax." Tierney pulled him down on the settee beside her, sharing a secretive smile with Siobhan. "It's not like anyone will ever mistake you for a—"

"Mongrel? Freak of nature?" Gulliver supplied, his cheeks bright with color.

"I was going to say a nobody." Tierney rolled her eyes. "Everyone in Lenya knows of the great Lord Gulliver O'Shea of Myrkur by now. And it won't be long before they're introduced to other Dark Fae."

"I don't think you understand what I'm saying, Tia." Gulliver crossed his arms over his narrow chest. "I am not, nor will I ever, return to the palace in Vondur. Period. I don't care if my life depends on it; I'm not going. I am going home to see my sisters. I miss them, but don't you ever tell either of them I said that or I'll deny it."

"Gulliver O'Shea," a familiar stern voice sounded at the front of the library. "I know the princess is your best friend, but you should have more respect." Riona stepped around a tall bookshelf, and Gulliver froze.

"Mom? I thought you went home already."

The room exploded into shrieks of "Gullie!" as two small, very loud balls of energy flew into the library, swarming around Gulliver's head. One of them pulled his tail, and the other wrapped her silvery-white wings around his middle.

"Niamh and Nora, what have I told you girls about flying inside? It's rude. And for heaven's sake, let your brother have some breathing room."

"It's okay, Mom." Gulliver hugged Niamh, the older of the two siblings, ignoring the way Nora fluttered around him, her wings flapping in his face.

"What did you bring us?" the girls demanded.

"You do realize I wasn't on a pleasure trip, don't you?" He eyed his sisters in mock seriousness.

"You still brought us something. We know you did."

"Girls, calm down or we will go straight back to Myrkur this instant." Riona elbowed her way into the fray, yanking Gulliver roughly into her arms. "I haven't had nearly enough hugs since you returned." She clutched him tightly in her arms.

"Every time I think about what you got yourself into, I want to break things."

"It wasn't actually my doing, you know," he muttered into her shoulder.

"I know. I was talking to your princess friend here." She managed to take her glare down a notch or two for Tierney's sake.

"You have no idea how sorry I am, Aunt Riona." Tierney's shoulders slumped as she avoided her aunt's silent reprimand.

"Good luck with your sisters." Riona patted Gulliver on the back. "I made a special trip to bring them here because they missed you so much. We flew the whole way back, and I was hoping it would tire them out, but you see how that's worked out." Riona moved to sit beside Tierney, folding her into her arms. "I was scared for you too, silly girl."

Niamh and Nora hurled questions at Gulliver faster than Tierney could keep up with the tiny Dark Fae girls. The smile on her best friend's face was worth the headache that was sure to strike any moment from the level of shrieking the girls were doing.

Tierney sank into the comfort of her aunt's embrace, feeling like the ten-year-old version of herself who fought in the war for Myrkur's freedom right alongside Riona.

"I ran into your father on the way in." Riona finally pulled back. "He's looking for you. That's as good an excuse as you'll get to escape the madness of Niamh and Nora."

"I'll walk you out." Siobhan leapt from the sofa, and the two women left Gulliver to his chaotic family reunion.

Tierney found her father in his study, the doors to the moonlit courtyard flung open to let the cool evening breeze in. She had missed the ice and snow of Iskalt. The temperatures were milder this time of year but still far colder than any she'd experienced since leaving Iskalt.

"You called for me?" Tierney sat on the chair beside her father's desk. It was her chair. Had been since she was old enough to crawl up in it on her own. It was where she had learned how to become the heir of Iskalt.

Lochlan sat back in his chair, turning to face her. "I'm proud of you, Tierney O'Shea." A hint of a smile tugged at his stern features. This was King Lochlan, not just her dad.

"I kind of made a mess of things."

"But you fixed it. And you did a beautiful job of bringing Lenya into the fold of the now five kingdoms. You're ready."

"Ready for what?" A twinge of uneasiness crept up her spine.

"To rule."

"Oh no, I'm not." She shook her head furiously. "Not even a little bit. Are you daft, old man?"

Lochlan chuckled at her reaction. "You know how I became King of Iskalt. I fought to take our kingdom away from my uncle, who had brought us to near ruin with his greed for power."

"Don't remind me of Uncle Callum." Tierney shivered, thinking of her kidnapper from another lifetime.

"It was my duty to our people to rid them of a cruel ruler and to give them an heir capable of leading them into a bright future. That was my job, and it's done."

"Are you dying?" she blurted, her eyes wide with fear. That was the only thing she could think of that would have her father talking about such things. And she was prepared to drag him to the Vondur palace this instant for a dunk in the healing pools to cure him.

"No. I'm perfectly healthy, but I've always known my time as king would be brief. I grew up in Eldur, unsure of my future. You have grown up knowing you would one day rule. You and I have worked together, right here, side by side as it should be. It was the way my father would have groomed me to take his place had he lived."

"If you're not dying, why are we having this conversation?" Her hands twisted in her lap as she tried not to sound as panicked as she felt.

"The fae world is changing, Tia. It's growing and evolving. And I believe Iskalt needs you more than it needs me. You are ready to be queen. You are so strong and wise. A little reckless, but you wouldn't be your mother's daughter if you weren't." Humor danced in his eyes along with something else she wasn't certain she'd ever seen there before. The respect of one monarch for another.

Tierney dragged in a steadying breath. "Are you ... abdicating?"

"Yes. I have done all I can do for Iskalt, and I don't want to spend the rest of my life under a crown that doesn't need me anymore. And I don't want to watch you waste your best days as a bored princess when you can bring the fire of youth and passion to our people who love you."

"But, Dad. No." Tierney clutched her hands in her lap to keep them still, staring into the fathomless blue eyes of the one man she respected more than any other. "You are a wonderful king. I cannot hope to follow in your footsteps. Not yet. Not for a long, long time."

"Sweetheart, that's just it. I don't want you to follow in my footsteps. I want you to forge your own path. You are the future of

Iskalt. You have always been the future. I have just been holding the crown for you until you were ready. The woman I saw down there fighting the fire plains and leading the fae to victory was every inch a queen. A queen I would be proud to serve."

"Are you sure you aren't ... old and addled? Because you aren't making any sense."

"I am not old or addled." His mouth narrowed into a thin line. "But I am determined. You are ready, and it's time to pass the torch to you. I will always be here to guide and advise you, but I am stepping down."

Tierney looked into his eyes and saw his resolve. Eventually, she nodded. "I'm scared."

"Don't be. I'll always be here to catch you if you fall."

Tierney lunged from her seat and threw her arms around her father. "I have to admit one thing, though. You were right."

Lochlan leaned back to study her face. "About what?"

"I need to get married. If you're going to abdicate, the kingdom will feel more settled if I am married when that happens. Our people need to see me as an adult, rather than the little princess they've watched grow up."

"My thoughts exactly." Lochlan crossed his arms over his chest. "And who do you have in mind for the role of husband?"

"You let me handle the whole husband thing." Tierney rose from her seat.

"Have you talked to Keir about this?"

"Not yet, but he'll get over it."

Tierney scoured the castle and the grounds, looking for Keir, but he was nowhere to be found.

Bursting through the doors of her least favorite pub in the

village, she was well on her way to angry. Had the blasted fae gone back home without telling her? If he had, he had better not get too comfortable.

"Your Highness?" The man behind the counter dipped into a stiff bow. "What can I do for you?"

Tierney's gaze swept the nearly empty room, dim and dingy, with only a few patrons tucked away in secluded corners. Her shoulders slumped in defeat when there was no sign of Keir's imposing figure anywhere. This was the last place she could think of to look for him. "A glass of your best Gelsi red." She sank down onto a barstool at the counter.

"Are you sure, Highness?" He gave her a wary look. "The stuff is potent, you know."

"I do, and I am certain." She sighed, trying to hang on to her anger so the tears wouldn't come. "Where in the fracking five kingdoms could he be?" she muttered to herself.

"Here you are, Princess." The man set a glass of her favorite red wine in front of her and she took a long draught. It wasn't sweet and refreshing like the Gelsi berry wine she couldn't drink if she wanted to access her magic. This was crisp and tart, and it went right to her head the way even a sip of the weakest Vondurian wine made Gulliver a drunken fool.

"Should I send to the castle for someone, Princess?" The bartender gave her a strange look.

"No, I'm fine." She took another sip from her glass, letting the magical intoxication wash over her. "I'm going to be just fine, I promise." She hiccupped and ran a hand through her wind-swept hair. A few scattered leaves fell out, and she scowled at them, wondering how she'd managed to get leaves in her hair. She must look a sight.

"Did ... did you know you're crying, your Highness?" The kind man gave her a linen handkerchief.

"No, I'm not." She sniffed. "It's the cold." She dabbed at

her face. "I'll have another please." She drained the rest of her wine and set the glass on the counter.

"How about an ale instead?" A shadow loomed over her. "I hear the red stuff is pretty potent."

"That's the point," she muttered, frowning at the bartender when he set two mugs of ale in front of her.

Tierney squinted up at the newcomer, her vision only slightly blurry at the edges. "Keir!" Her insides warmed at the sight of him. "I found you!"

"I think I'm the one who found you." He settled down beside her. "Do you know how long I've been looking for you?"

"No, I've been looking for you." She scowled at him.

"I know. Everyone in the five kingdoms has seen you today but me." He took a long draught of ale. "I've been ten steps behind you all day," he explained at her look of confusion. "A metaphor for life with Tierney O'Shea if I've ever heard one."

"I know why I'm looking for you, but why have you been looking for me?" She sipped slowly on the ale, her mind still a little fuzzy from the heady wine.

"Um, you go first." He set his mug down, avoiding her gaze.

"Nu-uh, you go."

"You're impossible. You know that, don't you?"

"I've been told." Her mouth thinned into a tight smile.

"But," they both said at the same time, laughing as the tension eased between them.

"But," Tierney continued, "for a little while there, I thought you might have left for Lenya without saying goodbye."

"I'd never do that, Tia." Keir leaned in closer. "Saying goodbye to you would kill me."

"Good." She nodded, propping her elbows onto the bar and leaning in close. "Because I want you to stay."

"Stay?" He tilted his head in question.

"Yes. I think you should be my co-ruler. I'm a princess and

heir to Iskalt, so it's kind of up to me to make these decisions since most men wouldn't think of proposing to a woman like me. But I don't want a king consort for a spouse. I don't want my husband to be bored waiting in the wings for me to finish my job every day because my job is never finished—even as a princess, my work keeps me busy all the time. Now that ... well, let's not give the village too much to gossip about, but let's just say ... I'm going to be a lot busier soon," she whispered softly. "And whoever I marry, I want them to be part of my life in every way. And that means I need someone to rule with me. Maybe not in name. Not at first, anyway. The council would have an epic meltdown if I even mentioned it, but in the years to come, I want my husband to be as much a ruler of Iskalt as me. That's sort of how my parents did it, and it worked for them." Tierney paused to suck in a breath, and Keir leaned in to kiss her, his lips warm and soft against hers only for a brief moment.

"There, that shut you up." His warm breath brushed against her cheek. "Now, in all that absolute babble, I heard something about husbands and consorts in there. Was that Tierney for 'will you marry me'?"

"Yes, Keir! Yes, I will marry you!" Tierney flung her arms around his neck and kissed him.

"Wait. Wait a second." He pulled back. "In the years to come, I foresee the retelling of this moment going in the direction of pure fiction. For the record, I did not ask you; you asked me."

"I did not." Tierney's eyes widened innocently as a smile tugged at the corner of her mouth.

"Did too." Keir rolled his eyes.

"Did not." Tierney stuck her tongue out at him.

"Ah-hem." The bartender cleared his throat. "As a man married to the same woman for forty years, son, it'll be in your best interest to let her have this one." He gave them a toothy grin and refilled their mugs. "And may I be the first to offer my congratulations, your Highnesses." He swept into a courtly bow and left them to their celebrations.

"*Forty* years." Keir's eyes widened as he caught her gaze. "You think we'll make it that long?"

"Absolutely. Now, what was it you wanted to tell me?"

"Oh, it was nothing." He reached for his tankard of ale.

"You ran all over the palace and the village looking for me all day to tell me nothing?"

"Fine." He sighed. "I was looking for you so *I* could propose." He fished around in his pocket for something. "In Vondur, we have a tradition." He took her hand and slipped something around her wrist. "It's tradition for the future husband to give his future wife a gift that once belonged to his mother."

Tierney pulled her hand back to study the beautiful bracelet made of tiny silver vines tipped with lovely blue stones that seemed to glow with magic.

"It's beautiful, Keir. But how did you have this with you?"

"I brought it with me from home. I knew I'd work up the nerve eventually."

"You managed to hold on to it from Vondur all the way here? Through fires and storms and a shipwreck?"

"And don't forget the trek across a frozen wasteland."

Tierney gazed into his eyes, lifting her hand to touch his cheek. "I love you, Keir Dagnan."

"I love you too." His eyes burned into hers, and her cheeks warmed.

Clearing her throat, Tierney lifted her drink to tap against his. "And that is how we will remember the proposal."

EPILOGUE
GULLIVER

Six months later

Gulliver paced the hallway outside the queen's council room, trying not to stare at the intricately carved wooden doors depicting the history of Iskalt. It was only Tierney on the other side of that imposing door. Yes, she was a queen now. A queen who summoned him from Myrkur just weeks after his return from an extended stay in Iskalt during her coronation celebrations. But she was still his best friend, right? Did queens get to have best friends?

The doors opened and advisors and representatives from Lenya filed out of the room one by one, scurrying off in a dozen different directions like their lives depended on it. Most of them looked pretty agitated.

Gulliver's tail twitched behind him, and he took a few steps toward the doors, debating whether or not he was allowed to just walk in.

"Why is this so weird?" he muttered under his breath.

"Gullie? Is that you?" Tierney's head popped out into the hallway, and she was all smiles for him, like nothing had changed. "Get in here." She pushed the door open and shooed him over to the huge table where Keir looked at home.

247

Gulliver eyed the vacant throne at the apex of the room.

"I can't make myself do it yet." She plopped down into one of the seats at the table. "To me, that's my father's chair, and I get freaked out every time I try to approach the throne. It's still too weird." Keir put a hand on her arm, and she visibly relaxed, before he took his seat next to her.

Gulliver let out an easy breath. This was definitely still the Tia he'd always known, just with a calming presence at her side now. It was weird to think that the man who agitated her also soothed her.

"Well, sit down already." She shoved a chair toward him with her foot.

"Why did you summon me with the official-looking queenly parchment and wax seals? I thought I was being arrested when the guard showed up to deliver it."

"I haven't had to summon anyone yet, and I wanted to try it." She gave him her most impish smile.

Keir shook his head with a wry grin. "Why do we like her?"

"Love." She pouted. "You both love me."

"You wanted to try it?" Gulliver scowled at her, still stuck on that point. "Do you know how long the trip from Myrkur is? My saddle sores have sores, Tia!"

"Ew, I don't need to know that."

Gulliver shook his head and stood. "If you don't actually need anything, I'm going to go to the kitchens to get some snacks, and then I'm taking a nap. When the moon rises, I'm going to go find Toby to open a portal for me so I can get back home to my family."

"Sit." Tierney's face changed in an instant from his best friend in the world to a proper ice queen.

He dropped back into the chair without thinking.

"I do need you, Gullie. I called you here for a reason, but you have to swear not to tell another soul. Not yet."

"What's wrong now? Have you discovered another kingdom on the brink of war and destruction? Because if you have, I think I'd rather sit this one out if you don't mind."

"Not quite." She scooted her chair closer, until their knees were touching. "About a month ago, I received a top-secret disturbing report from my father—you know, Mom and Dad are on an extended trip right now. Mom thought it was best to get him out of my hair while I establish my authority as queen."

"And her authority as wife." Keir grinned at her and she rolled her eyes.

"Gulliver doesn't need to know that."

He definitely didn't. Gulliver could imagine it would be difficult for Tierney to take over when her predecessor was still very much respected and loved throughout the kingdom. Worse still with her father breathing down her neck. It was no secret that Lochlan O'Shea was happy to abdicate to his more-than-capable daughter, but at the same time, he wasn't the sort to step back and keep his opinions to himself. In the first weeks after her coronation, Lochlan about drove her insane.

"What did he have to say that involves me?"

"This is like code red stuff, Gullie. You cannot tell *anyone*." Tierney looked over her shoulder to make sure the doors were shut and they were alone.

"What's code red mean?" They both ignored Keir.

"Then, how about you don't tell me? I think I'd prefer that option." Gulliver tried to stand up, but she shoved him back down. "Seriously, Tia?"

Tierney ignored him, dropping her voice to a whisper. "Dad says this could be super dangerous."

"Okay. But what has that got to do with me?"

"You're the only one I can trust with this, Gul. We have to act quickly and quietly."

"Yep. Sure. Sounds good. You let me know how that works out."

"Gulliver." She sounded a little too much like her mother when she said his name like that.

"*Tierney.*" He tilted his head to the side. "What have you gotten me into this time?"

ABOUT
MELISSA A. CRAVEN

Melissa A. Craven is an Amazon bestselling author of Young Adult Contemporary Fiction and YA Fantasy (her Contemporary fans will know her as Ann Maree Craven). Her books focus on strong female protagonists who aren't always perfect, but they find their inner strength along the way. Melissa's novels appeal to audiences of all ages and fans of almost any genre. She believes in stories that make you think and she loves playing with foreshadowing, leaving clues and hints for the careful reader.

Melissa draws inspiration from her background in architecture and interior design to help her with the small details in world building and scene settings. (Her degree in fine art also comes in handy.) She is a diehard introvert with a wicked sense of humor and a tendency for hermit-like behavior. (Seriously, she gets cranky if she has to put on anything other than yoga pants and t-shirts!)

Melissa enjoys editing almost as much as she enjoys writing, which makes her an absolute weirdo among her peers. Her favorite pastime is sitting on her porch when the weather is nice with her two dogs, Fynlee and Nahla, reading from her massive TBR pile and dreaming up new stories.

Visit Melissa at Melissaacraven.com for more information about her newest series and discover exclusive content.

Join Melissa and Michelle's Facebook Group: Search for Melissa and Michelle's Fantasy Book Warriors

Follow Michelle and Melissa on TikTok at @ATaleOfTwoAuthors

ABOUT
M. LYNN

Michelle MacQueen is a USA Today bestselling author of love. Yes, love. Whether it be YA romance, NA romance, or fantasy romance (Under M. Lynn), she loves to make readers swoon.

The great loves of her life to this point are two tiny blond creatures who call her "aunt" and proclaim her books to be "boring books" for their lack of pictures. Yet, somehow, she still manages to love them more than chocolate.

When she's not sharing her inexhaustible wisdom with her niece and nephew, Michelle is usually lounging in her ridiculously large bean bag chair creating worlds and characters that remind her to smile every day - even when a feisty five-year-old is telling her just how much she doesn't know.

See more from M. Lynn and sign up
to receive updates and deals!
michellelynnauthor.com

**Join Melissa and Michelle's Facebook Group:
Search for Melissa and Michelle's Fantasy Book
Warriors**

Follow Michelle and Melissa on TikTok
@ATaleOfTwoAuthors

What's Next?

Coming soon: Look for Gulliver's story wherever you purchase your books

Queens of the Fae will conclude with Gulliver's Story in
Fae's Envoy, Fae's Enemy, and Fae's End